Distraction

A Steamy Small-Town Romance

Michele Lenard

CMFR

Copyright © [2022] by [Michele Lenard] ***

All rights reserved.

No portion of this book may be reproduced in any form or by any means, electronic or mechanical, including photocopying and recording or by any information storage and retrieval system, without written permission from the publisher or author, except as permitted by U.S. copyright law.

This is a work of fiction. Names, places, characters, and incidents are either the product of the author's imagination or are used fictitiously, and any resemblance to any actual persons, living or dead, organizations, events, or locales is entirely coincidental.

Warning: The unauthorized reproduction or distribution of this copyrighted work is illegal, punishable by up to five years in prison and a fine of up to $250,000.

No portion of this book may be reproduced in any form without written permission from the publisher or author, except as permitted by U.S. copyright law.

***

If you enjoy this story be sure to check out a sneak peek of the FREE novella The Long Route at the end of the book.

Contents

1. Cade — 1
2. Cora — 11
3. Cade — 21
4. Cora — 31
5. Cade — 41
6. Cora — 52
7. Cade — 61
8. Cora — 73
9. Cade — 85
10. Cora — 97
11. Cade — 111
12. Cora — 121
13. Cade — 133
14. Cora — 147
15. Cade — 159
16. Cora — 173
17. Cade — 189

18.	Cora	203
19.	Cade	219
20.	Cora	237
21.	Cade	247
22.	Cora	255
23.	Cade	265
24.	Cora	275
25.	Epilogue	285
26.	The Long Route	295

Chapter 1

Cade

I wrap my hand around the pint glass and take a sip, enjoying the tingle of the cool liquid as it slides down my throat. *Damn that's refreshing.* I don't know if it's the crisp flavor, or the way it seems to soothe my aching muscles, but there's something about a cold beer that just completes a bike ride. Bonus if that beer comes with a burger on an outdoor patio where I can appreciate the mountains I've been riding since I was a little kid. There are several things that can get tiresome in this small resort town, but the view isn't one of them.

"Hits the spot." My cousin Deacon exhales as he takes a sip. "I swear beer tastes even better after a ride. Why is that?"

"Some things you just don't question. Good ride." I raise my glass. Deacon snorts as he clinks his glass to mine. He's only been here a few weeks and hasn't quite built up his lungs for the altitude, but he's getting better each time.

Leaning back in the chair I tip my head toward the sun and let my body go limp, a reward for pushing it to the limit earlier. I may be hurting now, but to me that's a badge of honor. Something I earn by conquering the mountains that surround us, which people flock to my hometown to experience. They only get a sample though, whereas this is just another day for me. I kind of love having a life that other people like to try on, which is why I thrive on the sore muscles. They remind me of how good I have it.

"Rough ride, boys? You're looking a little winded." I lift my head to look at our server, Tiff, a fellow local who's always giving me shit. It's sort of our thing.

"I don't get winded. And the Columbine trail isn't that tough. You'd know that if you gave up that dance stuff you do and took up a real sport. Just say the word and I'll get you out of leotards and onto a bike." Tiff does ride, just not as often as she teaches dance at the local studio, which I've teased her about for years. Not because I think there's anything wrong with it, but because she's actually a great rider. That kind of raw talent is hard to come by and it depresses me to see it squandered.

"I wasn't talking about the trail. I thought maybe you'd found another way to wear yourselves out," she smiles coyly.

That almost sounds like an innuendo and coming from anyone else I'd respond to that with an equally suggestive joke since I'm a relentless flirt. But our parents are close enough that Tiff's like a little sister so I don't make sex jokes with her, and she doesn't usually make them with me. Since I'm not sure what she's getting at I ignore it.

"The snows gone, what else would I be doing besides biking?" I frown. "And don't tell me dance. I did all your barbie and tea party shit when you were little, I draw the line at dance."

"Same deal as always, Cade, you take a dance class and I'll go for a ride." I dodge the hand she tries to ruffle through my hair.

"Why would I waste my time doing something inside when I can enjoy all this?" I sweep my arm around, gesturing to the towering peaks that surround us.

"Chicken." She winks as she turns back to the bar.

"Back atcha." I smirk, knowing she's going to place the order for our usual post-ride fare.

When our burgers arrive, we dive in, and as we eat a steady stream of people stop by our table to say hello, asking which trail we just did, what news we've heard about management at the ski resort—there's a rumor it's changing hands—and whether we know that Shawn is selling the restaurant that's been in his family for three generations and moving to Oregon. That's the gossip this week, and of course we've heard all of it. In a town where all the residents know each other, there aren't any secrets.

After replenishing the calories that we burned with greasy burgers, fries and beer, we make our way slowly back to my truck. Neither of us are in a hurry to get home, both because the pace of life in a resort town is so chill, and because we don't have anywhere else to be. Plus, strolling around Main Street is one of my favorite parts of living here. The artist in me appreciates all the bright colors; buildings are blue, pink, red, virtually every color of the rainbow, sort of like the Painted Ladies in San Francisco, which is so much more interesting than plain old beige.

Walking through town is also a social experience, since you'll either run into someone you know, or just get to observe the spectacle of tourists oohing and ahhing over our 'quaint' little town. It's another example of people admiring what I get to experience every day, and I kind of get off on it. Makes me feel better about living in a town that doesn't have a bowling alley or a movie theater or anything besides the outdoors for entertainment.

We're halfway to my truck when Deacon elbows me. "Oh my gosh, cousin. Do you see that?"

I follow his gaze up the sidewalk to see about a half dozen ladies coming out of Trudy's wine bar. But these aren't just any ladies, they're tourists, and I'm a sucker for tourists. The female kind anyway. Tiff's little remark about getting a workout suddenly makes sense.

"There are so many." Deacon sighs as he takes in several pairs of smooth legs in towering heels. I roll my eyes at his dreamy expression, but only because he's being so obvious, not because I'm thinking differently.

It's early June, which means it's been a long time since the weather has been nice enough for women to wear dresses, and all these legs are a welcome sight after a long, cold winter. Not only that, but these legs are poking out of some dangerously short dresses, and they're clicking along the sidewalk in some seriously fancy shoes. That's how I know these are tourists. Local girls don't get this dressed up, and they don't hang out in large groups like this, mainly because there aren't that many of them.

Katah Vista is an amazing place to live if you're an adventurous guy like myself, because there is no shortage of things to do. Biking, hiking and kayaking in the summer, skiing and snowmobiling in the winter, nowhere else can claim to be such a great playground for grown men. Women, too, they just relocate here in smaller numbers, meaning the male to female ratio is way out of whack, hence my excitement over a group of attractive strangers.

"What do you think they're doing here?" Deacon marvels. He may be new to town, but as family, he's visited a lot over the years, so he knows the fancy dresses are out of place.

I take in the elaborate outfits and perfectly styled hair, the tiny purses that no one around here carries. It's all slightly over the top for an average Thursday unless there's a holiday or themed festival. "Bachelorette trip." A sly grin spreads across my face.

"This isn't Vegas." Deacon shakes his head, knowing full well our little resort town shouldn't be a draw for those types of events.

"No, but men have this misguided notion that a group of beautiful single women won't get into any trouble here. They think the ladies will enjoy the spa and the pool and the trendy restaurants up at the resort, and that they'll have a nice relaxing trip. So, they convince their fiancés or whatever to come here where they won't get out of control."

"Does it work? Do they stay out of trouble?" He glances skeptically towards the visitors.

"Hell no." I rub my jaw to camouflage the look I'm giving the eye candy down the street. "No one wants a tame bachelorette party, so it's not like they go home after dinner. Come on, they're waiting for us to make our move."

"How can you tell?"

"They're just standing on the sidewalk like they have nowhere to go, but they keep glancing our way. Let's go." I slap him on the back and start walking.

Up close the girls are attractive despite having too much shit on their faces, and the way they bat their eyelashes and touch our arms leaves no doubt they're just as interested in a good time as we are. The fact that my cousin and I are decent looking probably helps our cause, although I also hint that we'd be happy to play some party games, and I think that seals the deal.

Twenty minutes later Deacon's eyes are rolled back in his head, his chest rising erratically. "I love where you live, cousin. I may have to make it my permanent home."

I bite back a chuckle, wondering how he can manage to look content and pained at the same time as several hands roam over his nearly naked body, searching for the penis sticker the bride hid after the girls were blindfolded. If he does make this his permanent home, this isn't likely to be the first time we go out for a quick bite and end up as part of the entertainment for a bachelorette party.

Not that these parties are a regular occurrence, but this isn't my first, and it isn't likely to be my last. For some reason rich chicks love to have their way with us working class guys. I don't know if they do this shit as some sort of rebellion against their high society lives or what, but who am I to object.

After several rounds of games that leave us just as spent as our earlier bike ride, Deacon and I get dressed and join the ladies in the kitchen for some shots. There's the typical small talk, or as typical as can be after they've become pretty familiar with us. What do we do? How long have we lived here? The usual.

They're from Texas–not sure why but Texans love Katah Vista. Liz, the maid of honor, has been vacationing here for years, mostly to ski in the winters, and this is her family's house. Like I said, *the usual*, which means it's time to make our exit.

"You ladies aren't planning to stay in for the night, are you? There's a good band playing in town tonight," I suggest to get out of more small talk. After all, my cousin and I are the entertainment, not their dates, and we've already played our part. Besides, we have to work early, so a band would make it easier to slip away unnoticed.

"Ooh, dancing!" The bride claps her hands together.

"What kind of band?" Liz backs into me and rolls her ass against my junk.

I put my hands on her hips to hold her still. "Let's go find out."

It takes another twenty minutes–the girls refused to leave before putting more shit on their faces–but finally we make our way back to Main Street and head toward the pub that doubles as a concert hall.

"Why didn't we call a cab?" The annoyed bride dodges a crack in the sidewalk.

I turn my head in time to see her stumble in her fancy shoes. *Crazy rich tourists.* They're fun, but they can take a lot of patience.

"There aren't any cabs in this town. Hop on Deacon's back if you need a lift." I throw my cousin a sly grin, but instead of returning it he cringes. When I collide with a fruity-smelling wall the look makes sense.

I lunge forward, my arms shooting out to catch the source of the sweet scent before I consciously decide to move them. I'm able to stop my roadblock's momentum enough that she just sort of sinks to the ground, my grip on her arms preventing a hard landing. That doesn't stop her from uttering a little "oomph" as she goes down. I stifle a laugh. In my defense, it was high-pitched and kind of cute.

The bags she's carrying crash to the sidewalk. I cast a quick look in Deacon's direction, and he nods, acknowledging that he'll escort the ladies to the bar while I help clean up the mess. They walk on ahead, the bride leaning on him for support as she grumbles about her feet.

"Sorry, I didn't see you there." I scramble to pick up the groceries on the sidewalk and put them back in their bags.

"Yes, I got that you were distracted." The words are dripping with sarcasm, though the voice is amused, not cynical.

"You okay?"

"No damage." She rubs her arms, right where I'd been gripping her.

"What about your groceries? I'll replace anything that's ruined." I chase an apple down before it hits the street.

"Everything seems fine." Her slender hands dust off her pants as she twists to make sure she's clean.

"Okay, good." I finish collecting the spilled items and hold the bag out, getting my first real look at the woman I plowed into. And damn if she doesn't plow me right back. Blonde hair that hangs in loose waves halfway down her back. Almond shaped brown eyes framed by long lashes. A smattering of freckles on her nose. And full, pink lips, still plump even though they're pursed, studying me. *Damn*. I've seen a lot of gorgeous women in my day, but none of them compare to the one staring back at me, who's effortlessly beautiful. *Natural*.

I'm pretty sure this girl doesn't have an ounce of makeup on, which should make her a local, because they tend not to bother with that shit. Only I've never seen her before, and this is a face I'd remember. Tourist then? Normally that would excite me, but she doesn't strike me as the typical visitor, the kind looking for a home-grown boy to show her a good time. She seems too mature for that despite looking close to my age. Although, since I've never been one to act my age, who knows how old she is.

"You can catch up to your harem, I'm fine." She takes the bag from me. Again, the words are saucy, yet the voice doesn't hold any anger.

"Funny." I look her over, detecting the slender curves her t-shirt doesn't flaunt. "I'll have to tell my cousin. He'd get a kick out of that."

"Why? Is it his harem?" She cocks her head.

I bark out a laugh. "Bachelorette party. Close enough."

"Ah, I see how I could make that mistake. Well, enjoy." She adjusts her grip on the bag and turns to leave.

"You're new here." I gamble that she's not just passing through.

"What makes you say that?" A little crease appears between her brows.

Yep, not a vacationer. Only a new person would want to know how I can tell the difference.

"I haven't seen you before." I lean against the side of the building.

"You know everyone in this town?" Those brown eyes bore into me.

"Yes, actually." I give her my sexiest grin.

"And I suppose knowing you would work in my favor?" She surmises with a wry smile.

"It can." I'm creeping into dangerous territory. I don't mix with locals, but she's seriously cute. Maybe even a little feisty.

"Is this the part where I'm supposed to ask you to help out the new girl? To give me the scoop on the town and show me the lay of the land?" She blinks, feigning innocence. I like it.

"If you want." I stuff my hands in my pockets.

"Let me guess, you're the only tour guide around?" She rolls her eyes.

"Not the only. But I am the best." I give her my best casual shrug.

"Cocky."

"Honest," I correct. "Few people have lived here as long as I have."

"How long is that?" She gives me a critical once-over.

"All my life."

"What makes you think I need someone to show me around?" She purses those full lips.

"You're grocery shopping on Main Street." I tilt my head toward the building I'm leaning on.

"So?"

"So, you're paying tourist prices. Nona's a sweet lady and I can see why you'd want to shop in her store, but she marks everything up since her customers are mostly visitors. There's a better option a little further out of town. And they offer a local discount." I give her a conspiratorial wink.

"And that option is open at…" She checks her watch, "nine thirty at night?"

"Nope," I say, emphasizing every syllable. "So, you need someone to show you where *and* when to do your shopping."

"Well, thanks for the offer, but I think I can figure it out on my own." She smiles with false sweetness, amused. That's odd. Usually by now girls are batting their eyelashes and asking when I'm free. I'm intrigued.

I'm supposed to be out with a group of women right now, half of whom know me pretty intimately after the night's festivities, yet none of them are anywhere near as interesting as the woman in front of me. Despite talking with those women over some drinks I don't know anything about them. In just a few minutes with this one I can tell she's witty enough to bait me, confident enough to show her real face instead of the one she wants people to see, and responsible enough not to be swayed by my flirting.

That last part is sort of annoying. This little back and forth is kind of fun, and I'd like to keep it going. Even if she won't cave, just teasing her gets my adrenaline going. Right now, it sounds more entertaining than babysitting what's sure to be a rowdy group, even if that could get me laid again. *Shit, where did that thought come from?*

It's on the tip of my tongue to correct this woman, to tell her she does need me to learn her way around so I can keep this dialogue going. Only she's not acting like every other girl I've met, which is throwing me off my game. Her words suggest she's turned off, yet her tone suggests curiosity, and I'm not sure how to handle that. I'm used to a solid green light, and this girl is more like yellow. We may not have stoplights in this town, but I do know yellow means caution. In that case, it's probably safer to back off. That's ok though. I can work with caution.

"Suit yourself, neighbor. See you around." I nod goodbye and continue walking toward the bar, a move that usually leaves them wanting more. I don't feel her eyes on my back as I leave.

Chapter 2

Cora

The rhythmic beeping from the backhoe is more distracting than I anticipated.

Uncle Rick warned me to expect noise, though when I made arrangements to spend the summer here, I thought I'd be out exploring during the day, and using the quiet nights to write my thesis. What I hadn't counted on is that June in the mountains isn't the same as June on the coast, so mornings and evenings get pretty cool. Cold even. That means no exploring until the afternoon sun warms the air, which in turn means schoolwork has to get done in the mornings if I want to get outside at all.

I look at all my notes, spread over the desk in front of me. I can't make much sense of them right now, not in any meaningful way, so I jot down the primary points of my thesis, adding bullets about which supporting information fits best under each section. It's the most that can be accomplished with this racket, but by the time lunch rolls around a few hours later a plan is taking shape.

After a quick salad I grab my hiking gear and head out to the car Rick left me, thinking to explore a trail that leads to a little cave in the foothills above town. But when I get to my car, I see it's blocked in by the trailer that was used to transport the backhoe. *Dammit.*

The machine seems to be sitting still off to the side and somewhat behind the house. I make my way toward it, gripping the straps of my backpack to keep it in place as I navigate the jumbled ground.

Rounding the corner of the giant contraption I run into a wall of muscle, eerily reminiscent of the one I encountered last night. This time there's nothing covering it, and I get a very up close and personal glimpse of just how smooth and sculpted it is. Two strong arms reach out to pluck me out of thin air before I hit the ground. The touch is surprisingly gentle despite the obvious strength of their grip.

"We've got to stop running into each other this way." A deep, silky voice washes over me. Yes, I'm aware silky is a strange way to describe a man's voice, and no, I don't want to change my description. I actually feel the words slide over me, same as I did last night, teasing goosebumps to the surface of my skin.

I take a breath and try to focus on the words, not the playful tone they're spoken in, or the mouth that speaks them. This one is dangerous. Between his voice, his leanly muscled frame and a face that's so perfectly constructed it's borderline angelic, he could have me eating out of his hand if I'm not careful, and I don't have time for that kind of distraction. I need to keep my guard up.

"You mean you've got to start paying attention to where you're going." My tone is more playful than I intend, so I cross my arms in front of my chest.

He smiles, amused. "This one's all on you, honey. What are you doing wandering around my construction site?"

"Your site?" I take a half step back.

"Yeah, mine. That surprises you?" The corner of his lip rises playfully.

"Kind of. I figured you for a bartender or something, not someone who gets up early for work."

"How do you know I was up early for work?" He's toying with me, and it's giving me butterflies. I'm kind of a sucker for his sexy little grin, especially covered in the light scruff that suggests shaving is optional.

"Can't miss the racket you're making out here." I gesture to the massive yellow vehicle.

"Well, if you knew I was out here making noise why didn't you come say hi earlier?" His blue eyes twinkle.

"Why would I assume it's you making noise?" I purse my lips, trying to keep my eyes on his.

"I'm the only guy in town with this machinery." I know he's referring to the backhoe, but he's leaving another implication unspoken, and that makes me take notice of the broad shoulders that are just about eye level, the V that disappears beneath his low-slung jeans. He has the body of a man, all angles and hard planes, but a mischievous demeanor that suggests he knows how to have a good time. I hate that I'm curious.

"I guess it's a good thing I don't know you then. I'd hate to distract you from doing actual work." I placate him with a saucy smile.

"And here I thought you were stalking me." He leans against the giant beast as his eyes roam over me.

"I think you'd like that actually, but I just need you to move the trailer for your *machinery*." I jerk my thumb toward the trailer. "It's blocking me in."

"Blocking you in? Wait, you're Rick's niece?" His brows disappear under the sun-kissed brown hair that's a tad too long without being sloppy. Hair that looks really soft.

"That's me." I'm enjoying his obvious surprise when a male voice rounds the backhoe and interrupts.

"I grabbed you a burger for lunch, cousin, extra pickles…" The dark-haired man pauses when he sees me. "Uh, hi. You're the girl Cade met last night. How'd you know he'd be here?"

I shoot a questioning look toward the man who's run me over twice. "Oh my gosh, you actually have people that stalk you." The guy is hot, but no wonder his ego is inflated. A grin teases the corner of his lip, which makes my belly flutter a little, dammit.

"I wasn't looking for him. And we didn't actually meet," I correct the dark-haired man. "Your friend here ran me over but never told me his name."

"You didn't tell me yours either." The shirtless one, Cade, stuffs his hands in his pockets, drawing my gaze to his perfect abs.

"Looked like you already made a dozen new friends, no need to add my name to the mix." I dismiss him with a little wave. "You wouldn't have remembered it anyway."

"I'd remember," he says softly, that hint of a smile still on his lips.

I find that hard to believe given that I'm probably pretty plain next to the women he was with last night… Although, he's certainly not looking at me like I'm plain. I'm not sure if that's genuine or a good act, but it makes my breath catch in my throat all the same.

"So, you remember the names of all your new friends?" I raise my brows.

"They weren't my friends, just people passing through town." His eyes meet mine through the wisps of hair falling around his face. I know he's trouble, but the flutter in my stomach is making the case that I should ignore that fact.

"And you were showing them around?" I borrow his term from last night.

"Just being hospitable." He manages to look bashful and mischievous all at once. He's really too beautiful for his own good.

"Of course." I have a pretty good idea of what he's referring to when he says hospitable, and while part of me wants to be offended, my libido is intrigued.

"Offer still stands." He interrupts my wayward thoughts. I'm vaguely aware of the other guy drifting away, so it's just us.

"What offer?" I squint.

"Showing you around." He holds my gaze, waiting.

"I can find my own way. I just need you to move the trailer."

"Yeah." He rubs the back of his neck. "That's not as easy as it sounds."

"Why not?" I frown.

"I need a special hitch for that trailer." He jerks his head towards it. "The truck with that hitch is on another job site right now."

"You're saying I'm trapped here? Did you not see the car when you pulled up this morning?" I clutch the straps of my bag so I'm not tempted to flail my arms like a lunatic.

"I saw it." He nods in affirmation. "But I didn't think you were supposed to get here until next week. Figured no one was around to drive it yet, so I sent the truck to another site."

"How can the only truck capable of moving that trailer not be attached to it?" I grunt.

"That truck has to move several trailers around to different sites. I can't leave it parked immobile all day when I need it for other projects."

"Great," I mutter under my breath. "How long?" I can feel my anger rising, which is a good thing because it distracts me from the butterflies. I really don't need to be experiencing those all summer.

"Today at least. Tell you what, take mine." He fishes in his pockets for some keys and holds them out to me.

"You're giving me your car?" I feel my jaw hanging open.

"Truck. You okay to drive one? It's likely a bit bigger than what you're used to." His blue eyes drift between the Subaru wagon that he's currently blocking in, and the massive pickup parked in the street. At first, I think he's making another lewd joke, like he did with the machinery comment, but when I look at him, keys extended, I realize there's no pun intended. He just wants to make sure I can drive such a large vehicle.

"You're willing to give me your truck? You don't even know my name, why would you give me a vehicle?" My words are skeptical, yet I find myself holding a pair of keys as I say them.

"We blocked you in. Seems fair." The sunlight glints over his broad shoulders as he shrugs.

"I'm a total stranger to you."

"Cade." He extends his hand.

I hesitate, knowing this is a bad idea, but it'd be rude to decline. The second my hand touches his, my hormones riot, and it takes all my strength to keep my knees from buckling. "Cora," I breathe. His forearm flexes as he shakes my hand, which draws my eyes up his arm and over his firm chest. It's just as perfect as his face.

"Pretty. Now we aren't strangers anymore." He smiles in a way that suggests we were never going to be strangers.

I drop his hand before the contact scalds me. "That's supposed to make me feel better about taking your truck? What if I wreck it?"

"It's insured."

"What if I have plans to leave town?"

"Looks like you're going hiking." He gestures towards my backpack. "And I've got plenty of people I can grab a ride from if needed. Plus, there's the town bus. I'll manage."

"Do you do this for all the people passing through town?" I draw my brows together.

"No. But you're not passing through." He stuffs his hands in his pockets again.

"I am though."

"You sure about that?" He studies me. "Rick seemed to think you'd be here awhile. At least the summer."

"That's still passing through."

"Stay here all summer, you're practically a local. Locals take care of each other." He grins as he leans a hip against the backhoe.

"Giving me your truck still seems excessive." I bite my lip and force my gaze toward the road where it's parked.

"Take it or don't, up to you. But that's the only way you're going on your hike today. Unless you want me to take you." He smiles coyly.

"Do you ever stop flirting?" I change the subject.

"This isn't flirting, this is being *hospitable*." He winks, drawing attention to his impossibly blue eyes.

"Is there a difference with you?" I squint at him.

"Not really." He laughs and his stomach ripples as it contracts. "Come on, Solo. Let's get you set up in my truck so you can do your hike." He takes a step forward and grabs my pack off my shoulders like it's nothing.

"Solo?"

"Yeah, you know, since you insist on doing everything yourself." He cocks an eyebrow.

"Oh. I thought that was supposed to be some sort of *Star Wars* reference.

"I'd like to think I'm more original than nicknaming someone after a movie character," he says over his shoulder as he walks toward the truck.

"What if I don't want to be called Solo?" I trail after him.

"Invite me on your hike and I'll have to find something else to call you." He slings my bag into the bed of the truck, the muscles in his arms rippling with his movement.

"Don't you have work to do?" I ask, exasperated.

"Nothing that can't be done Monday."

"You're incorrigible," I mumble.

"True." He opens the door so I can climb in.

I admit I'm enjoying this little banter we have going, but I really don't need the distraction of a hot guy this summer, especially one I think is the welcoming committee for any woman that sets foot in the town. I need to get away from him. I climb into the cab before he can help me with that.

"Your cousin doesn't seem to like the idea of you leaving." I nod toward the dark-haired guy who's now frowning in our direction.

"Sorta forgot about him." Cade chuckles, rubbing his neck as he peers up at me through wisps of blond hair. "I'm not used to having him around yet. Ah well, maybe I do need to get back to work. You know where you're going?"

"Yes, Lupine Bluff."

"That's a good one, you'll enjoy it. Watch out for the bats though."

"Bats?"

"Yeah, you know. Black rodents with wings." His stomach contracts as he tries not to laugh.

"I know what bats are. There are bats in that cave?" I wrinkle my nose.

"Sure. Their droppings are what turn the rocks all sorts of colors. Didn't know that little fact, did ya?" He cast me another suggestive grin. "Sure you don't want a guide?"

"I'm good. Bats aren't active in the day."

"Not usually, no. Have fun, Solo." He winks and moves to shut the door.

"Wait! How do I get your keys back to you?"

"Keep 'em." He shrugs. "I'll either still be here when you get back or I'll see you tomorrow."

"Tomorrow is Saturday. You work on Saturday?" I frown, worried I'm not going to get the two days of silence I'd been counting on.

"No, but it's a small town. I'll see you around one way or another." He shuts me inside the cab of his truck with a lingering grin before turning to head back toward the construction site. I watch him go, admiring the view. He's too beautiful not to admire. I am in so much trouble.

Chapter 3

Cade

Her eyes follow me as I walk away this time. That makes me smile, but it also makes me a little frustrated, because I thought for sure instead of going back to work, I'd be going hiking with her. I'm still not quite sure why that is, seeing how I felt her checking me out, and those lingering gazes suggest she liked what she saw.

I'm not used to a woman saying one thing with her eyes and another with her mouth, which makes Cora a bit of a mystery. That could be fun.

Cora. The name suits her. It's unique. Bold. Feminine without sounding frilly. Fuck, I've never thought twice about a woman's name and now I'm looking for a deeper meaning in hers. What the hell? But seriously, our interactions have me intrigued. And not just physically. That's a first.

"Two denials in two days? Not off to a great start, Cuz," Deacon calls from the bed of his truck where he's scarfing down his lunch.

"How can you say she denied me when she's driving my truck?" I jerk my thumb towards the retreating vehicle as I approach his.

"Because you're not in it. Your truck is going to round the bases faster than you are." He smirks around a mouthful of his burger.

"Shut up." I hop onto the tailgate and rifle through the bag between us for my food.

"I thought scoring chicks was supposed to be easy in this town."

"Tourists, yeah." I lick a drop of ketchup off my finger. "They come here looking for a good time and sex with a local boy falls into that category. But Cora's no tourist."

"Then why are you bothering?"

"Who says I am?" I take another bite, feigning disinterest.

Admitting that I'm curious about Cora could backfire in a big way. I can't explain it, but in this town if a guy zeros in on a girl for something beyond a casual fuck she instantly becomes intriguing to lots of other guys, like she puts off some sort of scent that says she's different. Special. Suddenly the girl that you had to yourself has a tsunami of admirers. It's one of the reasons I don't do locals – too much effort.

And, not to be a dick, but that's true of any girl, so if it's a girl like Cora, who is the most naturally beautiful woman I've ever seen, just hinting I'm curious about her will make her ten times more attractive to any male in a twenty-mile radius.

They'll catch on that there's something worth discovering under that pretty outer shell, and I'll have to compete for her attention. The worst thing I can do is let on that I'm intrigued, even to my cousin, who doesn't know all the nuances of this town yet and could say something to ruin my advantage.

Speaking of advantage, I might've ruined it myself by giving her my truck. Everyone in town will recognize it, and the beautiful stranger driving it will get tongues wagging.

"You expect me to believe you aren't interested in our pretty new neighbor?" Deacon pops a fry in his mouth. "You were ready to stick me with this project and take off."

"I was only going to make sure she learned her way around."

"Yeah, right." Deacon knows me too well to buy that, so I have to act fast.

"In case you haven't noticed, she's the niece of the guy who's house we're working on. The last thing we need is to get fired because we overstepped with his family." The words roll easily off my tongue, and once they're out I realize they make sense.

"You really weren't trying to flirt with her then?" Deacon studies me skeptically.

"I'm always flirting. But I really was trying to be neighborly. In fact," an idea forms, "I bet our client would appreciate it if we keep an eye on her. You know, keep the lions from pouncing."

"You want us to babysit this girl?" His lip pulls up in distaste. "No offense, but I'm not here to play babysitter. I'm looking forward to doing my own pouncing."

"You will, just not with her. And we'll discourage other guys from pouncing on her too. It's only a matter of time before they notice her. We'll just make sure to let them know our client would appreciate it if they leave his niece alone."

"Seriously? We just tell people to keep their distance and they'll stay away."

"Her uncle spends a lot of money in this town, and no one will want to risk that by treating his niece poorly." I pop a few fries in my mouth so I don't laugh at my own bullshit.

"Makes sense I guess," Deacon nods. "How do we do this?"

"If anyone asks what her deal is, we just say she's staying at her uncle's, and since we're working on his house, he asked us to keep an eye on her." This ruse gives me the freedom to talk to Cora without anyone reading anything into it. They'll probably think I'm getting paid to do it or something, which is fine because it will keep every other guy from trying to worm his way into my space. And that will give me time to figure out why she won't act on what her eyes say she wants.

"Okay, if you think this will be good for us, I'm in," Deacon agrees.

"Good. Now let's finish leveling this ground. I have a feeling the sooner we get this backhoe out of here the happier she'll be." I toss our empty bags in the nearby dumpster and climb back in the driver's seat.

Cora still isn't back by the time we're done for the day, which has me a little worried because the hike she's doing shouldn't be taking this long. I can't say that without drawing attention to my concern, so instead, I bite my tongue and head into town with Deacon for dinner.

We park on Main Street and start making our way to the bar, but as we pass our favorite outdoor patio I notice a head of light hair sitting at a corner table. I tell Deacon I'll meet up with him shortly and make my way over.

Cora's head is buried in a book, an empty glass on the table in front of her. The light is starting to fade, and there's a chill in the air, but she seems oblivious to it all. Until I pull out the chair next to her and she jumps, the scrape of the metal legs interrupting her concentration.

"Hey, Solo. You always do your reading in public or were you just avoiding the house?" I spin the chair so it's facing away from the table and climb on backwards.

"I like to read outside and it was a little noisy there. You probably want your truck," she starts to dig in her pack for the keys.

"If you give me back the keys, how will you get home?" I stop her.

"The bus?"

"Is that a question?" I cock an eyebrow.

She starts to answer then stops, and I know I've caught her.

"You don't know which bus to take." I can't stop the grin that pulls at my lip. There are several ways to play this, and all of them will endear her to me.

"I can figure it out," she grumbles, looking around to get her bearings. A small shiver ripples through her.

"I'm sure you could. But fortunately, you don't have to. Not tonight, anyway," I shrug out of the flannel shirt I'm wearing over my t-shirt and hand it to her. She hesitates a moment before accepting.

"What's tonight?" she threads her arms through the sleeves and wraps the shirt tightly around her.

"I'd say you could join me for a drink," I smile when she gasps, "but I already know you won't. So, I'm here to tell you to keep the keys. Until next week anyway. I can't get the trailer moved until then."

"I can't keep your truck all weekend," her eyes grow dark, like the color of chocolate, when she frowns.

"It's that or get a drink with me now and I'll drive you home later." I rest my forearms on the side of the chair and lean forward.

"Again with the hospitable stuff?" She rolls her eyes despite the corner of her mouth creeping upward. My persistence is getting to her.

"Just giving you the options as I see them."

"I'm not dressed for a night out." She looks down at her attire.

"It's Katah Vista, there's no dress code." Somehow, I manage to keep my eyes on hers instead of dwelling on how cute she looks wrapped in my clothes.

"Hey Cade, get you anything?" Lennon, the owner of this fine establishment, ruffles my hair from behind.

"Hi Len, busy today?" I drag my eyes away from Cora's and turn to look at her. The smirk she's wearing tells me she's angling for the scoop. Not to be left out, Tiff picks that opportune moment to join us.

"The usual," Lennon sighs. "Who's your friend?"

I'm tempted to be vague, to play with Cora's head since she obviously doesn't know my history with these women. But her little frown has me intrigued, so I decide to go easy on her. "This is Cora, Rick Gerome's niece. Cora, this is Lennon, the owner of Murphy's Pub, and Tiff, the little sister I never had."

Cora's eyes bug out for a second before she regains her composure and shakes their hands. "It's nice to meet you," she says.

"You're staying at Rick's place over the summer?" Tiff asks. "I always did like that house. Somehow it looks both spacious and cozy at the same time," she babbles, bubbly as always.

"That's the perfect way to describe it," Cora marvels.

"Well, Cade and his dad do good work." I dodge Lennon's hand as she reaches for my hair again.

"You built the house?" Cora gawks at me.

"My dad did, but I worked on it quite a bit, yeah," I nod. "I guess that makes now a good time for you to apologize for wondering why on earth Rick would hire me to work on his latest project," I bait her.

"I didn't wonder that." A sweet pink flush creeps over her cheeks.

"Yeah, you did. But I probably would've too if someone blocked my car in on the first day," I wink.

"Oh, Cade." Tiff shakes her head at me. "Is that why she's driving your truck?"

"How did you...?" Cora starts.

"Small town," Lennon answers before Cora can finish.

"It was an honest mistake." I look up at the ladies to make my case. "I thought Cora wasn't getting here until next week, so I didn't expect anyone to need the car."

"I guess that makes sense, seeing as how it's been sitting in the drive for so long," Tiff laughs.

"Exactly," I agree.

I can see the moment our exchange registers for Cora, because she stops pressing her lips together and lets them sort of fall open. Fuck, they look so soft, I have the sudden urge to touch them. Instead, I turn to Tiff.

"Thanks Tiff. Up until just now Cora couldn't understand how I'd be stupid enough to block in the car." I wink at her again.

"I didn't. I mean I never..." she starts to protest then abruptly looks down at the table.

"It's okay." I let her off the hook. "I should have double checked before parking the trailer."

Cora's face is so flushed it's almost the color of a cherry, making it hard to see her freckles, but I kind of like it. I don't usually see women blush, probably because the ones using a guy for his dick aren't likely to embarrass easily, but now that I'm watching it, it's fucking adorable.

"So, can I get you guys anything?" Lennon asks again.

I cast my eyes toward Cora. She's still too flustered to actually look at me. "How 'bout just the check?"

"You got it." She turns to head toward the bar, Tiff bouncing after her. Thank   god. Though neither of them mean any harm, they're chatty, and I don't need them chatting to the whole town about my conversation with Cora.

"So, what do you say, Solo? Are you coming for a drink or are you headed home?"

"Um." She bites her lip, still too embarrassed to look up.

I really want to cup her chin and force her to look at me so she knows there's no hard feelings, but I've already pushed the boundaries by giving her my shirt, and if I touch her in full view of everyone here the looking out for her excuse will be shot. Instead, I stand up and toss a few bills on the table. If I'm short, Tiff will just add it to my tab, and I'll settle it at the end of the month like I always do.

"I'll be at The Underground if you change your mind. See you around."

***

Despite being in a basement, The Underground is pretty spacious, with high ceilings and a half moon bar in the middle of the room. It is dark, there aren't any windows or anything, but I kind of like it that way.

The Underground draws a good mix of tourists and locals. There aren't any places specifically for one or the other, but there are a few places the tourists don't really know about, so if you aren't in the mood for small talk with a stranger you can go to one of those. Every once in a while I hit those up, but mostly I go wherever I can find some familiar and new faces. On a given day that usually makes The Underground my preferred spot, especially with Deacon in town, because he's looking for a good time. But tonight, I'm not as into it as I usually am. I'm too distracted wondering how long it will take for the pink to fade from Cora's cheeks, and whether she'll surprise me by showing up.

I spot Deacon at the bar, slowly sipping his beer as he watches the crowd. I know he's hoping to see the bachelorette party one more time before they leave tomorrow, but chances are they won't be in until later, if they make it at all. They were pretty hammered last night.

"Find your truck?" He slides the extra beer he ordered toward me.

"Sorta." I take a sip. "I told her to keep it through the weekend though, since I can't move the trailer before then."

He nods.

Dex, the bartender and owner of the joint, makes his way over to us. I have no idea if Dex is his first name, last name or a nickname, even though he's lived here nearly a decade. He's only ever referred to himself as Dex. He's probably the friendliest guy in town, but he's also pretty imposing, so no one presses him. "Who's the girl?" he wipes the moisture from Deacon's glass off the bar.

I knew this was coming, but sometimes it'd be nice to keep some things to myself for a change. To be anonymous.

I stare at him blankly.

He cocks an eyebrow.

"I'm just messing with you." It's pointless to play dumb, both about who she is and why she has my truck. Dex isn't a gossip by nature, but he practically lives in this bar, so he's surrounded by talk. That means I need to be careful about what I say. "She's Rick Gerome's niece. I blocked the Subaru in the drive thinking she didn't get here until next week, so I loaned her my truck."

"She's here all summer?" He grabs a lime and a knife from the counter.

"Supposed to be." I sip my beer.

"What for?"

It occurs to me then that I have no idea what Cora's doing here, and I'm not sure how I feel about that. Usually, I don't take much interest in what a pretty woman is doing in town—they aren't around long enough for me to care—but I've probably talked to Cora more than anyone else has, and I have no idea what her plans are.

She doesn't have a job in town, and given that she's related to Rick, she probably doesn't need one. On the surface that means she's here for some fun, but she's turned me down for that twice. Plus, usually when girls come here for fun they come in packs, not by themselves. Is she hiding from something? Someone? Why else would she be here all alone?

"Not sure. She's pretty quiet. Kind of independent." That much I know is true, I just don't know why.

"Hmm." Dex nods absently.

I sip my beer.

"She's a looker." He studies my reaction.

"Yep," I agree. It'd be futile not to. "But we're supposed to keep an eye on her so she's off limits to everyone."

"Too bad." Dex shakes his head and goes back to cutting limes. "Don't get many women that pretty around here." Just like that he moves on from the subject of Cora, but his comments play on repeat in my mind. No one will buy that I'm looking out for her if I don't know why she's here, only now I want that question answered for myself, not because it's part of my ruse.

Chapter 4

Cora

I spend the weekend locked in the house for two reasons. One, since the guys didn't work over the weekend, I had two whole days with no distractions to break my concentration, and that allowed me to make some good progress on my thesis. And two, I was too embarrassed to even think about leaving.

I'm well aware that news travels in a small town, and a new person would probably draw attention. But a new person driving Cade's truck even after she accused him of being stupid enough to leave her without a car—well, I didn't want to face that.

Between coming from money and living in Uncle Rick's miniature mansion for the summer, I look like a spoiled rich girl, and the way I regarded Cade a few days ago probably only ads to that assumption. Yes, I was kind of standoffish in the beginning because it's obvious he's trouble, and I didn't want to encourage him. But I never meant to be downright rude or superior, and I don't know how to make it right.

Taking him up on his offer to show me around could work, assuming he'd even want to after I judged him so poorly, but that idea still has me a little leery. I'm way too attracted to that man to trust myself in his company for an extended length of time, even knowing that I wouldn't be the first or last girl to cave to his charms.

I could clean his truck for him, if I knew where to find a car wash, or even just a hose and a bucket, which I don't. Buying something is always an option, though that requires leaving the house, and it would just make it look like I was buying his forgiveness. What else is there?

All I know about him is he works construction, drives a truck, likes to flirt, and would give you the shirt off his back, literally, which I'm somewhat ashamed to say I wore all weekend because it holds his woodsy scent. But none of that answers the question of how to say sorry I acted like an entitled bitch.

By the time Monday morning rolls around I haven't come up with a solution, and for lack of ideas I go with the old adage about the way to a man's heart being through his stomach. Not that I want to get to his heart or anything, but maybe going through his belly is a good way to make an apology.

I hear voices in the backyard just before eight, and spot Cade and Deacon walking the property. Cade seems to be pointing out different spots in the yard, maybe where they're supposed to dig, and Deacon is nodding along. I guess it's now or never.

The guys stop cold when they see me approach and give me a puzzled stare. Shit, this feels really awkward now.

"Um, hey. Thanks again for the truck and I'm sorry about the mix up with the trailer last week. I should've realized you had no way of knowing I'd need the car. So, I uh, made breakfast, if you want it." I hold out the tray of food.

Cade's blue eyes roam over me, curious and somewhat amused. His cousin is the first to recover. "Sweet, I only had cereal this morning." He comes to me and grabs one of the burritos and tears into the foil wrapper. "They're still warm. Breakfast on the job, hot coffee," he takes a mug, "man, I love this town."

Cade stalks forward slowly, studying me. He hasn't said anything, so I can't tell if he's still mad, and that makes me nervous. I'm pretty sure I'm blushing under his gaze. Hopefully, since it's pretty chilly, he'll attribute my color to the air and not my mounting embarrassment.

"Thanks, Solo." He takes the tray from my hands.

"Solo?" his cousin asks around bites.

"Cora," I correct.

"Deacon."

"Why don't you head back inside?" Cade nods his head toward the door.

Wow. Okay, still mad. I feel like I've been dismissed from my own yard. Maybe I deserve that? But my feet won't move. I was sort of hoping for him to acknowledge my apology, if not forgive me altogether. My words must've been more insulting than I realized.

Cade sets the tray on the ground and turns back to face me. "You frozen in place or too bundled to move?" His eyes roam over me and the wintery clothes I'm wearing.

"I...what?" I stutter.

"You're shivering. You're not used to the weather here, so there's no need to stay out here and turn blue while we eat. I'll bring this back later." It occurs to me then that I am shivering, which only adds to my embarrassment since the two men are standing outside in little more than jeans and Henleys. I nod silently and turn back to the house, feeling like even more of an outsider than I did just a few minutes ago.

Back indoors, I straighten up the kitchen then curl up on the couch with my book, because my mind is too riled to concentrate. Clearly, I'm not Cade's favorite person, which is bound to be an issue considering he'll be working on the house damn near every day, and I can't avoid him all summer. If every exchange is going to be as awkward as the one we just had, then avoiding him should be the goal. Why does that thought make me feel sad?

I'm not here to socialize or make friends. I'm here to work, ideally without the distractions I'd have if I was back home. For the most part I haven't had many, which is good. It's what I wanted. Although truth be told, the distractions Cade has provided have been some of the most interesting parts of my stay so far.

Even though talking to him sort of infuriates me, it makes me feel alive, too. Yeah, he's cocky and somewhat arrogant, but he's also kind of considerate. Endearing. It's clear underneath the cocky exterior is a genuinely nice guy, and while I don't want to get too close to him, I don't want him to be a stranger either. After all, he's basically the only person I know here.

No one has been unfriendly, far from it, but no one has offered more than a few pleasantries either. While I thought that's what I wanted, after talking to Cade a few times I realize some conversation is nice. If the person I'm most likely to see every day doesn't want to talk to me, who else is there?

A knock on the door jogs me back to the present. I make my way to the back door, expecting to see the tray sitting on the stoop, but instead I find myself facing Cade, tray in hand.

"Okay to come in?" he asks.

Dumbfounded, I take a step back to give him room. He carries the tray to the sink and sets it down.

"Thanks for breakfast. That was a nice surprise."

"Sure. Yeah. Glad you liked it." I shut the door and wring my hands together.

"I loved it. I don't usually get a hot breakfast before work. You didn't have to go through all that trouble over the truck." He rests his hip against the counter.

He loved it? He didn't seem so excited when I brought it out.

"It wasn't trouble." I pretend to study my hands so they aren't hanging awkwardly by my side. "And it wasn't just about the truck. I mean, I know breakfast doesn't really make up for implying it was stupid to block the car, but I really am sorry for the mix up with the trailer."

"Why would you have to make up for anything? Did you think I was upset?" His gentle tone gives me the courage to look at him.

"Yes."

"And you wanted to make it up to me with breakfast?" He sounds astonished.

My stomach does a little flip. I'm not sure if that's because he's making me nervous or because he's staring at me kind of in awe.

"I wasn't sure what else you'd like." I offer a little half shrug.

"No one's ever made me breakfast before." He smiles, not one of those panty melting ones but a genuine, appreciative smile. "But it really is fine. I'm not upset."

"You rushed me back inside earlier." I point a finger at him.

"You were cold." He stands up straight and crosses his arms, which makes his shirt pull tight across his chest.

"And you paid my bill and left me sitting at the café on Friday."

"After I invited you to come to the bar, Solo." Those deep blue eyes dare me to disagree.

"You were serious about that?" My jaw drops. "I'd just insulted you in front of the whole town."

"Insulted me?" He laughs, throwing his head back. "Did you run around telling everyone what an idiot I was to block your car in?"

"Well, no." I draw my brows together.

"Did you even tell anyone why you were driving my truck?"

"No."

"Then how did you insult me?" He grins, entertained. That's not the reaction I was expecting.

"I insulted you because I *did* think it was stupid to block the car. Up until I found out it had been sitting there unused for weeks." I feel myself blushing under his gaze.

"It was stupid. I knew you were coming but I didn't really pay attention to when. Blocking the car is on me. You shouldn't be worrying about something I brought on myself." He shoves his hands in his pockets with an amused grin.

"Yeah, but then I drove your truck around, and everyone saw me, so I might as well have run around telling everyone what happened." I avert my eyes, tucking a lock of hair behind my ear when it falls in my face

"This town has seen me do worse than block a car in the drive and lend my truck out, trust me." He smirks. Then without warning he turns serious, "Is that why you stayed hidden away all weekend?"

"What?" *How did he guess that?*

"I know you didn't leave the house all weekend or someone would've told me they saw my truck. Did you shut yourself in here because you thought I was upset?"

He's looking at me with sympathy now. *Great*.

"I had work to do," I mumble without thinking. Shit, could I sound any more pathetic? I mean, I'm not usually intimidated, but thinking that the whole town would have a bad opinion about me did lead me to cower inside the house.

"What kind of work?"

"Oh, um, my thesis," I say distractedly.

"What, like for a PhD?" He looks at me curiously.

"Yes."

"Hmm. In what?" He leans back against the counter and crosses his ankles.

"Environmental Science."

"And what do you do with that?"

"Study the effect of climate change and development, find alternative energy resources, monitor the health of soil and plants..." I trail off, looking to the yard outside.

"That makes you embarrassed?"

"What? No!" My gaze snaps back to his.

"Then why are you blushing?" A hint of a smile crosses his lips, telling me I'm busted.

"I'm not used to talking about myself. And most people think it sounds boring." I chew on my lip.

"Is it boring to you?" he asks.

"No."

"Then who cares what anyone else thinks." His hair sways as he shakes his head.

"Easy for you to say," I exhale. "Your family probably isn't wondering why you'd choose to work outdoors and eat sack lunches in ratty clothes when you could have a fancy office and designer suits and wine with lunch every day." I smack my hand over my mouth as soon as the words are out.

That really makes it sound like I'm at odds with my family and I'm not. We get along great, they just don't follow why I'd choose to work outside the family business, especially in a job that doesn't offer the same luxurious perks they enjoy.

Cade chuckles. "Maybe not. But my family, hell the whole town, is probably wondering when I'm going to take an interest in running the family business instead of putting in my time and going to look for some fun. I know how it feels when there's too much outside interest in your life." He locks eyes with me and holds my gaze.

He says that so casually it sounds like it's no big deal to have people second guess your actions.

"That doesn't bother you?" I search his face for signs that this is one of his 'hospitable' moments to make me drop my guard.

"Nah. It's my life, the only person I need to worry about is me." He pushes off the counter and takes a step toward the island. "Besides, in a small town, people always have an opinion or think they know your business. You'll never survive if you let that get to you."

"Huh." I turn that over in my mind.

What he says is kind of intriguing. Although my family doesn't understand my choices, they've never disagreed with them. You could make the argument that they support them since they're paying for my education. Yet for some reason, I always feel like I have to justify myself. I guess maybe that's why I blush when talking about my degree. I wonder if people will respect my choice or think I'm wasting my time. But Cade's right, it's my time. I should spend it how I want and not worry about what anyone else thinks. Wow, who knew the town flirt could offer such great insight?

"You seem surprised. Didn't think we'd have that in common, did you?" He rests his forearms on the counter with a coy grin.

"What? No." I feel my face heating up again.

"You sure? You kind of wear what you're thinking on your face." He arches an eyebrow as he laces his fingers together.

"Fine. I was surprised you can relate." I move to the island and take a chair across from him, a silent apology for making another bad assumption.

"Why?"

"Because your conversation setting seems to be permanently on flirt. Or tease. I thought that was because you didn't take things seriously, and I expected you to make light of my feelings instead of relating to them."

"I would never make fun of how you feel," he says softly, studying his fingers.

"Not make fun of, make light of. You know, try to make me laugh or something." I wave a hand dismissively. "But you bring up a good point. You genuinely don't live your life for other people, and I respect that. I need to learn how to do that."

Now it's his turn to be surprised.

"I'm not sure taking a page out of my book is the way to go." He shakes his head slowly back and forth. A warning.

"Why not?"

"I have no real goal except enjoying life. You probably don't want to mimic that considering you're trying to earn a PhD."

"But I might enjoy my own goals more if I'm not worrying about what others think of them." I reason with a little shrug.

"Still not sure that's a good idea, Solo." He stares out the window, a distant look on his face. "The art of not giving a fuck doesn't really lead to success."

That's a weird way to look at things. Living your life for yourself doesn't mean you don't care about anything.

"I didn't say I wanted to stop caring, I just want to care less about what people think. Like you said, it's my life." I point to my chest. "If I'm happy with my choices that's all that matters."

"Yeah, okay," he relents. "Do what makes you happy. I better get back to work." He pushes himself off the counter and heads toward the back door.

"Wait," I cry and run to the table by the front door, returning with his keys. I hold them out to him, but instead of taking them he just stares blankly ahead.

"I can't get the trailer moved until tonight," he says flatly.

"I don't have anywhere to be today." I jiggle the keys.

He reluctantly takes them, his fingers brushing lightly over mine. I inhale sharply at the contact and hold my breath to see if he notices. If he does, he doesn't comment, just pockets the keys and turns toward the door.

"Thanks again for breakfast," he says quietly as he steps outside.

Chapter 5

Cade

Deacon and I make plans to meet at the town concert after work, leaving me just enough time to run home for a quick shower. That doesn't really make me feel clean, though. It only washes off what's on the surface. My insides are just as murky as they've been since this morning.

At twenty-five years old, most people are starting to make something of themselves. They've got some value beyond just swinging a hammer and showing girls a good time. I don't. Up until today, that didn't bother me, but knowing that Cora sees something of value in me gives me a sense of responsibility I've never felt before, and that has my stomach in knots.

I don't know if I'm feeling guilty that she sees something in me that isn't there, or if I'm scared she'll figure out she's wrong about me. Either way, for the first time in, maybe ever, I'm questioning the way I live my life.

Blowing out a frustrated breath, I jump in my truck and head toward town. My thoughts don't usually run this deep, and it's stressing me out. I need to relax with some good music and good beer, which they serve in the park. And food.

I swing by the market on my way to town looking for something pre-made to take with me. After grabbing a sandwich, I head for the snack aisle for some chips, nearly colliding with Cora as I round the corner. What the hell? I've lived here my whole life and never physically run into anyone, but I've yet to go a single day in her presence without running into her, like she's a damn magnet. A beautiful, captivating magnet.

"You're getting better at that, you didn't run me over this time." She smiles brightly, like she's legitimately happy to see me. *Shit*. I try to keep my own expression blank, so she can't tell I'm happy to see her too.

My first instinct is to flirt, maybe congratulate her on being able to find the market without my help and insist she'll need me for something else, but that would only invite more conversation, and I shouldn't encourage anything that will make her think I have redeeming qualities.

"Guess this old dog can still learn a few tricks. Pretty soon I won't get in your way at all." I start to walk around her.

"You're not in my way." She looks at me curiously, like I'm not making any sense. Maybe to her I'm not, but I'm trying to be good here.

"Oh, good. Well, see you around then." I nod and try again to move past her, but she stays still.

"Something wrong? You're not usually so anxious to get going." Those chocolate eyes search mine.

"Just running late." I should've realized by this point she's used to me prolonging our conversations instead of dodging them.

"Oh, okay. Bye." Her eyes drop to the ground.

She sounds disappointed. *Is she disappointed?* Before I can dwell on that further, Dex comes down the snack aisle and slaps me on the shoulder. I suddenly hate living in a town so small you can't make it out of the store without seeing someone you know.

"Is this our new neighbor?" He looks at Cora appreciatively. He'll respect the warning I gave him, but that doesn't mean he won't take note of how pretty she is.

"Yeah. Uh, Cora, this is Dex." I point to the big oaf. "He owns The Underground on Main Street. Dex this is Cora, Rick Gerome's niece." Reminding him who she's related to can't hurt.

"Welcome to Katah Vista." He holds out his hand and she shakes it. "How do you like it so far?"

"Um, fine I guess. I haven't explored much though." Her eyes cut to mine a fraction of a second before she focuses on Dex.

"Do you have anyone to show you around?" He didn't cross the line, but I know he figures if Cora does the asking he's free to say yes, so he's trying to nudge her in that direction. She's exactly his type, feminine curves, natural beauty, so I can't let that happen. I'm about to jump in when she responds.

"I'm good. If I need any help, I can always ask Cade." That makes me unreasonably happy, and it's all I can do not to let my face show it.

"Ah good." Dex's expression remains neutral, although I hear the slight disappointment in his voice. "So, you'll be joining us for the concert?"

Shit. I didn't see that one coming. Cora looks at me, her deep brown eyes searching. There's no way around it, I'll have to invite her, and if she comes, I'll have to stick close to her to keep up the ruse that I'm looking out for her. It might not be necessary since I decided not to keep her for myself, but I don't want her to latch on to anyone else. They're no better than me, so by keeping them away from her, I'd be doing a good thing.

I smile at her without any ulterior motive. "There's music in the park every Monday. You're welcome to join."

"Cade, you didn't invite her already?" Dex arches his brows. Stupid prick wants me to suffer for being the one who gets to 'look out' for her. He knows I'm more predator than protector, and that this will be hard for me. Dammit.

"I didn't think I'd get off work in time," I explain, more for Cora than for Dex. "Do you want to come? I can grab another sandwich." I hold mine up for her inspection.

Cora looks from me to her half full cart to Dex, and suddenly I know exactly what she's thinking. She's going to do the opposite of what she normally would, because she's trying to live for herself and not for other people.

Yesterday, she would've gone home to work like a good student, but today the thought of spending another night alone in that big house holds no appeal. Today, she believes a little break is okay. God, I hope following my stupid example doesn't take her too far off course.

"Yeah, I'd like that." She smiles warmly.

"Great," Dex says. "See you over there." He heads for the register, leaving me alone with Cora.

"You want to finish shopping?" I point to her cart.

"I'm not sure the food will keep in the car." She chews on her lip.

Fuck, that's adorable.

I scan the items in her cart. Nothing looks too perishable. "Remember it gets cool in the evenings, so everything you have will probably be fine. Why don't you check out and I'll get another sandwich?"

"Okay, yeah." She nods bashfully and turns the cart toward the registers.

"Anything you don't like?" I ask.

"Not really," she says over her shoulder.

"Okay. Meet you out front."

I find Cora outside and load her into my truck to drive into town. Even though it's pretty big, with just the two of us it feels confining, like we're sitting on top of each other. I focus on driving.

"What band is playing?" I feel her eyes on me as she makes small talk.

"I don't know." I keep my baby blues glued to the road, where they should be. "I never really pay much attention to who's playing since there's a different band every week, and none of them are exactly big names."

"Are they local?"

"Some." I stare straight ahead, deliberately averting my gaze from her legs. "Some are from other parts of the state, but these are free concerts, so you don't usually see a name you recognize. It's really more of a giant community picnic with background music than an actual concert."

We pull to a stop along the road a few minutes later, and Cora offers to take the food while I carry a blanket and a cooler. Curious eyes follow us as we make our way toward my usual spot, left of center stage toward the back, where most of my friends are already seated. After spreading out the blanket, we take a seat, and I point out the rest of the group.

"Deacon, you know." I point to my cousin. "Then Dex." He raises a drink in salute.

"How do you know him?"

I can't help the grin that creeps up. "Dex showed up here one day about ten years ago. He's a few years older and was already out of high school, but my friends and I kept running into him on the mountain when we'd skip class, and in exchange for showing him where to ride he'd let us hang out at the bar until the big crowds came in around nine or ten."

"How old were you?" Her eyes grow wide as she does the math.

"Fifteen. He didn't serve us or anything, but he might've pretended not to notice when we'd sneak a beer. Mostly, we just played pool and hung out somewhere other than our houses."

"Next, is Ryder." I point to the average-sized guy sitting next to Dex as the band starts playing. "He lives here but he's on the circuit, so he travels a bunch during the winter."

"Circuit?" She leans in to speak so I can hear her over the music, but I barely register her voice over the sweet scent of oranges on her skin.

"Yeah, he's a snowboard racer."

"You mean like going around the poles?" She scrunches her nose, highlighting those cute little freckles.

"More like speeding down a narrow track." I exhale to keep her scent away from me. "Blake used to be on the circuit," I point to the tall and lean guy next to Ryder, "but he blew his knee and only skis for fun now. And mountain bikes. He works at the resort on the mountain." I leave out that he works as a masseuse and likes to brag about all the hot women he gets paid to touch.

"Last, there's Finn and his wife, Ally." She follows my arm to the couple sitting to her right. "Finn works up on the mountain, and Ally has a store on Main Street. They moved here a few years back when he took over operations at the resort."

"You manage the whole mountain?" Cora's wide eyes register shock. Finn is sorta young for such a big role.

"For now." He offers a weak smile.

"The family that owns the resort is selling it, so we're expecting big changes. Any word on the new buyer?" I sit up straight so I can see Finn over Cora's head.

"Nothing confirmed, but I saw Carter Quinn here the other day."

"Whoa." Ryder whistles. "Dude's a legend."

"*Was*. Blew his knee a few years after I blew mine." Blake sips on his beer. "You thinking he might be the new buyer?" He looks at Finn.

"Family's got money." Finn nods absently.

"At least he has the right background." Ryder elbows Blake. "Guy who's raced for a living couldn't totally screw things up."

"Guy with too much of daddy's money can always screw things up." Finn shakes his head in warning.

I feel Cora's curious gaze lingering on me. "We've lived through new owners before. Some have money but no experience and let things go to shit, others throw a bunch of money toward the wrong improvements. You never know what you're gonna get," I say as I pass her a sandwich.

"No more work talk," Ally says in her mom tone. She isn't one, but she keeps us in line like she is. "Ideas for Pedal—go!"

The guys shout ideas as Cora leans closer than I'd prefer so only I can hear her question. "What's Pedal?"

"Every year there's a bike race to benefit a local charity." I prop my arms on my raised knees to keep them from brushing against hers.

"But they're talking about costumes. Don't racers have to wear a uniform, or a bib?" She frowns.

"If it were an actual race yeah, but this is one of those things where people pledge amounts based on distance. If you do five laps, you'll generate less than if you do ten laps, that sort of thing. You do as many laps as you can during the timeframe. And you can do it in teams. We usually all form a team."

Fun fact about Katah Vista, everything is done in costume. Parades, charity events, races, you name it, it's an excuse to wear something ridiculous. I'm not sure where that tradition comes from, but it's been around longer than I have and I was born here, so it's like part of the town DNA.

"You do this race?" Cora raises her thick eyebrows, astonished.

"The whole town does the race. Why do you think I wouldn't?"

"I can't picture you on a road bike." Her nose scrunches up as she tries, unsuccessfully, to picture me on a road bike, drawing my attention back to those cute little freckles.

"You got me there." I can't help grinning at her since she's right. "But this isn't a road race. Well, not entirely."

"Where do you race then, if not on the road?"

"All over." I gesture to the town around us. "Some of it's on paved road, some on gravel. And it's not a winner take all race, remember, so no one rides anything for speed. You ride for comfort. My bike has a nice comfy banana seat."

That makes her giggle.

"What's so funny over there?" Dex's booming voice interrupts.

"I was just describing my bike to Cora." I sip my beer.

"You tell her the seat's big so it can fit your giant cock?" Ryder snorts. Cora's full lips drop open.

"Is that any kind of way to talk to our new neighbor?" I glare, shaking my head as if I'm offended.

The tiny smirk Cora shoots me says she doesn't buy my act for a second, but I'm committed to my ruse. Cora's not here for a good time or looking for the local hookup, so she doesn't need to know we're that juvenile.

Ryder actually has the decency to look ashamed. "Sorry," he mumbles.

"You should join our team this year, Cora," Ally suggests. "It'd be nice not to be the only girl for a change."

"What about Lennon and Tiff?" Cora squints at me, cocking her head to the side.

"That's a big day for the restaurant. They can usually only get away for a lap or two."

"There's no other women?" She turns her focus to Ally.

"These guys are too busy playing the field to have girlfriends." She points at each of us in turn.

"There aren't a lot of women who live here full time," I correct. We're both right, but I prefer my explanation because it doesn't make me look like the player I am. Cora probably already suspects that though due to my flirting, but I'd rather not draw any more attention to that aspect of my personality than is necessary. Besides, I'm not trying to play her, and I don't want her to get the wrong idea.

Ally can't object since what I've said is partially true, so she moves on. "I was thinking a *Game of Thrones* theme this year. You'd make a perfect Khaleesi," she suggests to Cora.

"Who are you going to be then?" I ask.

"Sansa, Queen of the North." She holds out a lock of her reddish hair as if to say 'duh.'

"Sansa always wears dresses, how are you going to ride a bike like that?"

"Hmm, good point." Ally chews on her lip.

I'm waiting for her reply when I feel a tap on my arm. I turn to look at Cora, trying not to notice she's close enough that I can see every freckle on her nose.

"What is *Game of Thrones*?"

Thank God I notice the anxious look in her eye before the laugh escapes my throat, because I'm pretty sure she's embarrassed by the fact that she doesn't know what we're talking about. I cover my near miss with a little cough.

"It's a TV show on HBO. Everyone battles for throne, and it's got tons of violence, sex, and dragons. You've never heard of it?"

She gives her head a quick shake.

"I'll show you how to find it," I offer without thinking. Shit, between working at her house, the bike race, and now showing her a popular show, I'm going to have way more contact with Cora than I planned to when I left her house earlier today. But how do I change course now? She seems like she's having fun, seems interested in the bike race, and it'd make me a huge dick to discourage those things because I need to keep my distance.

"Are you sure Sansa always wore dresses?" Ally quizzes me. "She was in a few battles."

"Pretty sure." I turn my attention back to Ally to keep my mind from going into overdrive.

"What if you fluff the dress over your bike?" Deacon wonders aloud. "Like, don't sit on it so the dress covers the entire back wheel. Could that work?"

"That's a lot of material dangling over the gears." Finn shakes his head. "I don't want it getting snagged and then she crashes."

"What if you have a frame for the dress?" Cora suggests.

"Say what?" Dex's lip curls up as his brows draw together. "How do you make a frame for a dress?"

"Ooh, I know what you mean." Ally claps her hands together. "Like a hoop skirt. We could rig something to the bike itself and I could drape the dress over it when I get on. Could you build me something like that Cade?"

All inquiring eyes bore into me, but one pair just looks flat-out confused. *Great*. Keeping Cora at a distance keeps getting harder, because I can tell she wants to know more, and that means telling her something that I don't share with many people.

"I have no idea," I tell Ally honestly. "I'm not sure what a hoop skirt is, and while I could build a frame around your bike, I don't how comfortable it would be for you to ride. I'm not sure you could get on and off around the frame, or even if I can make that frame detachable so it's not permanently stuck to your bike."

"If I have to buy a cheap bike that you build a permanent frame on, I can do that. I'd probably be able to reuse it with other costumes." Ally's eyes are about ten times bigger than normal. "Maybe you could even do two, so that way Cora and I can both wear dresses."

"Whoa, slow down, Al." Finn sets his hand on his wife's leg. "This is starting to sound like a lot of work, and I'm not sure Cade has that much time to commit. The race is in a month."

Ally's face starts to fall, but being that she's Finn's wife, and a friend, I hate to disappoint her. "Tell you what," I offer. "Find me a bike to play with and I'll see what I can do. No promises though, so you better have a backup costume."

"Of course, no problem," Ally beams. She *so* won't have a backup. And now I've got my hands full with two women.

Chapter 6

Cora

The concert was fun, and I had a good time meeting new people and talking about costumes for the bike race. I'm grateful Cade took me, but I can't shake the feeling that something was off with him all night.

First, he didn't flirt. Not once. Not even a double entendre or goading me by calling me Solo. He was polite, but reserved, and I don't know what to make of that, because it's so unlike the guy I first met.

Maybe that's not fair. I barely know him, so I'm not sure I'm in a position to judge if he's not acting like himself. But ever since he brought the breakfast tray back, he seems distant, not at all like the playboy I know he is.

Oh my gosh! That's what it is. I made breakfast, and he took that as a signal that I want something with him. He did say no one had done that for him before, so he must be reading more into that than I intended. I know he's not the relationship type, and he probably assumes I am, so he must be worried I want more than he can give. God that's embarrassing. And so not true.

Yes, I find him attractive, and yes, I do kind of enjoy when he flirts because it's a nice change from the serious, pointed conversations I'm used to having with my family and my professors. But that doesn't mean I want to claim him as mine. It just means I appreciate his company. And maybe that I like looking at him, because he is easily the most attractive man I've ever seen.

Oh, who am I kidding? Hot. The man is hot. He's all hard angles and planes, but his skin looks smooth and his hair soft, and as far as I'm concerned that's exactly the way a man should look.

Yes, I appreciate the view, but that doesn't mean I want an up close and personal look. I just want things to go back to normal, or my impression of it, where he's lighthearted and fun, and gives me a mental break by making me smile or laugh, or even cringe at his relentless flirting. Only he hasn't been here in two days.

The quiet I like. It's good for my work. It's the silence I'm starting to resent. Time to get out of the house.

I make the quick drive to the trailhead for Jasper Falls. It's another moderate hike, since I'm still acclimating to the altitude, but I'm interested in it because of the water. It's one of the alternative energy sources I've been exploring.

Having grown up near the water, I can easily sit for hours just watching it. Waves crashing, rivers flowing, there's a peacefulness to it, but there's a lot of power, too. I find it fascinating. And calming. As a result, any hike that leads to water is time well spent in my book.

The trail itself is mild, because the trailhead sits at a higher elevation than the town does, so there isn't a steep grade to reach the falls. But it is rocky and uneven, which forces me to look down where I'm stepping instead of at the trees lining the path.

After about forty-five minutes, the trail spits me out at the upper rim of a secluded waterfall. By the angle of the overlook, the water appears to be coming straight out of the rock, cascading down the cliffs into a little tide pool before it makes a steep drop to the bottom. The falls are the result of melting snow, and this past winter must have seen a lot of it because this is no little trickle. I take a few pictures then find a spot on a nearby bench to have a snack and listen to the water hitting the ground below.

The sound gives me ideas about how to use it for energy, and I let my mind drift to different things I might be able to power with it. But after a while, I forget about work and just enjoy listening to music that only the outdoors can play.

I'm not sure how long I sit, lost to the sound of the falls, before I realize the sun has moved past my bench. That's my signal to get moving. I want to be back at my car long before dark.

The descent is easy enough until I get to the rockiest portion, where the ground is extremely uneven. I have to pick my way around to find solid footing, and by going slow I'm able to do just that. But as luck would have it, a rock that first feels stable wobbles when I put my full weight on it, sending me crashing to the ground. The momentary discomfort of landing on my butt is nothing compared to the stabbing pain that shoots up my ankle, and the panic that grips my chest with the realization that I might be in serious trouble.

Taking a deep breath I probe the area that already seems to be swelling, wincing when I hit the source of the injury. It's painful but tolerable, so it shouldn't prevent me from getting down the trail, thank God. I do have a first aid kit with an Ace bandage, so I tenderly wrap my foot and put it back in my shoe. It's a tight fit, though it will have to do because the terrain is too rough to make it down the trail in my sock. I get up and take a few tentative steps.

My ankle can't support my weight very well, but since there are tons of trees around it's not too difficult to find a branch I can use as a walking stick. That's the good news. The bad is that I still have about a half mile to go, and my progress is slow. I'll be lucky to make it to the car before dark.

I shuffle rather than walk, making very little ground. At dusk I can just barely make out the parking lot by the trailhead, though I still have a big descent with several switchbacks before I'm finally down. My ankle is throbbing from the exertion, and I'm debating whether it'd be better to crawl the rest of the way when I spot a familiar figure heading toward me.

"Cora, what happened?" Cade jogs toward me, his normally smooth face lined with concern.

"What are you doing here?" I gasp, shocked.

"I saw your car, figured I'd make sure you got back okay since we're losing sun."

"You saw my car? What are you doing here?" I ask, still baffled.

"I went for a bike ride after work, further down the valley. I was on the way back and saw your car. What happened?" He zeros in on my ankle and frowns.

"I twisted my ankle. It's fine." Even though it's been Cade's fault he's had to catch me several times already, I'm still embarrassed to be the cliché new girl who's always in distress, and I hate that this is shaping up to be another situation where he has to "rescue" me.

"Doesn't look fine, you can barely put weight on it." He gestures to my walking stick.

"It's, yeah...it's sore. But I'm almost down." I take a step forward but can't contain the whimper that comes with it when pain shoots up my leg.

"Stop," Cade commands as he comes to a halt before me. "You can't walk. Give me your pack and I'll carry you."

"What? You can't carry me the rest of the way." I shake my head firmly.

"It's not that far and you're not that heavy." He reaches for my pack.

"It's far enough that your arms will get tired." I twist out of his reach. As far as reasons go, I know that's weak, but I can't think of anything else to dissuade him from carrying me. And I really, really don't want to be the damsel.

"Then I'll toss you over my shoulder, Solo. One way or another I'm carrying you down this trail, so you don't do any more damage to that ankle." He points toward my foot.

I think it's because he called me Solo that I relent, feeling a little like this is the Cade from last week instead of the one from the concert.

"Fine." I shrug off my pack and he puts it on, adjusting the straps so they fit comfortably on his larger frame. Then he scoops me up, one hand cradling my lower back and the other my legs.

"Put your arms around my neck," he grunts.

"See? I'm too heavy. You're grunting."

"I'm not grunting because you're heavy," he says with gritted teeth.

He takes a step forward as I lace my hands behind his neck, trying not to notice that I can feel his chest pressed against mine.

"Then why?" I push.

"Be quiet and let me concentrate. It's getting dark and I need to watch the trail so I don't take us both out." He sets his lips in a firm line, conversation clearly over.

I can do nothing but hang on as we make our way back down, only hanging on means my face is mere inches from his, and there's no way not to notice his strong jaw, and the hint of stubble lining it. Or the breath coming out of his full lips. Or the rapid beating of his heart. My ankle may be throbbing, but that's not the only body part giving me trouble right now.

We reach the parking lot as the last of the sun fades, leaving the sky a hazy purple. Cade sets me down gently next to the car so I can lean against it while he shrugs off the pack. That's when I realize mine is the only car here.

"Where's your truck?" I swing my head around, alarmed.

"Deacon took it. I told him to go on ahead while I waited to make sure you were okay." He fishes through the bag for my keys

"I'm sorry you had to do that." I close my eyes and lean my head against the car.

"No problem." He finds the keys and unlocks the door, then holds my hands to keep me steady as I sink into the passenger seat.

"You seem to be bailing me out a lot lately. I swear I'm not usually this helpless." I pick at a speck of dirt on my pants.

"I don't think you're helpless." He slides into the driver's seat and adjusts it to suit his height. "You were managing pretty well on your own, I just helped you get down faster. Now let's get you home and take a closer look at that ankle."

We make the drive in silence, and once we're back at the house Cade insists on carrying me inside. He takes me straight to the couch and gingerly removes first my shoe, then the bandage. He cups my ankle in his hand and pushes gently to find the source of the pain.

"Sorry, Solo," he says when I wince. "I know this hurts but I need to see how bad it is before I give you anything for it. Can you handle me looking?"

I grit my teeth and nod. He gives me a weak smile then turns back to my ankle, having me point and flex my toes as best I can. I'm not sure what that tells him, but he concludes that it's probably just a sprain that will heal with rest.

He grabs me some ibuprofen for the swelling then wraps my ankle again, 'to push the swelling out' he says.

"How did you learn to do all this?" I ask as he grabs some ice from the freezer.

"Everyone in this town knows how to do this." He grabs a dish towel to wrap around the bag of ice. "Guarantee every one of us has sprained or broken something, and most of us have done enough damage to require surgery."

"Have you?"

He sets my foot on a pillow and arranges the ice around it.

"Yep. Right knee. ACL." He shows me a scar lining his kneecap. "Most everyone here has a scar just like this. Or four little circles around your kneecap. These days I think they can fix it without having to open things up."

I shudder at that. "Why does everyone have these scars?"

He sits on the couch, just beyond my bandaged foot. "Having too much fun, pushing the limits," he shrugs.

"What limits?"

"All of them," he chuckles, the corner of his lip pulling up like he's reliving some adventure. "How fast you can go downhill, what's the biggest cliff you can jump off, what's the craziest trick you can throw."

"Everyone does this?" My brows shoot sky high. He nods. "Is there something in the water I should be aware of? I don't want to be brainwashed into thinking I can do any of what you just said."

"No brainwashing. It just comes naturally the longer you stay here." He says it so matter-of-factly I think he believes it.

"I don't get it." I sink back into the cushions.

"This is the ultimate backyard." He waves his hand, I assume to encompass the land around us. "Name an activity and you can find it here. Live here and you get better and better at those activities because you can enjoy them all the time, so much so you start looking for even more challenging things to do. More ways to push your limits."

I'm fascinated by this...by him. Terrified, but fascinated. The only boundaries I've ever tested are academic, pushing myself to understand the complexities of the environment, the science that gives the planet life, and how we might benefit from that without damaging things in the process. Here it sounds like people test their physical limits, to the breaking point if I understand correctly. On the one hand I get it, pushing your limits helps you grow. On the other, is any limit really worth a physical consequence?

"Let me get this straight. You deliberately try to do things you know might lead to permanent damage, just to see if you can do them? And most everyone in this town lives the same way?"

"Yep." He smiles proudly.

"So, if I want to stay in one piece I shouldn't stay here too long?" I mean that to be a joke, but his smile fades as if I've hit a sore spot.

"You said it, Solo." He exhales deeply.

Chapter 7

Cade

Damn she's got me all mixed up.

Cora's beautiful, and yeah, I want her, the same as I've always wanted beautiful women. But no other woman has given me a reason to wonder if there's more to life, more to me, than just having a good time. That's why I felt compelled to stop and check on her when I saw her car sitting all alone by the trailhead. I thought doing that would make me a good guy. Thank goodness she brings out that urge in me, I hate to think what could've happened if I hadn't found her. Although, the relief I felt was short lived, because carrying her down the trail was pure torture.

Having her body so close to mine felt right in all the wrong ways. She was injured, hurting, and I was trying not to get a hard on. She thinks I was grunting because she's heavy? I was grunting because I liked the feel of her in my arms, her breasts brushing against my chest with each breath. Her face was inches from mine, and her sweet orange scent filled my nose. It would've been so easy to kiss her, to see if those full lips are as soft as they look, but I'd be a total asshole to kiss a woman who's injured and stuck in my arms. Didn't stop me from wanting to, though. So, that grunt had nothing to do with her weight, and everything to do with lust.

She has no idea of the effect she has on me. How could she, when I don't understand it myself? There's just something about those dark, intense eyes and those cute little freckles that I can't get enough of. I see them even when she's not around, and when she is, I find it hard to leave. Prolonging my time with her won't do either of us any good, but that doesn't stop me from wanting to.

I should get out of here. Put some distance between us since my feelings are so jumbled. But what kind of asshole leaves an injured woman alone. Though, it's only an ankle sprain, she still shouldn't be putting weight on it. That means either someone has to be around to help her, or she needs crutches.

I have crutches at my place. They're handy to keep around, because in this town someone always needs a pair. But I'll be damned if I'm going to leave her to go get them. I should, but I won't, because with the crutches there's no reason for me to stay. And I want to.

Sooner or later, when I don't have an excuse to help her out, or the summer ends, she'll be out of reach. When that happens, I'll have to let her go. So, I'll worry about the crutches tomorrow, because tonight I'm going to take what I can get. What can I say? I'm a selfish bastard. A selfish bastard sitting so close, her toes are nearly touching my forearm. Pink toes, that are cute even though they're a little puffy. Fuck.

"You hungry?" I jump off the couch. "You probably need to eat something, right?"

"Probably." She sighs. "You must be hungry too. There should be a frozen pizza in there," she calls after me as I make my way to the kitchen.

I find the pizza and preheat the oven, but instead of going back to the other room I find myself poking around the kitchen, looking for something else to do.

I'm an asshole. I'm being totally selfish. Cora's the type of person who's proud of her independence, and I'm forcing her to rely on me. I'm taking pleasure in it. I like that she needed my help to get off the trail, and that she needs me to bandage her up and cook dinner. I like that she'll need my help to move around, at least for tonight. And I really like that those gorgeous brown eyes are looking at me with respect and appreciation.

I'm not used to women looking at me that way. Sometimes Ally does, like when I said I'd help her with her bike, but that's only because I said I'd do her a favor. Every other woman who looks at me does it with lust.

For years, I enjoyed the hell out of those looks. I'd see them and my dick would twitch, knowing it was about to have some fun. It didn't matter that the one and only thing women saw in me was someone to play with during their vaca. That's all I saw in them. Truth be told, I considered myself lucky that women only looked at me with desire, because I thought that was the best way a woman could look at you. Until the first time Cora looked at me with respect. And damn if that didn't make those looks of desire feel kind of empty.

I never thought I'd say that about a woman looking at me with pure lust, but there it is. It doesn't have the same effect that it used to.

The other night I saw a woman across the room watching me, and nothing happened. My dick didn't even twitch. She was hot, exactly the type of woman I'd usually consider an easy lay, and I didn't want any part of it. I feigned food poisoning and left early, wondering what was wrong with me. But it makes sense now, because a few minutes ago, when Cora looked at me like I was her hero, I felt something. Not a twitch exactly, but something. I liked it. My dick liked it. I kind of want to feel it again, which is why I'm hiding in the kitchen.

"Did you find the pizza?" Cora calls.

"Yeah," I reply as I open the fridge, looking for something to use as an excuse for hiding out in here. Lettuce. Some vegetables. Perfect. "I thought I'd make a salad to go with it. Sound good?"

"Sounds great," she answers.

I get busy chopping things up, which keeps my mind off my weird feelings, sort of. It's a mindless task, but the fact that I'm doing it at all feels strange because I've never made a meal for a woman before. I've never wanted to.

When everything's ready, I make her a plate and carry it into the living room. I get her set up with the food on her lap, then take my seat on the couch. I'm still aware of how close we are, but at least the meal is a distraction.

"Thank you," Cora says when she's done, reaching toward the coffee table with her plate. "I didn't realize how hungry I was."

I take it from her so she doesn't have to reach too far. "Tell me if you need something. I don't want you to move any more than you have to, okay?"

"Well, um, there is one thing I need help with." Her cheeks are turning pink, but I have no idea why, until she finishes her thought. "I have to use the bathroom."

Shit. I hadn't thought about that. How the hell do I do this?

"Uh, yeah. Sure. Do you just need me to get you there, or..." I rub the back of my neck.

"I can manage if you can help me get there." She's bright red now, and I think for the first time in my life maybe I am too.

I set my plate down and bend over to pick her up, cradling her to me the same way I did coming down the trail. She wraps her arms around my neck to hold on. It feels just as nice now as it did then, and I take a deep breath to control my heartbeat, but that only makes me more aware of how sweet she smells. *Dammit.*

Since I helped build this house I know exactly where to go, and instead of heading to the hall bath I head for the master.

"Where are you going?" she asks nervously.

"The master. There's more room for me to set you down." The toilet is in a separate room in the master, but the door to access it could be used to help her keep her balance while I'm not there.

"Hold on to the doorknob for support," I tell her as I set her down. She does, and when she's got her balance, I give her my arm so she can move all the way inside. "I'll be right outside, call me when you're done."

I watch as she closes the door then wait outside the bathroom to give her some privacy. Thank God she didn't need any more help than that. I have no idea how I would've handled having to help her undress. If she'd been in those skinny jeans that girls like to wear I probably would've had to step in, but hiking pants are roomy enough that she can manage on her own.

A few minutes later, I hear the water running and peek my head around the corner. She's made it to the sink—it's only a foot or two away from the toilet so she must have hopped over there and is washing her hands. When she's done, she looks in the mirror and fusses with her hair. I'm not sure what she's trying to accomplish with that, it looks fine to me, but I guess she disagrees because she gives a little groan before she turns away and catches me watching her.

"I'm a complete wreck." She gives a nervous laugh. "Sprained ankle, wild hair. I probably spilled pizza sauce on me somewhere." Cora snags the hem of her top in her hands and examines it. Finding it marinara free, she looks back up at me with an awkward frown.

I don't know how to respond. From what I understand, most women say things like this to fish for compliments…but Cora doesn't strike me as the type. Is she nervous or worried about what I'm going to think of her? If so, I don't see it. She's fucking beautiful, and the messy hair only adds to it and makes me want to mess it up more.

I worry my bottom lip between my teeth. Part of me wants to tell her that, to put whatever is making her nervous to bed, but I know it's not a good idea. Then again, how can I not? She's staring at me with those doe eyes, waiting for me to answer her, to say *anything*.

"We must have different definitions of 'complete wreck.' In my book, wild hair is referred to as *sexy as fuck*." It's the safest response I can think of, part silly, part serious, although I'm not sure she agrees, because all she does is stare at me open-mouthed.

"All set?" I ask.

She nods, so I pick her up.

"Where to?" I look at her for direction and find those chocolate eyes looking at me intently. I should've asked that before picking her up. Her face is just inches from mine, and I realize too late that we're too close. Practically breathing each other's air. I try not to move while I wait for her to respond, only she must be doing the same, because she's almost frozen in my arms. I need to look away, but that's futile. Instead, I just stare, taking in those flushed cheeks, her plump lips, the ragged breathing. *Shit*. I'm on the verge of doing something incredibly stupid when my phone rings and we both start.

I head for the couch and set her down, grabbing the bag of ice so I can refill it.

"Hey." I grab my phone and answer, trying to shake off that moment in the bathroom as I head to the freezer for more ice.

"Where are you?" Deacon asks. "I thought we were meeting at The Underground."

I check my watch and curse. "Sorry, I got held up. Cora twisted her ankle and I had to get her back home."

"Is she okay?"

"Yeah, I think so." I dump out the now watery ice and refill the bag.

"So, you coming out?"

"Not tonight, I'm beat." I exhale.

"Okay, well, I'll see you tomorrow then?" I can hear the disappointment in his voice, but Deacon's a grown man, he'll manage without a wingman for one night.

"Sounds good." I disconnect and make my way back to the living room with the ice, covering Cora's ankle with it and propping it on the pillow before I sit down.

"Did I ruin your plans for the night?" She bites the corner of her lip.

"If by plans you mean the same thing I do almost every night that I'll probably keep doing almost every night, then yes." I wink so she knows it's all good.

"Sorry." She cracks a weak smile.

"I'm not. Gotta change things up every once in a while, you know." I return it with a grin of my own.

"So, you get one free night and this is how you spend it?" Her smile is full now, sweet.

"Can't complain about frozen pizza and ice packs. Winter is coming." I wiggle my eyebrows.

"Huh?" She studies me confused.

"Oh, I forgot. You haven't seen *Game of Thrones*. You get HBO here?"

"Yes."

"Okay." I grab the remote and find the show. "Need anything before I start? How's the ankle?"

"A little sore," she admits through clenched teeth.

I look at her foot on the pillow next to me, noting that her toes are still a little puffy. "We probably need to prop your foot higher to get that swelling out." I look around for another pillow just as Cora starts to shift positions. "Are you uncomfortable?"

"My back is a little stiff."

My hands are gently lifting the pillow under her ankle before I can give them permission. "Scoot toward me and lay back." She has no choice but to follow my lead, scooting toward me so her foot is resting on the pillow in my lap. I try not to focus on the sigh I hear as I press play.

***

The brown eyed princess fades from my view as the sunlight pulls me from my dream. I don't usually remember my dreams, and if I do, I usually can't make sense of them. As the room comes into focus, I understand exactly what was in my head. I'm still on the couch, Cora's small foot resting on my lap, *Game of Thrones* playing on the TV in front of us. Well, that's better than thinking my brain conjured up a princess out of nowhere.

My back is stiff from sleeping upright, and I stretch as slowly as possible so I don't disturb Cora, who's breathing deeply beside me. She looks so soft and innocent snuggled on the couch, her hands curled beneath her chin. The corner of her lip ticks up, almost like she's trying to smile, and I catch myself doing the same as I watch her, wondering what she's dreaming about. For a brief second, I wish I was lying next to her so I could breathe in her orange scent, but I shake my head to clear the thought before it can stick. I should be thinking about how to keep my distance instead of wishing I could get closer, especially after staying the night.

I look around the room for a clock, curious about the time. The sun is up, but its overcast, making it hard to guess the hour. I lean back as far as the couch will allow and fish my phone out of my pocket. Just after seven. I text Deacon to grab me some clothes and the crutches from my garage since there's no point going home before coming back here to work.

The weight in my lap shifts and I turn my attention to Cora. Her eyes flutter a few times before she winces, telling me her ankle is still tender. I reach out my hand to steady her but think better of it and pull back, because I'm not even sure she realizes I'm here.

"Morning," I say softly. She stiffens, like she's surprised to hear my voice, then relaxes when her eyes connect with mine. I like that too much.

"How's the ankle?" I ask.

"Sore," she whispers.

"Can I take a look?"

She nods.

I gently lift her leg and take off the bandage. The swelling has gone down some, and its slightly discolored, but not the nasty shade of purple I was expecting. That's a good sign.

"Looks like we got some of the swelling down, and it's not bruised." I turn her ankle slowly to get a good look while trying not to notice how soft her skin feels on my fingers. "The sprain itself probably wasn't that bad but walking on it after didn't help. You should keep it up when you're sitting and put some ice on it throughout the day. Overall, though, it looks pretty good."

I re-wrap her foot, then stand and offer her my hands. "Think you can put weight on it?"

She puts her hands in mine and pulls herself to stand, gingerly setting her bad foot on the ground. As she shifts her weight to the injured foot, she grits her teeth.

"Looks like we should keep you off it another day or two," I say more to myself than to her.

"How?"

"There's probably an old pair of crutches at my place. I asked Deacon to see if he can find them before he comes over."

"Okay." She pulls her bottom lip under her teeth. "Do I have time to clean up before he gets here?"

"You don't need to clean up for Deacon," I say, mildly annoyed.

"Not for him." She rolls her eyes. "For everyone he'll tell about me needing to be rescued. I can't change the fact that I was helpless last night, but I don't have to look the part."

I don't think she needs to do anything, but those brown eyes are pleading, and I know that's because her independence is important to her.

"You're catching on to how things work around here." I give her a wink of approval.

I carry her first to her room so she can get fresh clothes, then to the bathroom so she can clean up. Holding her isn't necessary—she could've hopped along—but I can't seem to stop myself from milking every opportunity to be close to her. While she's busy, I brew a pot of coffee and scramble some eggs, and when she hollers that she's done I bring her to the kitchen for breakfast, sitting her at the breakfast bar with her leg propped on a nearby stool.

"You didn't have to do this." She flushes as she takes in the plate of food before her.

"We've gotta eat." I shrug.

"You've done so much already. I never meant for you to have to take care of me like this." She blinks sheepishly.

"I don't mind," I reply, hoping my tone doesn't convey that I actually enjoy taking care of her. Just in case I change the subject. "Did you see any of the show last night?"

"I think I was out before the end of the first episode. Which character did Ally say I should be?" She takes a bite of her eggs.

"Khaleesi. I'm not sure she was in the first episode. I don't think I was awake for all of it either." Before I can add anything else there's a knock at the door and I go let Deacon in.

"Wow, nice place." He whistles, taking in the walnut cabinets and stainless-steel appliances in the chef's kitchen. "Did you make breakfast again?" He looks at Cora.

"You're carrying crutches, why?" I rest my hands on my hips.

"Oh, yeah. Sorry. Can't think straight when I smell food." He grins.

I dish him a plate and he digs in while I adjust the crutches for Cora's height.

"Ever use these before?" I ask her.

"Never. But they're pretty self-explanatory, right?"

"Yep, just try not to let them rub against your armpit when you use them, the skin can get irritated. Do a quick lap and let me make sure you're good." I pass her the crutches and help her to her feet.

Cora does as I ask and makes her way around the kitchen, slow but steady. "Great. You're all set. I'm gonna change and then get to work," I tell them both as I grab my clothes from the counter where Deacon dropped them.

When I'm done, I head back to the kitchen to find that Deacon has cleaned up and is already outside. Cora is still sitting at the breakfast bar, a distant look on her face that makes me want to blow off work.

"Don't forget to ice." I remind her when her gaze meets mine.

"I won't." She nods.

I grab a piece of paper and pen from the kitchen desk and scribble my number on it. "If you need anything or if your ankle feels worse, call me." I hold out the paper.

"I'm sure it's fine. Thanks for everything." Her face turns the sweetest shade of pink as she takes it.

"I mean it, Cora." Her head snaps up when I say her name, and I take a step closer, so she has to look up at me. "I want you to call me if you need anything."

"Okay." She blinks.

"I'll check on you later. Take it easy today." I kiss the top of her head as I make my way past her, and immediately want to kick myself for it, because it was way too intimate and yet not intimate enough for the night we just shared.

Chapter 8

Cora

Holy hell. I know that kiss wasn't supposed to mean anything, but it sent shivers down my spine all the same, just like every other time Cade has touched me.

I know his intentions aren't sexual. They're all to take care of me, but the way he cradles me close to his chest when he carries me through the house, or how his fingers lightly trace over my ankle to check the sprain, well...They may not be sexual touches, but they are sensual, and they make my whole body tingle. I still don't know how I fell asleep with my body on edge like that, especially considering what happened in the bathroom.

I'm not certain, because I was admittedly tired and my ankle was uncomfortable, but I think he wanted to kiss me when he picked me up. He was staring at me so intently, almost like he was trying to make up his mind, and if we hadn't been interrupted by his phone, I think he would've. And the crazy thing is, I wanted him to.

I've been telling myself it's a bad idea to get involved with him, or anyone, when I'm here to work. Well, getting involved beyond being just friends anyway. Except, I'm having a hard time looking at him as just a friend right now. Maybe it's the way he looks at me, this crazy combination of awe and heat. Or maybe it's the way my body responds from his innocent touch. Even though he's a flirt, a playboy, and so *not* the type of guy I should be interested in, I think I'm crushing on him. I can't help it, he's unbelievably hot. But beyond that he's a good guy.

I still can't believe he came looking for me last night, and on top of that skipped his plans to take care of me. No strings attached, no ulterior motive, which I wouldn't have put past him given his flirtatious nature, but all he did was take care of me, making sure I was safe, fed, and comfortable. That's not the behavior of a guy who *'lives to have fun'* as he's told me. That's the behavior of a guy who has a good heart under that pretty, aloof shell.

So, yeah, Cade has some layers that run deep, and that should scare me, because when I thought he was nothing but a flirt, he was safe. *Fun*. Nothing that I would get hung up over. But knowing there's a big heart under the surface, well, that's dangerous. That's the kind of person I could fall for. And I can't fall for Cade. Not when my future plans don't involve staying in Katah Vista. And especially when the guy in question has a track record of being nothing more than a good time.

Still, it's hard not to imagine what it would've felt like if Cade kissed me. The way my body responds to him physically, the butterflies and tingles and racing heartbeat, who wouldn't want to experience more of that? Who wouldn't be tempted to forget, even for a night, why some things should be forbidden?

Whoa, I need to come back to reality. Just because I'm tempted by Cade doesn't mean he is by me. For all I know, he can make any woman feel like they have a moment with him, and I was just the one he happened to be with last night. That's what I need to remind myself of when my body starts to pull my brain off track. And maybe I would've, if voices hadn't drifted in through the open window, where the guys are staking out the perimeter for the new patio.

"Seriously dude," Deacon grunts. "We've gone out every night since I got here, but in the last week you've only been out twice, and you went home early. What's up?"

"I've had shit to do," Cade says.

"Like what?"

"Working on Ally's bike," he trails off.

"Pfft. Like you can't do that in a few hours," Deacon scoffs.

"I don't even know how to do it yet. I mean, what the fuck is a hoop skirt, and how do I put it on a bike?" He sounds so confused I can't help but smile.

"If you don't know what a hoop skirt is you haven't been spending time on Ally's bike," Deacon mutters.

"Well, do you know what it is?"

"Yeah, it's a skirt shaped like an umbrella that starts at your waist and goes all the way down to your feet."

"How the fuck do you know that?" Cade demands.

"I studied design."

"Landscape," Cade's frustrated voice interjects.

"You still have to take other classes. And fashion was a good class to pick up girls."

"That explains it," Cade mutters. I chuckle into my palm.

"So, why aren't you coming out with me?" Deacon demands.

"You really need me to help you pick up girls?" Cade's tone holds a challenge.

"Of course not," Deacon scoffs. "But having a wingman doesn't hurt, and I need a wingman this weekend, there's supposed to be another bachelorette party coming through. Maybe they need *entertainment*."

Bachelorette party? Entertainment? What can that mean?

"We'll see," Cade says.

"We'll see? What is wrong with you? How are you not drooling over the idea of getting your dick wet?...Oh *shit*!" Deacon's voice rises. "That's it, isn't it? You have somewhere you're already getting it wet, don't you?"

I don't realize I'm holding my breath until I hear his response.

"My business cousin." I don't have to see Cade to know his jaw is locked tight.

"Since when? You've never kept your social life secret from me before. Is it Cora? You spent the night last night. Tell me it was Cora," he presses.

I feel my jaw drop down to my toes, but apparently it didn't make a sound because the guys go right on talking.

"Don't talk about her like that," Cade warns.

"Why not? She's hot, I bet you'd love to hit that."

"Of course, she's hot. But don't you remember what I said about looking out for her? She's got shit she wants to do with her life. She's too good for the guys in this town," Cade says with authority.

Too good for the guys here? I apologized for acting like an entitled bitch, but does he still see me that way?

"Lots of women have stuff they want to do with their lives, that's never stopped you hooking up with them before," Deacon grumbles.

"Cause they wanted a hook up. Cora's better than that. If she's into a guy it's for more than his dick. And any guy that's into her better be into more than her pussy, which means no guys in this town are worthy."

Well, that's crude. And oddly *sweet*? I think?

"So that's your deal then? You like her." Deacon makes it sound like an accusation.

"Of course, I like her. Who doesn't like it when the client cooks us breakfast on the job?" Cade reasons.

"That's not what I mean and you know it."

"Fine. I *respect* her, so I'm not going to treat her the same as all the other women who roll through here. Get it?" Cade huffs.

"I get it. She doesn't want you, so you *respect* her," Deacon goads him. Cade doesn't take the bait.

"I respect that she doesn't see me as something to fuck," he says evenly.

"How do you know that?" Deacon sounds genuinely curious.

"Cora doesn't have an ulterior motive when she talks to me, she just...*talks*," Cade explains.

Huh, I thought the same thing about Cade just this morning.

"Just cause a woman won't use you to stroke her pussy, doesn't mean she doesn't want you to do it," Deacon points out.

I slap my hand over my mouth. That's actually not untrue, even though I'm trying not to go there.

"Maybe not." Cade's voice drifts softly through the window. "But I'm not going to disrespect Cora by treating her like a hookup when she doesn't treat me like one."

"Okay, cool. So, you respect Cora, which means she's not getting your dick wet, so you're free to hunt for the bachelorette party this weekend," Deacon insists.

"Damn you've got a one-track mind. How the hell are you the one with a degree when you can't even focus on work for, like, two minutes?" Cade complains.

"It's a gift."

Cade chuckles, a cross between annoyed and amused. "Well, 'give' me a hand so we can finish this and break for lunch. I need you to take me to my truck so I have a way to get out of here later."

"I can just take you home."

"I can't leave without checking on Cora and I don't want to interfere with your prowling."

"You'd rather play nurse than find someone who can deep throat? Who are you and what have you done with my cousin?" Deacon demands.

Either Cade answers too softly for me to hear, or he doesn't have one to give.

***

"Come in," I call when hear a soft knock on the door. Cade pokes his head in, his searing blue eyes seeming to relax only after they've settled on me.

"How are you feeling?" He moves toward the couch where I'm lying down, ankle propped up.

"Okay." I look at my puffy foot. "I still haven't put much weight on it yet, but the swelling is down, and it doesn't hurt as bad as it did."

"Want me to take a look?"

His touch would only bring back the tingly feeling that I shouldn't pursue, but that doesn't stop me wanting it. "Sure."

I hold my breath as Cade's fingers slide over my skin, so he doesn't see how much his touch affects me. It's so tender, and for a moment I imagine he's touching me like that because he wants to, not because my injury forces him to be gentle.

"It does look better. You've been icing it all day.".

"Yes." I nod solemnly

"Good girl." He smiles, and my heartbeat accelerates. How is it he can take care of me and turn me on at the same time? *Good grief,* I'm in danger. Is it possible to have a heart attack, triggered by your libido? I want him to stay, not to take care of me but just to be here, because the thought of being by myself seems so depressing. He's already done enough though, and having him here will make me want more than just his company.

"Thanks again for taking care of me. I really appreciate everything you've done."

"You kicking me out?" He looks at me warily, almost like he's sad I'm giving him permission to go.

"No." I shake my head. "But I know you canceled plans last night, and I don't want you to feel like you have to do that again. Or like you have to take care of me."

"We talked about that. I didn't miss anything I haven't done hundreds of times before, and I don't mind taking care of you." His blue eyes look sincere, but I'm not sure I trust them.

"You shouldn't feel like you have to," I say softly.

"I don't." His brows draw together, like he's not sure what my point is.

"Yeah, but Deacon was expecting you--" I start to remind him, before I think better of it. I'm not supposed to know, and I cringe at my slip up when his head swivels to the window that's still cracked open.

"You heard us talking." It's not a question.

"I didn't mean to." I feel the heat rising in my cheeks.

He sits on the couch, right where he slept last night, and rests his elbows on his knees. "I'm sorry." He hangs his head. "I don't feel like I have to take care of you, and I really don't mind doing it. I was just trying to make Deacon feel better about leaving him on his own. I didn't mean any offense by what I said."

"You didn't offend me."

"I was kind of crude." I see him wince even though he's still looking at the ground.

"Maybe, but I think you were trying to give me a compliment." I smile so he knows I'm not offended.

"I was." He casts a sideways glance at me, like he's uncertain of his response.

"Why?"

"Why give you a compliment?" He looks confused.

"Why do you think I'm better than the guys in this town?" I hold my breath.

"Cause I am one," he replies, like that makes all the sense in the world.

"Am I supposed to understand what that means?" I frown.

"The fact that you don't is exactly why you're too good for us." He shakes his head.

"I still don't get it." I lean forward, though I can't get any closer with my leg propped between us.

He runs a hand through his hair, like he's frustrated, or trying to decide what to say.

"Things are different here. Women are different."

"How?"

"Well, for starters there aren't many, and the ones that are here usually don't stick around for more than a season." He exhales as he sinks back into the cushions.

"Why is that?" I'm genuinely curious.

"Remember, this place is like every little boy's fantasy backyard. Guys flock here for that shit. Girls not so much." He chews on his lip, staring at the blank screen on the TV in front of us.

"Okay, so? I'm still confused by how that makes me too good for guys in this town. I like back yard stuff."

"Of course, you do," he mutters to himself. "Anyway, my point is the area has mostly male residents, so when chicks come to town, we shoot our shot and don't expect to stay around to snuggle, if you catch my drift."

"Are you saying you use female tourists for sex?" I frown.

"It's...*mutual*. The women who come here tend to be in the market," he admits, though he still doesn't look at me.

"So, you and every other guy in town have casual sex with strangers that come through and that makes you guys not worthy of me?" I borrow his term from earlier.

"Bingo." He picks at a speck of mud on his pants.

"Well, that's stupid," I blurt.

"What?" He turns to look at me and I swear his eyes are wider than normal. *Bluer.*

"You think I haven't had one-night-stands?" I balk. It's not really my thing, but I've done it, and right now I feel like saying that might be important to him.

"Uh." His eyes dart around the room as if he's looking for an escape. "I think I'm afraid to answer that," he deadpans. I can't help but laugh.

"Guys don't have the market cornered on casual sex, you know." I cross my arms and lean back against the cushion behind me.

"Well, obviously, or else we'd all be gay," he snorts. "But you don't have that look about you."

"The 'I want to use you for my pleasure look?'" By tossing his words back at him he knows exactly how much I overheard earlier.

"That's the one." He nods absently, turning his attention back to the mud on his pants.

"Like you said, it's not really my thing. But just because it's not, doesn't make me better or worse than the people who like casual sex.

Especially when those people give up a sure thing to help me." I dip my head to see if the movement will force him to look my direction.

"Are you complimenting me now?" He cocks an eyebrow in my direction.

"I am." It's impossible not to smile when he looks at me like that.

"You think I'm a sure thing?" A sexy smirk tugs at his lips.

"That wasn't the compliment." I try to scowl but I can't because that look is making me laugh. "Only you could turn a genuine compliment into something dirty."

"I'll take that as a compliment too." He winks just before he stands up. "And now that I know you appreciate my dirty humor, it's time to go before I take it too far. Besides, as you heard earlier, I have no idea how to attach a hoop skirt to a bike, and the race isn't too far off."

"Why you?" I blurt.

"Huh?" He looks confused.

"Why are you building her bike?"

"Oh," he says, and I swear he turns a little pink. "I do some welding."

"That sounds interesting."

"Yeah, I guess. Keeps me entertained." He stuffs his hands in his pockets.

Entertained. Deacon talked about entertainment earlier, and I remember thinking that was strange, but it's not my business so I leave it alone. Plus, I get the sense Cade just shared more than he intended to, and if he wants to share anything else, he can do it in his own time.

"I'd love to see your work." I hint.

"Yeah? Okay, maybe I'll show you sometime." He smiles, although this one is different. It's not laced with innuendo, it's genuine. Thoughtful.

He seems to rock forward, like he's going to come closer, but instead he gives a little jerk of his head. "Have a good night, Cora." He turns toward the door.

"You too," I call after him.

When the door clicks shut, I let out the breath I'd been holding for most of our conversation. I should be disappointed that Cade is every bit the playboy I suspected he was, but honestly, I'm not bothered. How can I be when he was so honest about it? When he let me see more of what's beneath the surface?

Chapter 9

Cade

I head straight to my garage when I get home, desperate for something to keep my mind off the things Cora said earlier, and my little studio is the perfect outlet. There's something about the process of creating things that gets you outside of your own head, which is exactly what I need right now.

Most people would look at my studio and see just clutter, but I see it as organized chaos. It's full of old tools, metal scraps, and discarded wood from our job sites, random things that I've collected and assemble for fun.

I rarely have a goal when I start messing with materials, I just look at what's available and piece it together. Sometimes it turns out to be a sculpture, sometimes a piece of furniture, but I never really know what the finished product will look like until it's done. Trying to build something specific for Ally will be a new challenge, but I'm kind of looking forward to it.

First, I have to figure out this hoop skirt thing, so I google it and scroll through the different images that come up. It really does look like a tall umbrella, and I now understand why the girls think this shape will keep their dresses from getting caught in bike gears. But to really make sure the fabric doesn't get caught I'd have to make this hoop frame just as long as the downward stroke of the pedal, which will make it difficult to even get on the bike. I have no idea how to do that just yet, but I have to admit Cora's suggestion makes a certain amount of sense now that I understand what she was saying.

And now my thoughts are back on Cora, dammit, exactly what I was hoping to prevent by coming in here to work.

I'm still freaked out by that conversation we had at her house tonight. I had no idea she could overhear Deacon and I talking, and if there's any conversation I didn't want her privy to it was that one. I mean, not only did Deacon allude to my fondness for pussy, I specifically mentioned *her* pussy. Just knowing some of what she heard makes me cringe, and I'm stunned she wasn't pissed by it. I'm even more shocked she doesn't seem to hold it against me.

Of all the things we could talk about, tourists using me for my dick was the last topic I thought we'd cover. It's like all she has to do is look at me intently and all my secrets pour out, and then she fucking compliments me for them. That's why I had to get out of there, because the one secret I can't share is that I'm starting to like her. *A lot.*

I've never known anyone like her before. Someone who doesn't judge, who sees things in me I don't even see in myself, who talks to me without an ulterior motive and wants to know more about me. She wants to see my welding for God's sake. No woman has ever asked to see that before. No woman I've slept with even knows it's my hobby.

That never used to bother me. I mean, it's not like knowing stuff about each other is a requirement for making them come. Anatomy is anatomy and once you learn how to make one squirm, you can make them all. Not knowing about their personal lives is what makes everything casual and keeps the strings *unattached*. But I have to admit, knowing that Cora doesn't like, but has had casual sex makes me even more curious about her. Why doesn't she? Did she have a bad experience with it? Is it some kind of moral or ethical choice? Or does she know something I don't, like maybe there's something *better* than casual sex. Like actually knowing someone, or gasp, actually liking them changes the game.

Okay, now I've officially lost it. Casual sex has always worked for me and there's no need to question that now. I need to get my shit together and stop thinking about stuff I can't have.

I grab a pad of paper and a pencil and start doodling. After several false starts I hit on a design that sort of resembles an oversize birdcage covering the back half of the bike. If I could create an opening that swings on hinges, maybe there's a way Ally could open the frame and still climb on the bike. She'd have to fluff her dress over the birdcage part as she climbs on, but in theory that would keep the material from hitting the gears. It's not exactly pretty, but it could work.

The problem is distributing the weight evenly, so the finished bike isn't off balance. Plus, I have to make sure the extra framework doesn't make the bike so heavy Ally can't pedal it. This is not going to be an easy project, not only because I'm winging it, but because I don't know if I can get the right materials to make it happen. Ideally, I could use old bike parts, but it's not like those are in huge supply. I'll probably have to swing by the local shops to see if they have anything they can donate to the cause. It's too late to go scavenging now though, so I work on my sketch to help me pinpoint some of the materials I'll need.

***

A few days of rain kept us from getting much done at the Gerome place, which means I've successfully put some distance between me and Cora. That hasn't stopped me thinking about her and questioning why easy hookups suddenly don't sound so appealing.

I go for a morning ride to get outside and clear my head, pedaling one of my favorite trails that weaves through a giant field of wildflowers before dropping into the trees. I've ridden it so many times I practically float over the terrain, which is oddly peaceful despite the fact that I'm moving at a pretty good clip. After wearing my body down, I shower and head into town for lunch and a quick beer, then hit up the bike shops to see if they have any more scraps I can pick up.

I strike out at the first shop but have some good luck at the second, scoring a few busted pieces off a frame made from carbon fiber. That's the ideal material, its durable but lightweight, and it's usually expensive as fuck, but since the bike it's on is beyond repair the tech lets me have it just to get it out of his way. I promise to bring him a six-pack next time I swing by, a typical thank you for hooking someone up in this town, then start making my way back to the truck. But I have to pass Ally's store to get there, and she doesn't let me sneak by.

"What's that you've got?" she asks as she comes to stand in the doorway. I head up the walkway, holding out my find for her review.

"Well, miss Ally, this here might be part of that bike you want me to build you," I tease her.

"Ooh!" She claps her hands together. "I knew you'd figure it out. How long until it's done?"

"Hold up." I put my hand up to stop her little celebration. "I'm still not sure I can get it to work, so don't get your heart set on that dress costume."

"You'll figure it out, I know it," she insists, completely ignoring my warning as she turns to head back inside. "Speaking of, think there's any way you can build more?" She casts a mischievous smile over her shoulder, because even though she knows it's a ridiculous request she's still asking.

"Hell no." I follow her inside to the register, where Lennon's sitting with a cup of coffee. "I'll be lucky to finish yours. Why, does Lennon need a dress?"

She gives a curt shake of her head. "Nah, I'll be working."

"I'm surprised you aren't doing that now." Girl works way too much.

"Coffee break." She holds up her mug as if she has to prove her point.

"Who else needs a dress then?" I turn to Ally.

"Well, most of the male characters wear capes, and Khaleesi wears a dress a lot too." She rests her arms on the counter and leans forward, smiling with exaggerated sweetness.

"Yeah, but Khaleesi doesn't *have* to wear a dress and in this instance she can't, because I can't make another bike that fast. I barely have enough parts to make yours," I remind her.

"But wouldn't Cora look great as Khaleesi in a dress?" Ally pouts. An image of Cora in one of those sexy warrior dresses flashes before my eyes, and I have to agree it's an appealing sight. But I can't admit that to Ally.

"I don't know." I shrug. "All I know is I can't build another bike so everyone else is in pants. Got it?"

"Fine." Ally plops into a chair next to Lennon behind the counter. "Is your costume ready?"

"I don't know, is it?" I cross my arms and pin her with an expectant look.

"Why are you asking me?"

"Because you assigned everyone a role. And because I'm making your bike, so you can make my costume." I point at her and smirk.

"Ugh, fine, I'll get you a costume. Want to be Drago with your princess?" She sits up straight, eyes fucking twinkling with excitement. I swear Lennon's eyes get bigger as she registers Ally's enthusiasm.

"I don't have a princess." I lean my hip on the counter, dismissing that comment with what I hope is indifference. "And I may be tall, but I'm not three hundred pounds of muscle like Drago. Make me something else."

"No." She shakes her head, studying me with a critical eye. "I've seen you without a shirt, you can pull off a slim version of Drago."

"I'm not doing a couples costume with Cora." I give her a hard look.

"Who said anything about couples? This is a group costume. Although it's interesting your mind went to couples. I thought there was something between you at the concert." She bites the corner of her lip and gives me a knowing grin.

"There was nothing between us." I shake my head firmly. "I'm one of about five people she knows here, nothing else."

"So, you didn't spend the night at her place the other night?" Lennon prods. Damn Deacon and his habit of getting dinner at Murphy's.

"I took care of her after she sprained an ankle, and I slept on the couch," I ignore the unspoken plea for gossip, leaving out the part that Cora slept on the couch too.

"And I bet you did that out of the goodness of your heart." Lennon lays her palm on her chest, mocking me. She knows me too well.

"Of course," I deadpan without taking the bait. Tiff is the only one who can successfully bait me. "When have I ever not helped a friend in need?"

"Touche." Lennon grins, because that's actually true. "Speaking of, isn't that your friend headed this way?" I turn as she gestures to the large window overlooking the sidewalk where Cora is passing by. Shit. Any hope of her missing us is dashed when Ally darts for the door.

"Hey, Cora. Just the girl I wanted to see. Come here so we can talk about your costume." Ally beams.

Cora starts at the sound of her name, then smiles brightly when she recognizes Ally. I swear my breath hitches just a bit when I see that toothy grin. It's so...*real*.

"Hi," Cora breathes as she steps inside and sees me for the first time in days.

"All better?" I ask, since she seems to be walking just fine. Plus, those are the only words I can safely say in front of Ally.

"I think so. Better enough for a few errands anyway." She bites her lip sheepishly, like she should've got my okay before walking on it. *Fuck*, she's adorable.

I catch the girls watching our exchange too closely. "Good. Well, I'll leave you guys to it." I push off the counter and nod as I pass by her, almost making it to the door before Ally reaches out and grabs my arm, halting my getaway.

"No way. You have to help."

"Help with what?" I cringe, resisting the urge to yank my arm free.

"Picking costumes. I have a few options for both of you." She pushes Cora and I further into her shop. I grit my teeth and head back to my spot at the counter, which gives me a clear view of Cora taking in the shop. She wanders around, admiring the odd garment, oblivious to the wicked smile Ally's sporting as she pulls things from the racks.

"Cade's being difficult and says he can't make two bikes so I can't put you in a dress." She rolls her eyes dramatically, trying to make me jump to impress Cora. When I don't budge, she turns back to the racks. Cora smiles at me apologetically, like it's her fault Ally is berating me even though we both know it isn't, which makes me like her even more.

"These pants with this top, and these pants with this top." Ally instructs as she hands Cora two options. "Dressing room is through there." She points to a little cubby with a curtain hanging in front of it.

Once Cora is tucked inside Ally turns to me. "Your turn," she says brightly.

"What can you possibly have for me in here?" I balk. "This is a woman's store. Besides, all I need is a pair of pants, right?"

"Not just any pants." She shakes her head as she rifles through the racks, yanking something brownish off the hook and thrusting it at me triumphantly. "Suede pants. They were supposed to be *in* last winter, but I didn't sell many. These are one of the biggest sizes I carry so they might actually fit around the waist."

I hold them up to me, realizing she might be right about that. "What about the length, they barely go below my knees."

"So, we'll put you in boots. That'll totally work for Drago." She gives me a once over, envisioning the final look.

I check the tag on the pants. *Holy shit!* "I'm not paying a hundred bucks for this goofy costume," I protest.

"Of course, you're not," she assures me. "These haven't sold in ages so I might as well just put them to good use and give them to you."

I'm about to object again when Cora comes out of the dressing room in a pair of skintight cream pants and a sleeveless blue top that does sort of resemble a classic Khaleesi outfit. It's not revealing in the least, but it hugs every curve like it was made for her, and I'm helpless to ignore how long and lean her legs look in those pants, and the swell of her breasts under that top. I take a deep breath and will my body not to react.

"What do you think?" Ally turns to me. I'm uncomfortably aware of all three women studying me, waiting for my response.

It takes me a second to find my voice. "That's a pretty good option," I choke out.

"Your turn." Ally pushes me toward the dressing room, giving me a much-needed excuse to leave the room. I offer Cora an apologetic smile as I squeeze past her. She gives me one back, which makes me feel a little better about this whole thing.

I pull the curtain closed and strip out of my clothes to pull on the suede pants, trying not to focus on the scent of oranges that lingers on Cora's clothes, or the hint of pink lace I can see poking out from where those clothes are hanging on a nearby hook.

The pants actually fit well in the waist but are a bit baggy in the legs and only come down to around my calves. I have an overwhelming urge to strangle Ally as I look at myself in the mirror, and decide I'm done playing her little game. But before I can change back she yells that I'm taking too long and demands I come out. Fuck it.

"Nice try, Ally, but there's no way this will work. I look like a half-naked German soldier, and no way I'm doing a race like that."

Ally circles me, inspecting the pants. "I can fix that. I can take out the extra material in the thigh so they don't balloon out, maybe loosen them in the calf so they hang flat," she says mostly to herself as she tugs and pulls at the pants. I chance a look at Cora, expecting to see her fighting a laugh over this ridiculous outfit, but instead her eyes seem glued to my waist, where Ally's currently fussing with the pants. And instead of laughter I swear I see something like interest, or desire. It's the first time Cora's looked at me like she wants me, and even though

I like that she hasn't looked at me that way before, I really like that she is now.

"Can I take these off now?" I grumble, desperate to get away from Cora's gaze.

"Let me mark the alterations first. Cora, why don't you try on the next outfit?"

Cora scrambles into the dressing room while Ally sticks pins in the pants, turning me toward the dressing room while she works. That's why I'm staring right in Cora's direction when she comes out again, wearing a pair of pants similar to the ones I have on, but with a tiny scrap of a top that shows off her smooth shoulders and flat stomach. It's a sexy look without taking away from her sweetness, exactly how the character she's mimicking first appeared in the show. Suddenly, Khaleesi is my favorite character of all time, which has nothing to do with the actress that played her and everything to do with Cora. I have a feeling that from here on out, every time I watch an episode of *Game of Thrones*, I'll see Cora telling John Snow to bend the knee.

Fuck, I'd bend the knee if she asked me to.

Cora freezes the moment her eyes find me, and I watch her gaze linger briefly on my hips before traveling up my stomach and over my chest. I feel her stare skimming over me like she's touching me, tracing the planes of my skin. It makes me hot and tingly at the same time, like some overeager teenager with no restraint. I hold my breath and will my cock to stay still, because there's no denying that I like the way she's looking at me. A lot. And I really like the way her breasts rise and fall as her gaze travels over my body, like she's imagining what it would feel like to touch me, same as I am her. And if I'm looking at her anywhere near how she's looking at me, I have a feeling we're on a collision course.

I have an overwhelming urge to touch her, even now, with Ally and Lennon standing right here, which I might have done if Ally hadn't snapped me out of my trance.

"Oh wow. You two look perfect, like you actually belong in the desert with Drago's tribe. Do you see it?" she asks Lennon.

"Spot on." Lennon grins over the top of her coffee mug, her raised brows daring me to disagree.

"Cora hasn't seen *Game of Thrones,* she doesn't know what we're supposed to look like." My voice sounds kind of hoarse in my ears.

"Well, actually, I watched a few episodes this week, and yeah, this could work." She gestures between us as her cheeks turn pink.

"Excellent." Ally beams, evidently proud of both her work and her little setup.

She dismisses Cora, who makes a beeline for the dressing room to change, and once she's out of sight I finally get a full breath. Holy shit that was intense. I've never been so on edge just looking at a woman, or watching a woman look at me, which is crazy cause lots of women have looked at me before, and it never had this effect. The girls are smirking at me. I guess I'm not the only one who felt the tension just now.

"I give it another day. Maybe two," Ally says softly.

"What?" I rest my hands on my hips.

"You know." She pins me with a look that says, 'don't bullshit me.'

"Nope," I whisper, shaking my head. "No way. I'm not going there. She's a sweet girl."

"So?" Lennon arches an eyebrow.

"So, I have no business getting involved with a sweet girl," I grit.

"That sweet girl wants you." Ally ignores the warning in my tone.

"If she does, it's because you paraded me around half-naked in front of her," I hiss.

"I don't think it is." Lennon shakes her head. "She was into you before she got a look at you shirtless. And I'm guessing you know that, since you went out of your way not to talk to her."

"I didn't do that," I object, but before I can say anything else Cora emerges from the dressing room. She avoids eye contact as she makes her way to the counter, though her cheeks are still flushed. I offer a weak smile as I pass her and take my turn changing, getting into normal clothes as quickly as possible.

Why would Lennon say I avoided talking to her? I asked how she was doing, told her the costume looked good, I think. There wasn't much else to say, especially in front of an audience. And Cora didn't say much either, so how am I the one that avoided talking?

When I come back out, Cora's gone, which I'm both relieved and disappointed by. I toss the pants to Ally and tell her I'll trade the bike for them when we're done, effectively ending all conversation. Much as I love them, whatever I say to the girls will be repeated to Finn and Tiff at minimum, and I'm still not ready for them, much less the town, to know my business.

Ally doesn't let me off that easily. "Sweet might be good for you," she calls as I shut the door.

Chapter 10

Cora

I'm going to get whiplash trying to keep up with Cade's moods. One day he's flirty and mischievous, the next sweet and caring, the next virtually indifferent with an undertone of lust. I know that doesn't make sense, but that's Cade in a nutshell. Nothing he does makes any sort of sense to me. And the worst part, instead of running away from that confusion the way I should, I find myself wanting to run to it. To figure it out. As if I could.

I put my bags in the trunk and shut it just as Cade strolls into the parking lot, which makes my heartbeat accelerate. A quick glance down the aisle and I see his truck parked a few spaces away. Strange I didn't notice that until now. Although admittedly I was a little distracted by the memory of his bare chest and the thoughts it inspired.

I'd seen him without a shirt before, the second time he knocked me over, and I remember thinking then that he had a great body. But I wasn't focused on that because my guard was up. I saw a guy who knew he was hot, liked to flirt, and I assumed that was the extent of him. I judged him by how he looked and decided I didn't need to know any more. But after getting to know him a bit, after learning some of who he is and realizing the flirty playboy is only a part of the whole package,

I'm not afraid of noticing how amazing his body is. I'm not afraid of what that might lead to. Nervous maybe, but not afraid. I'm actually a little curious about it.

Cade stops cold when he sees me, briefly, and I can't tell if the look on his face is one of relief or unease. But it's gone before I can decipher it, and he strolls slowly forward and meets me at my car.

"You survived your first costume fitting with Ally," he teases.

I know this is Cade's way of talking without talking, because flirting is common ground for him, but I'll take it over the stilted conversation in the store.

"That's a common occurrence?" I fight the urge to smile.

"At least three or four times a year." His blonde hair sways gently as he nods.

"What can you possibly have to dress up for so often?" I laugh.

"The bike race, Fourth of July, Halloween." He ticks off his fingers with a sly grin as he goes. "This town likes its costumes."

"I'm not sure if that's sweet or concerning." I bite my lip, taking in what looks like part of a bike dangling from his hand.

"A little of both, probably."

"And you dress up for all of them?" I search my brain for any memory of costumes during my past visits but come up empty.

"Ally would have our heads if we didn't."

"What did you do before Ally?"

"Huh?" He cocks his head.

"You said she and her husband moved here not long ago. What did you do before you had a costume designer?" I joke.

"Probably wore the same costume for everything, I guess." The bike floats up as he shrugs.

"That's part of her costume?" I gesture toward the bundle of metal in his hand.

"Maybe, I don't have it completely figured out yet. But the hoop skirt suggestion gave me some ideas, once I figured out what that was." He rubs the back of his neck.

"Can I see it?" I'm legitimately curious about what he's doing, but I also want to keep talking to him, since he's at least talking right now.

My request catches him off guard. I can see him debating what to say, and it makes me wonder if it's too personal. But that's silly. He already told me he does some welding, and no one at the concert seemed surprised when Ally asked if he could build her bike. So why is he wavering?

"Yeah, sure." He finally exhales, and I let out the breath I didn't realize I'd been holding. "You can follow me."

We pull out of the lot and I follow him to a neighborhood about five minutes out of town. The houses are smaller her and feel homier than where my uncle's house is. That neighborhood is for vacationers, people that want space and quiet to relax, and this place has more of a community feel, with a park around the corner, and kids running everywhere.

We pull up to a cute little bungalow with a front porch spanning the length of the house, and a long drive leading to a garage in the back. Cade gets out of the truck and starts heading to toward it. There's a regular door to the side of the garage doors, and he holds it open for me to walk inside.

There are high and low cabinets around the perimeter, with what looks like a butcher block counter covering the low cabinets, although it's hard to tell under all the tools resting on it. There's also a massive table in the middle of the space, with several stools underneath it. I recognize the mask you wear when welding, and what I think is the welder itself, but nothing else looks familiar. It's just a random bunch of parts and pieces, although it does look like things are grouped together by size and shape.

In the corner closest to the garage door, it looks like there are several finished pieces. One resembles something like the tin man from Wizard of Oz, only rounder, because it's made with mostly gears and pipe and standing on a block of wood. It also looks like there's a bench of some kind. A bike frame with a bustle of sorts is resting against the center table, and I'm guessing this must be his creation for Ally.

"It's, uh, kind of a mess." He clears a space at the table. "I don't have many people in here."

That statement makes my heart flutter, but I try to ignore it.

"Shouldn't it be a mess?" I ask as I take in the clutter. "I mean, a clean workshop would mean there wasn't much work, right?"

The corner of his mouth ticks up like he's fighting a smile. "True, but this isn't work. This is just messing around."

I wander over to the man made of gears and look to Cade for permission. He nods, and I pick it up, turning it over in my hands to see all of it. It's not overly large, a little over a foot tall, but its heavy. Solid. There's one large gear for the torso and a smaller one for the head. Straight rods are used for the arms and legs, but they're put together at angles that suggest movement, like the little man is waving his arms as he strolls along, or maybe dancing. Even though there's no real expression coming from the gears it feels like this portly man is happy.

"You like it?" Cade asks.

"I do," I mutter, tilting it to look from another angle.

"Why?"

"He looks like he's enjoying life," I say without thinking, then immediately backtrack. "I mean, I know that sounds stupid, it's just a bunch of gears. But he looks sort of fat and happy." I shrug, thoroughly embarrassed.

When I finally meet Cade's eyes, I find he's staring at me intently.

"What?" I laugh nervously.

"That reminds me of my grandpa. Fat and happy is a good way to describe him." He shakes his head, almost like he's confused. Or amused. I can't tell which.

He takes the sculpture from me and turns it over in his hands, studying it. "He was a tinkerer, hence the gears, and the older he got the fatter he got, which he blamed on my grandma's cooking. But he was always moving. Always smiling. He's the one who taught me how to weld."

"He sounds interesting."

"He is. He lived here until he started to have trouble breathing and had to move to a lower elevation. Left me this house and his workshop when he moved..." he trails off, looking around the room before his eyes come to rest on the sculpture in his hands, then me.

Suddenly, the air around us is so thick with emotion I can't breathe. The way Cade's looking at the sculpture, at me, is overwhelming, and I don't know how to react. So, I grasp at the first thing that comes to mind.

"Show me the bike," I blurt.

His gaze lingers on me for a few seconds before he puts the fat man down and turns to the bike. "I was going for sort of a birdcage, like a frame that drapes over the back half of the bike, but that didn't leave much room for Ally to get on. I thought about a door that could swing open on hinges, but that would trap her on it," he rubs his hand over the back of his neck, which I now understand is his way of working through what's on his mind as he speaks.

"Right now, I think I've got it so the dress can rest on this frame and not get caught in the tires, but I still think I need something for the side of the bike to keep it from getting caught in the gears." He sighs heavily, looking at his work.

"I think it looks good so far." I inspect the frame. "Like a bustle."

"A what?" He looks at me curiously.

"A bustle. It's that thing that makes it look like a woman's butt juts out behind her." I mime the silhouette of a bustle with my hand, but all I get is a curious and slightly intrigued look. "You know, Cinderella," I prompt. Still nothing.

I pull out my phone and google bustles, showing Cade the images that come up. He looks between those and the frame he's added to the bike and cracks a smile. "I guess it does kind of look like that. And now your little," he waves his hand behind his butt, "makes sense." He laughs.

"Cinderella wasn't a good reference?" I squint up at him.

"Not for an only male child, no." He shakes his head with an amused grin.

"So, what's left then?" I gesture to the bike.

"Ah, I guess a few more supports for this bustle, but maybe lower so Ally's whole leg isn't caged in," he rubs the back of his neck again. "I won't really know until I get something on there."

"Can I watch you? I mean, if you're going to do something now?"

"I'm not ready to put anything on the bike yet, but I can show you something else, if you just want to see how it works," he offers.

"Yes," I practically shout. He chuckles.

"Ok, gimmie a sec to see what I have to work with." He digs through different drawers, picking out some gears and what looks like pieces of thin metal pipe. One long piece he leaves straight, but the shorter ones he puts through some sort of press so they start to bend. When he's got everything where he wants it, he grabs a stool and sits down as he places the mask on his head.

"Best not to come any closer." He warns as he gives his head a little jerk and the mask falls over his eyes. There's something about the casual movement that makes my stomach flutter, and I kind of want him to lift the mask up so he has to do it again. Then he turns on the welder, and it's hard to see anything else.

He positions two pieces of metal together and holds a third tiny sliver of metal above them. The welder seems to melt it, binding the separate pieces along the seam he's creating. He repeats the process over and over, attaching smaller curved pieces of metal to the one longer piece. The garage heats up as he goes, but I don't notice the temperature because I'm so focused on his hands.

They're covered with bulky gloves, but they're steady, moving almost delicately to avoid missing a spot or straying off course. He's absolutely still except for his hands, and I don't know if that's how it always is or if it's because he's working with small materials.

The process is slow, but not so slow that I can't see it come together. The smaller pieces sticking off the large straight piece sort of resemble leaves, and I'm guessing he intends to use the large gear as a flower. When he raises his helmet, I'm almost disappointed, because I really want to see the finished product. Then I notice the spark in his eye, and I feel my heartbeat pick up.

"Want to try?" He holds the tools out.

"Me?" I squeak. "But it's so pretty. I don't want to mess up your flower."

"You won't mess it up, I'll help you."

He hands me a pair of gloves and an apron of sorts and adjusts a mask to fit my head. Then he guides me to the stool and stands behind me, placing the welder in my hand. I try to breathe normally with him pressed against my back, but there's no stopping my heartbeat from accelerating, which it seems to do every time he gets close.

"We're going to attach the stem to the back of this gear. The gear is our base metal, and this is our bond." He gives me a sliver of metal like what he was melting earlier. "We're going to bond the stem to the gear. Hold the bond metal where we're going to connect the two, and we'll melt that to join the two pieces together. Got it?"

I nod, and the mask drops down to cover my face. It wasn't intentional, but it makes him laugh. "Why do I get the feeling you're going to be a natural at this?" I catch his grin right before his own mask falls into place.

Cade turns the machine on and positions his hands over mine to help keep them steady. Together we move the bond metal to the parts we want to stick together. The heat coming off the welder makes the room stuffy, and it's kind of nerve wracking to see sparks flying around as we work, but welding is kind of a rush, and I'm almost giddy when I see that the two pieces we forged together do resemble a flower.

"Wow." I lift the front of the mask for a better look.

"Nice work." He admires our effort while I take off the gloves and flex my hands. "I've never made a flower before, but it turned out pretty well."

"You've never done this before?" I hold up the flower.

"Nope."

"What do you usually make then?"

"Whatever comes to mind." He takes his own mask and gloves off and goes to hang them on the far wall. "I just take what I have available and piece things together for fun. The bike is the first thing I've done with an end goal in mind."

"So, this flower just came to you from looking at what was lying around the shop?" I marvel.

"Yeah." He shoves his hands in his pockets.

"I can't imagine looking at a bunch of different parts and putting them together to make something new," I compliment him.

"They don't always turn out this nice," he chuckles. "Half the stuff I throw out because it never turns into anything. But sometimes I get lucky and things fall into place."

"Like your grandpa sculpture?" I tease, except Cade must not see the humor because his expression turns thoughtful. Somber.

"Exactly like that," he says softly, almost distantly, except the look in his eyes is anything but distant. Its penetrating, seeming to look inside me instead of at me. I feel self-conscious under his gaze, but not because of its intensity. Because of its uncertainty, like he doesn't totally understand what's happening, and doesn't know what to do about it.

I'm helpless to do anything but return his stare. I don't know what's happening either. I can't explain why being with him feels so comfortable after such a short time, why his past doesn't scare me, or why he seems to open up to me in a way I don't think he does with others. So, we stand there, suspended in time, just watching each other. Waiting.

I have no idea how to move. What to say. It's too late to pretend this hasn't turned into a moment, but I don't know what to do about it. So, I wait, until he finally takes a step. And another. And another. Until he's standing right in front of me, and I have to look up to see into his cloudy blue eyes.

"You know, you're the first person to see a happy guy in those gears." He takes the mask off my head and sets it on the table.

"I am?" My heart is beating so loud I barely hear my own response. He's so close, towering over me. I almost feel like prey. But the look in his eyes isn't menacing. It's gentle.

"You see a lot of things other people miss, don't you?" he says more to himself than to me.

"What do you mean?" I exhale a shaky breath.

"Situations, people." He tucks a stray lock of hair behind my ear. "You see into them. Just don't be fooled by what you think you see in me. It's not real."

"What do you think I see?" I search his murky gaze.

"Something that isn't there," he says softly. "I'm not as good as you want me to be."

"You want me to believe a guy who's honest and fun, who takes care of the people around him, including a woman he just met, is bad?" I dare him to explain away his attributes.

"A guy who's only ever used women for sex is bad." The words are spoken without emotion, but the look on his face is sad. Almost regretful.

"That's not who you are." I shake my head.

"It is," he insists, fingering my hair again. "You just don't want to believe that about me."

"I believe using women for sex is something you've done. That doesn't mean it's all you are," I say softly.

"How can you be sure? You barely know me." He searches my eyes, looking for the lie, I think.

"I know enough," I whisper.

"Saying shit like that about me makes me want to believe it." He rests his forehead against mine. "It makes me want to kiss you, even though I shouldn't."

"I won't stop you." I breathe, because right now there's nothing I want more.

Cade pulls back slightly and cups my face in his hands, brushing his thumbs over my cheeks. His blue eyes are filled with a mixture of wonder and lust, so intense my breath catches in my throat. He traces his thumb gently over my lower lip. I close my eyes and sigh, and then I feel Cade's lips on mine, soft and sweet. His kiss is tender, almost reverent, like this is a dream he doesn't want to wake from, so he's careful not to move too quickly.

"Fuck you taste good," he mumbles against my mouth. "So sweet. So, fucking soft."

His words are dirty and endearing at the same time, and hearing them makes me gasp. Cade takes advantage, flicking his tongue against my lip to coax mine out. His strokes are light, the barest of friction, yet the most fulfilling kiss I've ever experienced.

I assumed Cade would be a good kisser, but I expected those kisses to be passionate. Hungry. Not slow and gentle, like he's savoring the contact. Savoring *me*.

Cade's mouth brushes delicately over mine as his hands caress my cheeks, my jaw, my throat. His touch is sensual, patient, like he could spend hours doing nothing more than exploring my mouth, learning my taste.

I've never been kissed like this before. Never been made to feel cherished, like my touch is a precious gift, but that's exactly what Cade's doing to me right now, making me feel as though kissing me is the most profound sensation he's ever experienced.

It's profound for me to, so intense and intimate I can't contain the emotion building inside me. I sigh, a lustful, dreamy little exhale that makes Cade freeze and pull back slowly. His jaw is locked tight as his eyes roam over my face, lingering briefly on my lips before meeting my gaze, searching. Waiting. His breathing is shallow, like it's taking all his energy to stay in control, and while the gentle exploration we just shared was perfect on so many levels, it's no longer enough. I want more. I break our stare to look at his lips, and his restraint evaporates.

Cade lifts me off the stool and sets me on the table, putting my face level with his. He casts my apron aside and spreads my legs wide so he can step between them, pressing our bodies together as he crushes his mouth to mine. He moves urgently, hungrily, threading his fingers in my hair and tilting my head where he wants it so his tongue can slide against mine. This is the passion I expected from a man with his experience, and while I don't want to think about how he got that experience, I'm not complaining about its benefits.

Whereas our first kiss was sweet and tender, this kiss is carnal. Demanding. Lips and tongues and teeth clashing together furiously now that we've given into our desire. Both kisses are intense in their own way, but while Cade had me melting earlier, he now has me burning up.

His mouth clings to mine, his tongue stroking feverishly against my own, coaxing a moan from deep in my throat. He responds in kind, deepening the kiss.

I slide my hands up his arms, over his shoulders, into his hair, relishing the feel of the soft strands sliding through my fingers. I swear he growls under my touch, clutching my head in his hands and pulling me closer.

Heat explodes through my body, traveling from my mouth, past my chest, and settling between my legs. It's been several months since I felt the sweet ache of desire, sensed the press of a man's erection on my center. I rock my hips forward to relieve the pressure building there and feel the extent of Cade's need. Flames shoot through me as I grind against his length, the friction causing me to moan against his mouth. I want more of that.

I rock forward again and...

Cade utters a strangled groan and steps back so our bodies are no longer pressed together, although he's still holding my head in his hands. He presses his forehead to mine.

"Fuck, Cora," he pants. "I wasn't supposed to do that. You shouldn't have let me touch you."

"I wanted you to touch me." I heave, just as breathless. "I want you to keep touching me."

I feel his head shake slightly. "Don't say that to me. It's hard enough to resist you as is."

"Why resist?" I gasp.

"You know why." He traces his fingers along my cheeks.

"I don't." I shake my head.

"Yes, you do. Your first instinct about me was the right one." He drops his hands and takes a step back.

"What are you talking about?" I frown.

"You thought I was an outrageous flirt. Don't deny it," he adds when I start to shake my head. "I know what you saw. It's what everyone sees. And you were right not to. Just because you see more than a flirt doesn't make me good for you. I fuck people for fun, nothing more. You deserve better."

"You didn't kiss me like it was just for fun," I protest.

I can tell I've tripped him up because he doesn't answer right away. He seems to be reliving that kiss, what it meant. But either it meant nothing, or he doesn't want to acknowledge it did, because he shakes his head dismissively and says, "It was just a kiss. I've got a lot of experience with that," he adds for effect.

That comment was meant to sting, but it doesn't make me hurt as much as he intends. It makes me sad, because I know it's his way of trying to make me see him like he sees himself. What he doesn't understand is that I can't unsee the good parts of him. It doesn't matter what he says to push me away, I'll still see the whole picture instead of the parts he thinks I should focus on.

I want to make him understand that, but I know years of being regarded as a plaything have conditioned him to believe that's all he is, and it will take time for him to trust that I really do see more than that. If I push him tonight, he'll just retreat further, so while it breaks my heart to see him doubt himself, or think that he made a mistake by touching me, the best thing I can do now is leave. But I won't leave quietly.

"If you have that much experience kissing then you should recognize the difference between simply touching your lips to someone else's and tasting them. Getting lost in them. I know the difference. Make sure you do before you make decisions about what I deserve."

Cade's eyes track me miserably as I get my bag and head for the door. I don't know if my words make any sense to him, but I do know that was not the kiss you give someone for casual fun. Now, I have to help him understand that.

Chapter 11

Cade

As soon as she's gone, I lean back against the counter and rub my hands over my face. That was...I have no fucking idea what that was. Impulsive. Insane. *Perfect*.

I've kissed girls before, lots of times, but it's usually a meaningless prelude to other things. A warm-up to get the blood flowing. Once the clothes start coming off it's done, because there's other things to do with your mouth. And let's be honest, casual hookups aren't about kissing, they're about coming, so it never meant much to me. *Until now.*

I never knew kissing could be so intense, especially the soft, slow kind. I totally got lost in it, forgetting all the reasons I shouldn't be doing it and focusing only on the feel of her lips on mine, soft and plump and perfect. I think I could've left it like that, slow and sweet, all night. It was hot, yeah, but not in the sense that it made me want to race ahead to the good stuff. I didn't know kisses could be like that, and in some ways, I liked it even more than the urgent, hungry kissing we shared. And that was definitely everything I hoped it would be.

If I thought slow and sweet was hot, well, urgent and needy was hot as fuck. That one did make me want to get to the good stuff, but only because it got me so hard so fast, not because I wanted to skip the kissing and go straight to getting naked.

Usually that's the way it works for me, a little hot and heavy necking to get things running and then plunging deep into whoever I'm with. But with Cora I liked feeling turned on without the urge to take it further. Just feeling aroused, feeling her pressed up against me while we devoured each other, I could've done that all night too.

So, yeah. I know we didn't just kiss. It was more than that, like Cora said. What I can't figure out is why she didn't storm out when I said it wasn't anything special.

That was shitty of me, but it was the only thing I could think of to get her to take me off the damn pedestal she put me on. I tried telling her it was a mistake to think of me as a good guy, but the stubborn woman didn't listen, and for a second, she made me believe she was right. Being the selfish prick I am, I don't regret that, because it led to the hottest kiss of my life. Hell, I think it ruined me. But I'll just have to consider myself lucky that I got to touch her at all, because it can't happen again. And that's what really scares me.

Cora said she wanted me to touch her, and that's a temptation that will be hard to ignore. I'm actually shocked I was able to stop myself just now, and I'm not sure I can do it again, which is why I can't even let it start. I have zero idea how I'm going to accomplish that since I'll be seeing her again in just a few short hours. Fuck my life.

***

There's a ton of work happening at the Gerome house today. Deacon has a few guys working on the new patio, and I've got a crew framing the garage and laundry room, which we're trying to have done by the end of the week. We're not off schedule, but it's not impossible to get the occasional snow in June, and the faster we work now the better we can accommodate weather delays that might come up.

The activity is good because as long as I'm moving or concentrating on the job I can't think about Cora. Plus, I suspect the increased number of bodies on site is keeping her inside. I know this reprieve won't last indefinitely, but for today I'll take it.

These are the kind of days when I love what I do. Sunny but not scorching, a group of guys laughing and joking while we work, music playing in the background. It's part social while still getting shit done. These are also the kind of days that make me dread taking over the company one day.

If I'm the guy in charge, I won't get to have these days often. I'll be checking in at different job sites to make sure things are going smoothly, spending more time in my truck than outside. I'll have to manage paperwork shit, like insurance and payroll and scheduling. At some point, I'll even have to be the one trying to solicit work.

I'm not afraid of those tasks, but I'm afraid of them taking the fun out of what I do. I actually like building stuff, whether it's houses or the tinkering I do in my studio, I like working with my hands and making something out of parts and pieces. I especially love doing that outside and with a group of guys who keep me entertained. The boss doesn't get those perks, so if I have it my way, I won't be stepping into that role for as long as possible.

I know the town thinks I'm either too lazy or too focused on having fun to take work seriously, and they assume that's why I haven't taken an interest in running things. That's not *entirely* true, but their opinions didn't bother me enough that I felt like I had to correct them. I've never had someone to anyone to answer to or impress, so what was the point? Let them confuse my preference for working with my hands as a lack of motivation, it didn't matter to me. Still doesn't, truth be told. Except when it comes to Cora.

She makes me want to care, because even though I know I'm not good for her I don't want her to think I'm a total fuck up. I don't want her, a girl who comes from money but is busting her ass to build a career, to think I got my job handed to me and I'm going to ride my dad's success for a living. I don't know why it's important to me that she doesn't see a total screw up when she looks at me. Maybe I don't want her to be embarrassed about being attracted to me. Who knows? But for some reason I don't want to be the lazy local guy in her eyes, which means I'm actually starting to think about what comes next. Whether I'm ready to give up days like today in order to take a bigger role in the company.

Fuck, this woman has me in knots, and all I've done is kiss her. I need to get it together. Nothing is going to change today, or tomorrow, or maybe even this summer. I just need to concentrate on the job and try to enjoy it like I usually do.

By the time four o'clock rolls around, we've made enough progress that I feel comfortable letting the guys go. There's enough daylight left that they can do something outside, and since that's why we live here I want to give them the opportunity to enjoy it. Besides, it makes for a happier crew when you give them a break here and there.

We get everything packed up and I head out with the last of the guys, so I'm not left on site alone. I do a quick ride myself, because floating over the trail on a bike has a way of quieting my mind, then head into town for the weekly concert.

I make my way to the crews' usual spot and come to a halt. Cora's sitting on a blanket next to Ally, and now I really am fucked. Why did I ever introduce her to my friends?

I take a seat between Deacon and Dex and we shoot the shit about which trails are open—since some of the higher ones aren't accessible until enough snow melts—and which we've ridden recently. This is usually one of my favorite conversations, but I'm only half listening, because the rest of the time I'm trying to eavesdrop on the girls.

For the most part, they aren't saying anything interesting. Something about the clothes in Ally's store, and maybe going on a hike later in the week. Then Ally has to go and bring up the bike race.

"Okay guys, only two weeks left until the race. Did you all finish your registration?"

There's a chorus of yesses.

"We have to register?" Cora's freckles group together as she scrunches her nose.

"Of course, it's a race," Ally replies.

"I thought it was for charity, not a real race."

"It is, but you still have to register. I think that's where most of the money comes from because the town is too small to really get a bunch of people pledging money for laps. Most of them ride in the race anyway, so they aren't going to pledge money toward someone else's laps."

"Oh, I guess that makes sense. How do I register?" She looks around the group for input.

"I'll take care of it," Dex offers, and I feel my whole body constrict.

"You don't have to do that." Cora smiles sweetly.

"I don't mind. You register at the post office and that's right next to the bar. I can do it tomorrow," he says casually.

Okay, that makes sense, but it still has me on edge. I told everyone I was keeping an eye on her, so Dex shouldn't have volunteered. But I can't object without causing a scene, so I pick up a blade of grass and pretend to study it while I stew quietly.

"Perfect." Ally claps. "I've ordered stuff for the costumes. Deacon and Ryder have tunics, and Finn, Dex and Blake get cloaks. I'm thinking we don't need to worry about cloaks getting caught in the bike since they're not closed in the front, make sense?" she asks no one in particular, but I know it's her way of asking me in case it means more welding.

"Should be okay," I concede.

"Great. And I'm still good on the dress for Sansa?" she prods.

"I'm on track. But don't get your hopes up that it'll be comfortable or pretty. It's strictly for function," I warn, because if there's one thing I know about Ally, it's that she likes things to look good, and this will not meet her standards.

"I thought it looked good," Cora volunteers, and I swear you could hear a pin drop even with the band playing in the background. *Great*.

"You saw it?" Ally gasps.

"Yeah, why?" Cora's oblivious to the eyes pinned on her.

"Cade doesn't show his stuff to anyone," Deacon says. *Traitor*. "Not unless its finished, and even then, he might not."

Though technically true, I don't keep people out because I'm sensitive or embarrassed about the work, I just don't invite them in because it's my place to unwind when I can't get outdoors, or when I need quiet. It's not off limits, but I don't encourage visitors either.

Cora looks at me with wide, guilty eyes, like she just divulged some taboo secret. She didn't, but the others will make a big deal of her being to the studio. I want to be pissed, because I don't need that drama, but it's not her fault. All I can do is try to diffuse this.

"I don't show you my stuff cause none of you has ever asked to see it," I say dismissively.

"Not true." Dex shakes his head. "I've asked if several pieces in your house were your work."

"You have." I nod, my jaw firm, a silent warning to drop it. "But you never asked to see what I'm working on."

"Semantics," he huffs.

"None of you like the studio." I try a different tactic. "You think it's hot and cluttered."

"That is true." Ally chews on her lip, throwing me a bone. "It's stuffy and kind of smells."

And now Ally's bike has earned some more of my attention, to see if I can make it look a little nicer.

"Well, what if I want to see then?" Deacon puts me on the spot.

"You don't need an invitation."

"How come Cora got one?" Damn, he's ornery today. I wonder what's got him so hung up on this.

I sneak a glance at Cora and find her staring at the ground, her cheeks flushed a deep pink color. I hate that she's embarrassed, but I like seeing her blush.

"She didn't. She asked to see it. And it was her idea how to build the damn thing anyway, so it made sense for her to take a look." I pin him with a glare that says, "back off."

"So, the bike is almost ready?" Ally gets us back on track, but I don't miss the way her eyes study me and Deacon.

"Yeah, almost ready," I soften my tone. "When you get your dress come over and you can try it."

Ally squeals and claps her hands, and it's hard not to smile at her excitement. She may be nosy, but she's good for a laugh.

"Hey." Finn waves his hand to get my attention and jerks his head toward the sidewalk. "Is that who I think it is?"

Deacon, Dex and I all turn in the direction he indicated. A dark-haired man is walking hurriedly past the park, giving everyone in his path a wide berth and avoiding all eye contact. Since no one is ever in a hurry in this town, there's only one explanation. He doesn't want to be noticed. But as a former professional ski racer and rumored new owner of the resort, he's out of luck.

"Sure, looks like it. I guess the rumors are true, huh?" I shoot Finn a questioning look.

"Don't look at me." He holds his hands up in front of him. "They don't tell me anything."

"You're the Director of Operations," Deacon calls bullshit.

"That means I make sure the lifts are running, the mountain gets groomed each night and enough employees are scheduled each day. They don't include me in anything else, including whether they're really gonna sell the place."

"I don't think we have to speculate about that anymore." I watch Carter Quinn as he fades in the distance, hoping he's up for the task ahead.

When the concert is over, Dex bribes us all with a free drink if we go to the bar, so he doesn't have to go by himself. I know he loves his job, but I'm sure it's hard to go off to work by yourself after hanging out with friends, especially when the night is still pretty young, and especially on a Monday, which usually isn't a busy night.

We all take seats at the bar and sip on our drinks while Dex does some housekeeping, washing glasses and stocking bottles. It's pretty laid back for about thirty minutes, when out of nowhere a group of twenty or so comes in. It's a mix of men and women, all in their early twenties, and no sooner do they step inside, Deacon cozys up to the cutest ones in the bunch. Without thinking, I jump behind the bar to help Dex with the rush, something I've done before when he unexpectedly gets slammed.

"Crap, the photography club," Finn moans. "I totally forgot they were in town. Sorry, man," he tells Dex.

It's not unusual for different organizations to have conferences or meetings in town, although it is a little early in the season for that. Finn usually gives Dex a heads up, since he works on the mountain and knows the big events coming up, but this one must've slipped his mind. It's no big deal, I don't mind slinging drinks once in a while, and it's good business for Dex. I do hope they make it an early night because that was my original plan.

The first several orders are easy, guys asking for beers, but the ladies are more indecisive. That doesn't bother me except for the fact that my idiot cousin is pushing some of them at me and making absurd suggestions about what they should order.

"My cousin makes a great Sex on the Beach," he tells one brunette.

"We aren't on the beach," she giggles.

"He could give you a Quick Fuck if you prefer." He winks at her.

"That's actually a drink?" A nearby blonde asks.

"Is it?" Deacon grins at me, daring me to object.

"Maybe the lady would be more comfortable with a Cosmo," I say, because it doesn't suggest anything, and it's easy to make.

"Where's the fun in that?" Deacon scoffs. "But you've made me rethink, cousin. We should make sure these ladies have Wet Pussys before we give them a Quick Fuck."

"Are we still talking about drinks, or what comes after?" The brunette bites her lip suggestively.

"Either. Or both," Deacon grins wickedly.

Dammit. A few weeks ago, I would've been totally into this scene and gearing up for what comes next, but right now I couldn't be more bored. I suppose the two women Deacon's entertaining are good looking, but neither of them do anything for me. Nada. Zilch...And honestly, I don't feel like flirting with them. With the way Deacon's throwing out sexy drink names it certainly seems like that's my goal, and the blonde's looking at me like she's into it. *Fuck*.

"Tell me when you're ready, I'm going to see if anyone else needs anything." I jerk my head towards the rest of our group sitting down the bar. Before I head in that direction, I sneak a quick peek at Cora. She's deep in conversation with Ally, but she suddenly looks up at me like she can feel me watching her. She doesn't smile or laugh or give any sign of what she's thinking. I hold her gaze for a second, trying to understand if it means anything, before Deacon interrupts.

"The ladies will start with a Pink Panty Dropper, and we'll see where the night goes from there."

I groan inwardly and make the drinks, doing my best to be polite without encouraging them further.

Chapter 12

Cora

"Disgusting, isn't it?" Ally says.

"What?" I sip my drink, a plain old vodka tonic, just like my grandma used to drink.

"You know." Ally rolls her eyes. "No wonder these guys are perpetually single, women literally fall at their feet."

I look down the bar to where two women are blatantly throwing themselves at Deacon and Cade. If Cade weren't standing behind the bar the blonde would be climbing him. I think under normal circumstances he'd let her, but according to Ally he's not acting normally. I want to believe that's because of me, but I can't let myself go there right now. Things are too fragile after last night, and I'm resolved to give him the space he needs to figure his shit out. Although, if I want him to realize that he's worth more than a good time, these women certainly aren't helping my cause.

"Do they do that to everyone, or just Deacon and Cade?" I'm slightly afraid of the answer.

"I think Deacon and Cade are the first choice, and let's be honest I get why. I mean, Finn's hot and I love him, but those two are on another plane entirely." She looks at the two men in question.

I nod, agreeing with her.

"But really any attractive guy in this town will get hit on by the women coming through. And they're only too happy to be noticed since there aren't many women here year-round." She gives me a sad smile, almost like she's apologizing for their behavior.

A flirty laugh pulls my attention toward the women, and I see one smiling and batting her eyelashes at Cade. He's smiling back, but it's not the flirty one he wore the first few times I met him. It's not even a genuine one. It's polite. Forced. It's not easy to watch women throw themselves at him after what we shared last night, but it's marginally better knowing that he's not enjoying it.

"Now this is interesting," Ally says, following my gaze. "Cade doesn't look like a man on a mission tonight."

"No?" I inquire.

"No. And I gather, based on the tension between he and Deacon earlier, that he hasn't been on a mission in a while." She pulls the straw between her lips, letting that little hint linger.

"By mission you mean…"

"Yes," Ally interjects. "That's exactly what I mean. And that's not like him at all. Neither is bartending."

"He doesn't bartend? He seems to be doing a good job of it. Whatever drinks they wanted he knew how to make."

"He'll help Dex out when needed, but he doesn't usually stay behind the bar, and he's usually close enough to be groped." She seems on the verge of elaborating but takes a sip of her drink instead.

"Women do that?" I gasp, my gaze shooting around the room. "Here?"

"I've seen it happen more than I care to admit. That's why I usually only go out when town's a little quiet. My eyes don't see things they don't need to see that way." She shudders.

I stifle a laugh. Ally in no way strikes me as prude, but she definitely doesn't like watching her friends get manhandled.

I look up to find Cade studying me. Apparently, I didn't do as good a job at containing that laugh as I thought. I watch him thoughtfully, curious about the almost pained look on his face, which Ally latches on to.

"Okay, that's like the third time I've caught you two staring at each other, not counting what happened in my store yesterday. Spill," she commands.

"Spill what?" I take another sip of my drink.

"Why Cade isn't acting like himself. He's practically stopped flirting, Deacon seems upset with him, which I'm guessing is because Cade is no longer acting as his wingman, and he's looking at you like some abandoned puppy. What happened?" She looks at me pointedly.

"Nothing happened. I mean, I think he's attracted to me, and I'm attracted to him, but nothing happened." Unless you count a couple of mind-blowing kisses, but much as I like Ally that doesn't feel like her business.

"So, he's acting pussy-whipped without getting any pussy?" Her mouth drops open

"Oh my gosh, you sound just like the guys." I try to contain this laugh by covering my mouth.

"What can I say, their caveman language has rubbed off on me. But seriously, you haven't...you know." She leans in closer, expecting some juicy detail no doubt.

"No! Honestly, we've mostly just talked." I shake my head.

"Mostly?" She arches a brow.

Of course, she'd pick up on that.

"Well, he did have to carry me down the trail after I sprained my ankle, and he made me dinner and slept on my couch after," I babble.

"But yeah, mostly we've just talked." I sip my drink, not sure what else to say.

"Well, I wouldn't have expected it, but maybe that's his kryptonite." She shakes her head, bewildered.

"His what?" I laugh.

"Kryptonite. Achilles heel," she offers when I don't react. "Downfall. Jeez I really am adopting their language. Anyhow, I wouldn't have thought anything could take Cade off the casual sex bandwagon, but apparently conversation does the trick."

"I haven't tried to talk him out of casual sex," I protest.

"That's not what I mean, and besides, I don't think Cade can be talked into anything he doesn't want to do. What I mean is you just talked, didn't you? No flirting, no games, just talking. And apparently, he likes that, or he'd be staring down the front of that blonde's shirt. Lord knows it keeps getting lower every time she leans against the bar." She shudders in disgust.

I can't say she's a hundred percent right, although her observation has some merit. Cade did flirt in the beginning, and I know flirting is his way of talking without saying anything meaningful, so he can keep people at arms-length. But we've had some conversations that went beyond flirting, and I think he enjoyed those. I know I did. So maybe actual conversation is what draws us together. Well, that and him being incredibly nice to look at.

I look over to where Cade's standing upright behind the bar, admiring the way his t-shirt hugs his chest just enough to hint at his physique without looking glued on. Despite the blonde practically laying on top of the bar to push up her cleavage he has a somewhat bored expression, but that doesn't detract from his piercing eyes and full lips.

The blonde rocks forward, pushing her boobs almost out of her shirt. I catch Ally's eye and we both dissolve into a fit of laughter.

"Are they all that obvious?" I ask, awed.

"That's tame. Remember, I've seen groping before." She grimaces as she turns her back on the display.

"Ugh." Now it's my turn to shudder.

Another round of our laughter grabs Cade's attention, and he excuses himself under the guise of needing to check our drinks.

"What gave you two the giggles tonight?" He rests his forearms on the bar and leans toward us conspiratorially.

"The peep show you were getting. I bet if you go back over there, she'll show her nipples." Ally smirks.

"I should probably cut them off." He exhales heavily. "They were forward enough before Deacon got them all riled up on sex shots."

"Sex shots?" My eyebrows shoot sky high.

"Yeah. Shots that are named after sex." He looks down at the bar top, and I swear I see a little pink in his cheeks.

"For real? And you know how to make them?" I'm intrigued. A little repulsed but intrigued.

"It's sort of a game we play to mess with tourists. Mostly bachelorette parties. They think it's hilarious." He gives a guilty shrug.

"Give her an example. Tell her what they ordered," Ally commands before closing her lips around her straw.

Cade takes a deep breath and lets it out while shaking his head slowly. "Pink Panty Droppers, Wet Pussys and Quick Fucks. You string the names together in a sentence that sounds raunchy but is actually a drink order."

"Oh my gosh," I nearly snort.

"That's not all." Ally grabs my arm and leans closer, giggling. "These morons compete to see whose sentence amounts to the biggest order."

I cover my nose in case my drink wants to escape through it. "Well, it could be worse. At least they're measuring success by the number of drinks and not the length of their tools." I crack up at my own joke.

That might be the vodka talking on top of the wine from the concert, but I haven't laughed like this in a long time, and it feels good.

Ally stares at me, stunned, before she cracks up laughing. "That would be worse."

I look to Cade and see him shaking his head, amused, I think, or surprised. He's never seen me tipsy, or very forward with what I say. It's hard not to join in now that I know the joke.

"Who's winning?" I ask.

Ally nods toward Cade.

"Ok, give me your best order." I lean closer so I don't miss a word.

"No." He stands straight and crosses his arms.

"Please?" I bat my eyelashes like the woman down the bar.

He shakes his head and sighs, like what comes next will physically pain him. Finally, he rests his hands on the counter and leans forward. "I'm looking for a Nympho to Tie Me to the Bedpost with The Leg Spreader and give me her Hot Pussy for a Quick Fuck, and after that Kinky Orgasm we'll have a Slow Comfortable Screw."

"Is that the winning sentence?" My jaw hangs open.

He nods.

"How many drinks was that?" I try to count them in my head as I tick them off on my fingers.

"Seven," he says evenly.

"That's all? There have to be more sex drink names."

"There are, but you can't just string a bunch of random drink names together. They have to make a real sentence." He exhales.

"Who's in second?"

"Ryder, with five." Cade wants to leave it at that, but evidently, he can tell I'm not going to let it drop because with another sigh he says, "I'm looking for a Clit-Licking Cowgirl to take me in her Deep Throat and give this Cock-sucking Cowboy a Blow Job to get rid of these Blue Balls."

I'm laughing so hard I can feel tears threatening to fall. "Oh my gosh, I had no idea drinks could be so filthy."

"We're talking about an industry that encourages a lapse in judgement, of course it's filthy." Ally scoffs, trying to contain her own laughter.

"I would've thought Dex would be in the lead," I muse. "He is the bartender."

"He's the scorekeeper. He has to make sure the drinks we order are legit," Cade says reluctantly.

"Have you ever played this game anywhere else? I mean, if you went to a different bar would they know what you're ordering?"

"I don't know." Cade seems surprised by the question. "Most of them are shots so a good bartender would know them."

"And let's not give these guys too much credit. I'm sure there are hundreds if not thousands of horny guys out there who play the same stupid game." Ally ads with an eye roll.

"Oh my gosh, that should be a bar game, or a theme night. Dex could host the sex drink championships and people from all over could compete for the title." I collapse into another fit of giggles with Ally.

"Jesus," Cade mutters. "Between your game show antics and Deacon's half-dressed new friends I'm going to have to cut off everyone in this bar."

"I think Deacon's half-dressed friends want you to undress them." Ally nods towards the group of three down the bar. Deacon's wearing a *'get your ass over here'* expression while the blonde is visibly pouting that Cade isn't watching her.

"Huh?" he grunts.

"Those girls aren't...I mean, he won't take advantage, right?" I ask.

"What? No, he'd never do that," Cade insists. "I haven't served them that much, and he wouldn't cross a line. But trust me, if those girls weren't interested, they would've walked right past him when they first came in. He's not giving them attention they don't want."

"Okay," I concede, because it does certainly look like they're enjoying themselves. Well, the brunette anyway. The blonde is still looking at Cade like she wants to lick him from head to toe, and it's not a good look. It's too desperate. If that's how women usually look at him, it's no wonder he needs a break from that.

"You aren't going to partake?" Ally goads him, and I feel my cheeks turn pink because I know she's using me to try to force Cade to talk. Not maliciously—I get the sense she'd like to fix us up—though I'd rather not be present while she tries to do it.

He shoots her a pointed look. "It's already past my bedtime on a work night."

"I didn't know you had a bedtime." Ally pokes him further.

"I wouldn't expect you to since you don't share my bed." He glares at her.

"Touché!" Ally laughs, letting him off the hook. I offer a weak smile, too embarrassed to do much else.

"You ladies need anything else, or can I clock out now?" he asks dryly.

"I'm good," Ally singsongs like she's proud of having pushed his buttons.

"Me too." I've got just the slightest buzz going on, and that's my cue to stop since I have work to do tomorrow.

"How are you getting home, Cora?" Cade asks, his tone suddenly gentle.

"My car is still over by the park."

"You're okay to drive?" He looks at me skeptically.

"Yes, I only had the one drink. Plus, walking back to my car will give me some fresh air." I reach for my purse to pay the tab.

"You're walking to your car? *Alone*?" A thin line appears between his brows.

"Are you worried I'll run into trouble?" I smile. Okay, flirt. I hold out a twenty.

"No. I'm parked that way too. I'll walk with you." He waves away my money and puts his own in the register.

"Oh. Okay." I stick my twenty in the tip jar instead, earning another frown from Cade.

He comes around the bar to meet me and we say our goodbyes, earning a sly smirk from Ally, and an annoyed glare from Deacon. Even though he seems on edge he's a total gentleman, holding the door open for me as we step into the chilly air.

"Looks like I may have to make Deacon breakfast again to get back on his good side." I steel a sideways glance at him.

Cade winces. "You saw that?"

"I have sort of been monopolizing your time lately," I continue without answering. "You really don't have to walk me to the car. We both know this town is safe enough for me to walk alone."

I know suggesting he can go back to the bar is a risk, but I have to give him that choice.

"What if I'd rather walk with you than hang out with Deacon and his new friends?" I'm not sure he meant to say that aloud, though I answer anyway.

"I'd be glad for the company, if that's what you really want."

He's quiet for so long that I start to wonder if he's ever going to answer. Just when I'm about to change the subject he says, "It is."

His sincerity renders me speechless. This is the second time in a week that he's given up a sure thing to spend time with me, and while I think the first time was part obligation to make sure I was okay, this time I've relieved him of any sense of duty. Knowing that he really does prefer to be with me gives me butterflies, and I shake out my hands. Time to change the subject.

"Who came up with the drink game?" I nudge his arm with mine.

"Ah, that was me." He rubs his hand over the back of his neck.

"You can't just leave it at that." I twist so I'm facing him, walking almost sideways so I can see his face. "What made you think of it?"

"I had to look up the recipe for a drink one time when I was helping Dex." He exhales. "I jumped behind the bar because he was swamped, kind of like tonight, and even though I didn't know how to do much else than pour beers I figured another set of hands would help him. Then this girl comes in asking for a fancy drink I'd never heard of, and Dex was too busy to jump in, so he told me to look it up. I found a book of drink recipes, and as I was flipping through, I found a couple that were…" He shakes his head, searching.

"Suggestive?" I supply.

"Yeah, you could say that." He chuckles. "The next time I was in the bar I grabbed that book and started reading it, then ordering these drinks just to piss Dex off. One time a girl overheard, and instead of being offended she seemed curious. So, I upped the ante and started ordering multiple drinks at a time, but instead of rattling them off like a list I dropped them into sentences. It sort of caught on." He shrugs sheepishly.

"I can't believe I'm admitting this, but I suppose it really does take talent to put all that in a sentence." I bite my lip, waiting for the suggestive response.

"I'm not sure talent's the right word for it. More like, too much idle time spent in the bar." He offers a weak smile.

"I can see why you like to hang out there. Tonight was fun." I press on, undeterred.

"Yeah?" he asks, genuinely surprised.

"Yeah. I haven't laughed that hard in a while." I grin just thinking about it. "It was nice to let loose."

"It is." He nods slowly. "And it was nice having you there. But this town has a way of making you focus on fun and not work, so don't let it sidetrack you." He turns serious.

"What do you mean?" I turn to face him as we reach my car.

"This town caters to people on vacation, which makes it real easy to think you're on vacation with them. Most people don't have college degrees because they're not necessary here. We work only so we can play, not because we want to have impressive careers. I know you didn't come here to play, so don't let the town mentality suck you in," he says, which I know has a double meaning. He's not just warning me about the town, but to steer clear of him to, like he's some kind of vortex that's bound to syphon off my ambition, my goals, and leave me with nothing. I refuse to let him think that about himself. He's worth more.

"The town mentality sounds kind of refreshing. Enjoying life and all," I say.

"It is. But you have something important you want to do." His gaze is almost pleading.

"That worries you?" I ask softly. "That I'll forget why I'm here?"

"Not forget, no. But get distracted, yeah. Maybe." His concern is endearing.

My heart beats a little faster knowing that he's worried, that he's put so much thought into it. Then again, all he's done since I got here is look out for me, so I shouldn't be surprised.

"I won't," I assure him.

"Good." He stands motionless in front of me, sort of like he did in his studio yesterday, and I get the feeling there's something else he wants to say, or do, but isn't sure how. Or if he should. Instead, he opens my door for me so I can climb in.

"Good night, Cora," he says softly.

"Good night," I say before he shuts it and leaves.

Chapter 13

Cade

It's another busy day of work, which normally makes the time pass quickly, but since I can feel the frustration boiling off Deacon it's making things move extra slow.

He hasn't said anything to me, and probably won't in front of the rest of the crew. He doesn't have to. I know he's pissed that I didn't play wingman last night, even though my absence probably meant he had them both to himself. He's not mad about having to soldier on as a party of three, he's mad that I left with Cora, who he knows I'm not sleeping with.

Okay, I may be slightly to blame for that. For years, I talked up how great it was to live here, probably sharing a little too much detail about how easy it is to score in this town. Now that he's here, he wants to live that way, with me by his side. That was the original plan, but when Cora rolled into town, things changed. My unwillingness to participate has to make him feel like I falsely advertised. I don't blame him for feeling like that, hell it was even a shock to me, but he could drop the snark down a notch. Jeesh.

By the time three thirty rolls around, I'm over his attitude. With the exterior framing complete I send everyone home and go to inspect the patio Deacon's been working on, hoping to clear the air.

"Looks good, cousin." I survey his work. "How long will it take to build the fireplace?"

"Couple days," he says stiffly as he straightens, clutching the broom in his fists.

"You doing the plants after that?" I squint to see him in spite of the bright afternoon sun.

"Depends on the weather. I'd rather wait until July so there's less chance of snow." He sweeps the last of the dirt off the patio.

I nod my head, agreeing with that logic.

"You ready to tell me what's on your mind or you gonna keep sulking?" I confront him, wanting to get this over with.

He seems to think about it for a second before turning to face me. "You talk a lot about none of the guys in this town being good enough for Cora, which should include you, but you're chasing after her like some lovesick puppy and ditching me to do it. You're being a hypocrite."

I chew on my lip, pondering his words. He's not wrong, but he's not right either.

"Not trying to be a hypocrite." I shake my head. "I know I'm not good enough for her. I keep trying to tell her that, but she doesn't seem to agree. Doesn't judge me either. I'm not used to that, and it's kinda nice. Makes it hard not to enjoy being around her."

"What do you mean doesn't judge you?" He leans on the broom, studying me.

"I told you, she doesn't look at me like some boy toy that exists for her pleasure."

"That's a good thing?" He frowns, clearly confused.

"I think so, yeah. It's never happened to me before." I shrug helplessly, because I don't have the words to explain it any better.

"She doesn't look at you like a play-thing and you're happy about that? Seriously?" He arches a brow as he leans the broom against the house.

"Yeah."

Deacon shakes his head with another huff, clearly unimpressed with my reasoning.

I try another angle. "When was the last time a woman looked at you like you might be interesting?"

"Fuck, I don't know," he grumbles. "Probably in school. One of my professors was a woman. And some people I worked on a project with. I went on a date with one."

"See," I tell him. "You grew up in a big city, went to college. You probably had your fair share of ladies who were interested, but did they treat you like the only thing you had to offer them was sex?"

"Are you kidding? I would love if they treated me like the only thing I have to offer is sex. That's living the dream, all the fun parts of a relationship without any of the work. That's why I'm here." He gestures towards the landscape around us.

"I get that." I lock my jaw and nod. "I lived like that for years, and you know how much fun I had. But that was before anyone looked at me like I'm more."

"So, you're telling me that because Cora doesn't want to jump you, you're fine to hang out with her and not try to screw her? Or anyone else for that matter?" He rests his hands on his hips.

He's trying to piss me off, because that would make his own anger justified. But I'm determined to keep the anger out of my voice. "Yeah," I admit, "Surprised the hell out of me too, but yeah."

"Don't you want to though?" he presses. "I mean, she's hot."

"She's gorgeous. And yeah, I'm attracted to her." I rub the back of my neck. "But I like just talking to her too. It's interesting."

"You're gonna do that all summer, just *talk* to her?" His eyebrows rise as he lowers his head, making it seem like he's looking down on me.

"I don't know. I keep trying not to do anything, but I keep bumping into her, and it's hard to walk away." I rub my hands over my face. "I know what I should do, but I can't make myself do it."

"So, come out with me. Have fun, take the edge off. Get Cora out of your head," he pleads.

"That's just it, cousin." I sigh heavily, willing him to understand. "Taking the edge off has no appeal anymore. I know, I used to live for that, but now it doesn't seem as fun."

"Are you seriously trying to tell me that sex isn't fun?" Deacon recoils.

"No. I just don't think it sounds fun with a random stranger that comes through town."

"That's what we were supposed to do all summer." He throws his arms wide, like he's got nothing to show for coming here. No reason to stay.

"You still can."

"Yeah, but it was fun to do together. Tell me that bachelorette party wasn't amazing." I swear his eyes are pleading for me to see reason.

"It was amazing." I placate him, though he's right. At the time it was.

"And you want to give that up?" he balks.

"Just because I'm taking a break from picking up tourists doesn't mean you have to. And it damn sure doesn't give you an excuse to be mean to Cora." I point an accusing finger at him.

"I haven't been mean to her." He crosses his arms defiantly.

"Deacon, she's not blind," I groan. "She sees you glaring at her."

"I was glaring at you, not her."

"Well, she doesn't know that." I throw my hands up. "She's still the client so you can't treat her like shit."

"Speaking of, isn't it a bad idea to get too close to the client?" He scowls, throwing my own BS back at me.

That's the other part of this fucked up situation I've been trying to avoid. I said that earlier, and it still makes a lot of sense, though there's a part of me that just doesn't care anymore. But I can't just ignore it. This is my dad's business, my future business we're talking about. And the Gerome's are good clients. I don't want to mess that up because of my interest in Cora. Yet each time I'm with her, I feel my resolve fading a little more, and I don't know how much longer I can hold out.

I'm still shocked I didn't screw up and start kissing her last night when I walked her to her car. I'm even more shocked she actually enjoyed hanging out at the bar and hearing about our stupid drinking games. Seeing her smile, laugh, and even throw down a few jokes made her that much more appealing, and when we were alone, I realized she once again didn't judge me for my immature antics. That made me want to push her up against the car and kiss the hell out of her like I did in the studio.

I think about doing that every time I see her, because I'm dying to feel her again. But between me being bad for her and her being the niece of our client, Deacon's right, getting too close to her is a bad idea. I know that. I just haven't been able to keep my distance.

"Yes, getting close a bad idea." I rub my face again. "I don't feel like I have control over it though."

Now that I've said it, I realize it's the truth. I keep trying to avoid her, but she keeps materializing everywhere I am, and when that happens, I'm powerless.

"That sounds fucked up." Deacon whistles.

"It is. It's all kinds of fucked up." I drop onto the retaining wall that surrounds the patio, exhausted. "I see her, and I'm tempted to forget that I'm bad for her or that it's reckless to get close to her. I'm trying to fight it, but..." I trail off.

"Okay, now you're freaking me out." Deacon's brow furrows. "You're talking like you're whipped, but there's no way that's true, right? I mean, you're the ultimate bachelor. This is just, like, a phase or something."

"I have no clue, cousin." I squint up at him. "If it's a phase it's the first one I've ever had."

"Maybe you just need to do this. Hang out with her, bang her, whatever, just get her out of your system so you can go back to normal." He sits next to me, a peace offering of sorts.

I take a moment to think about the merits of this idea. She's clearly in my system right now, and the harder I fight it the worse it seems to get. Maybe I do need to stop fighting this and see where it goes. Maybe that's how I get her out of my head. We do have all summer, which should be plenty of time to get my fill of her, and it's not like we have to be inseparable or anything, so it's possible I won't become a distraction.

The only thing I get hung up on is the fact that she's not a casual sex person, and I don't know how to be anything else. I'm not opposed to being monogamous, hell I've already thought about doing that for her, I just don't know if I'd want that long-term. But she is leaving at the end of the summer, so there's a limit on this thing, and maybe that's a good compromise.

We're both obviously attracted to one another, and I don't see that going away. I think it will only get worse, and I am getting tired of fighting it. I'm not sure I can do it the rest of the summer. I'm also not sure I could be a boyfriend type for longer than that, so having an expiration date could be the perfect solution. It would make us more than a casual hook up but less than a couple, I think. Friends with benefits, if you will. Best of all, an expiration date means it won't affect our relationship with her uncle, because I can't mess something up that can't be permanent to begin with.

I'm still not worthy of someone like Cora, not by a long shot, but if she's okay to slum it with a guy like me for a few months, who am I to object? We could hang out, get our fill of each other, and go our separate ways at the end of the summer. She'll move on to a successful career and I'll go back to my carefree lifestyle. This could work.

"Hello. Earth to Cade. What the fuck?" Deacon waves his hand in front of my face.

"Shit, sorry. I was thinking."

"Yeah, I got that," he grunts. "So, what are you gonna do?"

"I think you're right." I nod absently. "I think I should just do this and get it out of my system. Then when she leaves at the end of the summer I'll be back to normal."

"Okay, yeah. I mean, sucks to go it alone for a while, but it's only temporary, right?" he reasons, looking as scared as I feel.

"Of course. It has to be. She's leaving."

"Okay." Deacon puts on a brave face. "I mean, I still don't get it, but if this is what you gotta do, then do it."

Just then, as if I need a sign, Cora comes out of the house with her hiking gear. "Okay. Right." I exhale. "Let's see if this works."

***

"Solo, are you really heading out to hike all by yourself again?" I grin as I approach.

"Solo," she muses. "I haven't heard that name in awhile. I thought you'd given it up."

"Can't give it up until you stop doing things by yourself." I fall in step with her as she heads to her car.

"What's wrong with doing things by myself?" She casts me a curious glance.

"I won't be there to rescue you." I wink.

"Oh." Her shoulders slump forward. "And here I thought you wanted to keep me company." She tosses her pack in the back of the car.

"Who says I don't want to keep you company?" I lean against the driver's side door, blocking her escape.

"You." She pokes my chest. "You think I need a babysitter."

"I didn't say that." I hold my hands up in surrender.

"You implied it. If you want to come, come. But don't do it because you have some backward notion that I need a guide or a babysitter. I'm not helpless." She reaches for the door, determined to get past me.

Her independent streak is kind of hot, but she's damn defensive about it. I wonder why.

"I know you don't need a babysitter." I step back and pull the door open so she can get in. "I was only teasing about the rescue thing. What trail are you doing?"

She studies me for a moment, like she's trying to decide if I really am teasing. I must look convincing because she finally relaxes. "Highline."

"That's one of my favorites. Can I come with you?"

Her eyes search my mine. I've never asked to hang out with her before and doing so now seems to have made her suspicious. Eventually she relents. "Okay."

I swap my work boots for a pair of tennis shoes and grab a water bottle, then jump in the car with her. She's focused as she drives, never taking her eyes off the road. I don't know if that's just her personality or if I'm making her nervous, so I try to ease the tension.

"Why are you so determined to do things on your own?" I ask.

She grips the steering wheel tighter. Maybe that wasn't the best topic to bring up right now, but I am curious.

"That bothers you?" She glances briefly at me before turning back to the road.

"No. I'm just not used to that. People here are always helping each other out so I don't understand why having help makes you think you're helpless."

She takes a few deep breaths before answering. "I guess I'm sensitive to people assuming I can't do things on my own."

"Why would they assume that?" I frown.

She exhales heavily. "You're probably well aware, but my family has money, and that makes people think I get everything handed to me." She casts another quick glance in my direction, and I must pass some sort of test because she continues. "It doesn't help that I could have that if I wanted it. Most of us go into the family business, and while we have to earn our place to a degree, there will always be a place. Growing up people hated me because they thought I didn't have to work for anything, and I hate being seen like that."

That totally fits what I know about her, and in a way I can relate. My future has been handed to me, so I know how easy it is to just take it and not find your own way. It can't have been easy to turn all that down, and if I'm honest it makes me respect her even more. I hate that she worries about that though.

"You don't have to prove yourself to anyone."

"What does that mean?" A cute little crease forms between her eyebrows.

"It means people who assume you're getting a handout are just jealous that they aren't, and no matter what you do they'll assume you had it handed to you. So, don't waste your time trying to prove them wrong. Prove yourself right. Chase your dream." I shrug.

"Speaking from experience?" She regards me warily.

"Not really. I'm the guy that's going to take the career my family's giving me. I've never considered doing anything else. What didn't you like about your family's business?" I change the subject.

"I don't dislike the family businesses. Managing money means evaluating the different places to invest in, and that part is really interesting. But I thought building something instead of financing it would be even more interesting." A slight smile tugs at her lip.

"What made you pick environmental science?" I ask as she pulls into the trailhead.

"An intro-level science class in college. There was a unit on the environment, and we covered climate change, alternate sources of energy… I got hooked." She blushes adorably when she says it.

Once we're parked, I grab her bag from the car, but instead of handing it to her I strap it on. She scolds me for trying to take care of her again, but I just smile and start walking. This isn't being protective, it's just good manners.

We walk in silence for several minutes before she finally gets over my chivalry. "You hike this trail a lot?" she asks.

"Bike it, usually." I give her a hand to scale a bumpy section.

"You bike *this*?" These rocks are more like steps. How can you possibly bike this?"

"Years of practice." I chuckle, forcing myself to let go of her fingers as she gets her balance. "If you know where to place the tires all you have to do is keep pedaling and the bike rolls over the rocks. And the whole trail isn't like this, just a few sections, so most of the time you're pedaling on even terrain."

"So, when you bike this, you ride up and then turn around and come down?" She looks over her shoulder at the trail we've climbed so far.

"Sometimes. I usually do the whole loop though, which is about ten miles. I prefer riding the back part of the trail down."

"Why?"

"Well, this section is fun with the big drops," I gesture to the rocks we're stepping over, "but it's more technical so you have to watch your speed. If you ride the trail the way we're hiking it you have a steep but short climb to start, and more of a rolling hill to finish, so you get more speed and sort of float down the trail."

"Huh," she mumbles. "So, you bike this trail all the time, do you ever hike it?"

"Not for years, no." I shake my head.

"Why now?" She glances at me sideways as we trek along.

"Uh, because you're hiking now?" I thought that was obvious.

She stops and looks at me. "No, I mean why did you ask to spend time with me now? You've never done that before. I didn't think you wanted to."

"I wouldn't say I didn't want to." I rub the back of my neck.

"Were afraid to then," she presses.

I nod, because there's no point denying that. "I told you why."

"What changed?"

I'm not really sure what she wants me to say here. All I know is I'm tired of fighting this, and that I won't stop her from taking a risk on me if that's what she really wants.

"You told me not to make decisions about what you deserve." I lift my shoulders.

"I told you that days ago, why are listening now?" Her pretty brown eyes bore into mine, but I can't tell if that's because she's confused, upset, or just plain curious. I was hoping the fact that I listened would be enough, but I guess I have to admit everything. Fuck it.

"I like you. I think you like me. I'm tired of trying to ignore that or tell you it's a bad idea." I hold her stare, hoping that makes it easier for her to believe me after I spent so long trying to push her away.

"You don't think you're bad for me anymore?" Her brows draw together.

"Of course, I'm still bad for you," I tell her honestly. "I'm still the selfish guy who lives to have fun and has no idea how to be with just one girl. I can't for the life of me figure out why that doesn't bother you, but I don't think it does. You know what you're getting with me, and if that's what you want, I won't stop you, because I damn sure want you."

"You want to sleep with me," she concludes.

"No. I mean yes, I do, ever since the first time I saw you. But that's not all. I just want to be with you." I rub my neck. "Only you. For however long you're here."

By the look on her face, she's just as stunned by that admission as I am, though I meant every word. I want her, and if she feels the same, I'm not going to block it anymore. The question is, does she want me, or did I screw this up already? I can't tell.

She's too quiet as she climbs up to stand beside me. What is this woman thinking? The silence is eating me alive and I'm not sure I can take it much longer. Cora worries her lip between her teeth falling deep in thought, likely overthinking it. Either that, or she's convinced I've lost my ever lovin' mind. I drag in a deep breath, pull her to me, and kiss her, hard enough to forget whatever was making her quiet and hopefully convincing her to forget how I've screwed up.

Chapter 14

Cora

Pleasure. That's all I feel right now. Cade's lips are just as soft against mine as they were the first time, and it feels so good I can barely breathe. Barely think. If he wasn't holding me up, I'm sure my knees would've given out by now.

He's kissing me like I'm the first woman he's ever tasted, and it makes me wonder if I am. I mean, this is not the type of kiss you give a stranger, it's the type you give someone you cherish.

Cade pulls his tongue back and lets his lips linger on mine, my face cradled in his hands. It's so tender, so soft, I want him to take me in his arms and never let go. I don't know if he's asking me to date, I'd be surprised if he can even put what he wants into words, but if he wants more than just sex, if he wants to be with only me, well, yeah. I'd like that.

"Cora, did I say something wrong?" He strokes my cheek, a panicked look in his eyes.

"What? No. I just, I wasn't expecting you to say all that," I stutter.

"Sorry." He licks his lips. "I told you I didn't have any idea how to do this. I shouldn't have kissed you."

"You should always kiss me," I tell him.

"I...what?" His brow furrows.

"If you want to be me with me you should definitely kiss me. All the time." I put my hand over his.

"So, you really want this? You really want to be with a guy like me?" His blue eyes search mine.

A few days ago, I would've said no. I was singularly focused on reaching my goals and getting involved with a hot guy who had a somewhat rocky past wasn't on the agenda. Since then, I've come to know more about Cade as a person, and there's no denying the spark between us. I know it can't become anything long term, since I have no plans to stay here beyond the summer. But right now, with this man, yeah, I want this.

"I do want this." I nod.

"Thank fuck," he growls.

His relief makes me laugh, but its quickly cut off when he presses his lips to mine. Though I feel the tension in his limbs, taste his desperation, he handles me gently, his full, soft lips caressing. Savoring. Claiming. And in that moment, I want nothing more than to be his, for as long as he wants me.

***

The rest of the hike is comical. We're both too high on excitement and lust to do much besides look at each other and smile, like we're lovestruck teenagers on a date. And for Cade, who's never really done anything non-sexual with a girl, this might actually be his first. That thought makes me kind of giddy. To think, he may never have experienced the shortness of breath, the racing heartbeat, when the accidental brush of a hand evolves into clasped fingers, the way ours are now. He may never have felt the butterflies that accompany such an innocent but sensual touch. The selfish part of me hopes that's true, so that I can be his first.

When we get back to the car, Cade comes around to my side to open my door, but before I get in, he presses up against me, pinning me between his body and the car.

"I don't want this day to be over." He brushes his lips over mine.

"Me, either." I gasp for air.

"I want to take you to dinner, but I don't want to see anyone besides you tonight." He plays with a strand of my hair.

"Not ready to ruin your playboy rep?" I waggle my eyebrows.

"It's not that." He shakes his head, an almost pained look on his face. "It's that it won't be just us anymore. This town is too curious to leave us be, and I want you to myself."

If we were anywhere else, I'd find this weird, a lame excuse to keep me as some sort of dirty secret. Given the quirks of a small town, I think I know what he's saying.

"What are you asking?" I whisper.

"Come home with me? We could order dinner and just hang out."

"What if I cook? It's probably my turn, since you made dinner the last time we ate together." I trap my lips between my teeth and look up at him.

"Frozen pizzas count as making you dinner?" He seems amused by the idea. "All I did was turn on the oven."

"You still fed me. Now, it's my turn to feed you." I let my fingers slide from his chest to his stomach, and it's only after I see the mischievous smile on his lips that I realize the alternate interpretation of my words. But instead of being embarrassed by it, I'm intrigued. *Turned on*.

We stop by Cade's long enough for him to shower and change, then head back to my house so I can cook dinner. I get out all the ingredients for spaghetti with meat sauce and a side salad, then set a pot of water to boil while I brown the meat.

"What can I do?" Cade asks.

"Chop vegetables for the salad?" I hand him a cutting board.

Cade gets to work dicing peppers and tomatoes while I stir the sauce. We work together silently for a few minutes before he abruptly stills. "I forgot to get wine."

"I have some, it's over by the bar," I nod toward the wet bar between the kitchen and living room.

"I should've thought of that." He rubs his head, eyes cast downward.

"It's no big deal."

"It is though. I'm already screwing up." The knife angrily hits the cutting board.

"Why would you think that?"

"Because you're cooking our dinner instead of me taking you somewhere nice, and on top of that I forgot the wine. You deserve better than that." He looks at me with a sad smile

"I thought we agreed you were going to stop worrying about what I deserve." I point the spatula at him in mock anger.

"I can't help it." He wipes his brow with his forearm. It hits me then that this is probably the first time he's cooked a meal with a woman, and he's nervous. It's sweet. And kind of hot.

Setting the spatula down, I step into him and wrap my arms around his waist, though I have to lean back to see his face. It's tan and smooth and perfect, except for the tiny little crease between his eyebrows. "Tonight, isn't about what we deserve, it's about what we want. I want you. What do you want?" I challenge.

"You," he grunts hoarsely. "I want you too."

Standing on my toes to reach his lips, I brush them softly with mine, hoping to put him at ease. He stands absolutely still, letting me control the pace, though I feel the restraint behind the stillness, like he's just barely holding on. It's thoughtful. And endearing. And not enough.

I trace his bottom lip with the tip of my tongue and am rewarded with a strangled growl as he finally caves and reaches around my waist to haul me against him, crushing his lips to mine.

What started as a slow burn, turns to an inferno as he devours me, teeth and tongues clashing desperately as we try to get our fill. Apparently, I'm just as desperate for him as he is me because my body is reacting before my mind can catch up.

He grips my ass firmly, tugging me to him, so I wrap my legs around him and hang on, savoring the pressure of his body flush with mine. The friction makes me wet, and I start to rock my hips against him to relieve the ache gathering between my legs.

"Jesus, Cora," he heaves. "I'm trying to be good here. I can't hold back if you do that."

"Then don't hold back," I breathe.

"I'm not supposed to fuck you this soon. What about dates? What about dinner?" he says through gritted teeth.

"Turn off the stove. Food can wait."

A wave of lust washes over his face, and I know in that moment he's done fighting. "You're offering to let me eat you instead?" He reaches over to turn off the burner.

"Oh," I whimper as a flood of moisture pools between my legs. "Yes."

"You like the sound of that?" His eyes go wide, like he's shocked by this admission.

I nod, panting.

"What do you like? The image of my head between your legs, or my words?" He kisses my neck.

"Both." I don't recognize the husky tone in my voice, but he must like it because he chuckles and palms my ass in his hands, helping me grind slowly against him.

"Damn that feels good." His head falls back as he groans. "I think you could make me come just like this."

"I could come like this too," I whisper. "But I want more."

"More?" The gleam in his eyes says he's up for that. "Do you want to watch me suck your swollen little clit into my mouth until you scream? Or feel my cock filling you?"

"Everything."

"You're sure?" It's his final warning. "If you take me to your bed, I'm not stopping until you're shaking beneath me."

"I know." I grind my hips against him again, because I can't stop either.

"Where to?" he asks, stalking in the direction of the bedrooms.

"Second door on the left," I mumble between kisses.

Cade holds me pressed against his cock as he walks us toward my bedroom, loosening his hold only when he sits on the edge of the bed with me in his lap. For a moment, he just looks at me, as if trying to accept that I really want this, before gripping the hem of my shirt and lifting it slowly over my head.

I'm still wearing a sports bra from the hike, though it's a feminine one, with strips of fabric crisscrossing between my breasts in a somewhat geometric pattern. It's dim in the room since the sun has gone down, but that doesn't stop Cade's eyes from flashing with lust as he traces his fingers over my bare skin.

"I like this," he says huskily.

"It's just a sports bra," I dismiss. But he's intrigued, brushing his fingers over the swell of my breasts, which are visible between the straps.

"It gives me the sweetest glimpse of your tits. I feel like there should be a bow here," he tugs gently at the thin straps holding the cups together, "so I can untie it and let them spill into my hands."

I take a shaky breath as his finger follows the curve of my breast. He smiles mischievously as he watches my chest rise and fall, dragging his finger from the side of my breast to the center, where my puckered nipple is straining beneath the fabric. I don't even try to contain the moan his touch elicits when his finger lightly circles it.

"Did you feel my cock move when you moaned? I've never heard such a sexy sound, and I haven't even touched you yet. Not really. Let's see what kind of sounds you make when these gorgeous tits are bare." He pulls the sports bra over my head and sits back to admire my body. I don't have enormous breasts, but they are round and full, and as Cade cups them in his hands, I have to admit they fit his grip perfectly.

"Damn, Cora." He licks his lips as he brushes his thumbs over my nipples. I inhale sharply. "You're stunning. Put your hands on my legs and arch your back. I want to see you. All of you."

I feel myself blushing under his heated gaze, but do as he asks, arching my back and thrusting my chest forward. He helps hold me in place with one hand while running the other up my side and over my left breast, between the two, up and over my right breast. Occasionally, he squeezes, molding them to his touch, but mostly he just runs his hand over them like he's committing every curve to memory.

My body tingles everywhere he touches, and I shamelessly arch into his palm, needing him to take me higher. Without warning he leans forward and sucks a nipple into his mouth, and I scream his name.

He releases my nipple and flicks it with his tongue before biting down gently and pulling it taught. I can't stop my hips from bucking, searching for the pressure or friction that will ease the ache in my core.

"God, you have the most perfect tits. So round and firm and sensitive." He strokes them. "I wonder if they're sensitive enough to make you come? Have you ever come just from having these played with?"

"No," I pant.

"Hmm." He pulls my nipple back into his mouth and sucks it slowly. "We're gonna have to try that later. But right now, your pussy is desperate for attention, isn't it? You want to show me how wet you are, sweetheart? Stand up and take the rest of your clothes off."

Normally, I'd balk at being called sweetheart in such an expectant way, but Cade is absolutely right. I do want him to focus on my center, and right now I don't care what pet names he gives me as long as he touches me where I need him most.

I rise off his lap and let my shorts and panties fall to the floor. Cade sits there on the edge of the bed, drinking me in.

"Every inch of you is spectacular, Cora. I've never seen anyone so beautiful." He says it softly almost reverently, and while it sounds like the sort of line Cade would feed any naked woman, there's no trace of insincerity in his gaze. Only awe. "Come here. Let me taste you."

"What about you?" I whisper as my gaze wanders over his frame.

Cade seems to register for the first time that he's still fully clothed. He pulls his shirt over his head and tosses it to the floor before standing up to shed his pants. When his erection is free it springs upward, slapping against his stomach before coming to rest parallel to the ground. Holy. Crap.

If I thought Cade was beautiful shirtless, he's a masterpiece naked. Broad shoulders, muscled chest, lean stomach that showcases a smooth six pack, and a sexy V pointing toward his long, thick cock.

He sits back on the bed and beckons me to him, spreading his legs wide so I can stand between them. At this height, his head is level with my breasts, and he fondles them gently before dropping his hands to my hips and issuing more commands.

"Touch yourself, Cora. Show me how wet you are."

I've never touched myself in front of anyone before, but I can't stop myself from slipping a finger between my legs. I slide it back and forth once, twice, before Cade grunts, "Show me."

I hold my finger up for his inspection, and they glisten in the dim light of the room. Cade brings my finger to his mouth and sucks them clean. His eyes flutter closed, and I put my free hand on his shoulder to keep my knees from buckling.

The moment my finger leaves his mouth, he scoops me in his arms and lays me on the bed, spreading my legs wide so he can look his fill. He traces a finger over my slit, groaning as he makes contact.

"You're dripping, Cora. Do you always get this wet, or is it just for me?" He toys with my sex.

God, he's arrogant, but with good reason. Between his words and his touch, he's got me more primed than I've ever been. I'm desperate to come, but I'm desperate not to, because this simmering ache is the hottest thing I've ever experienced, and I don't want it to end.

"I...I don't know," I admit. "I can't remember being this turned on before."

"I've never been this turned on before either. I'm so hard it fucking hurts. Just like you, huh? You're so turned on you ache. Does this make it better?" He slides a finger slowly inside me, and I sigh, relieved to feel the pressure of his finger inside me. "It does, doesn't it. I'm going to take that need away soon, but first I need another taste."

Cade lowers his head between my legs and begins gently flicking my clit with his tongue. My hips buck violently at the contact, and he presses my legs firmly to the mattress to keep me still.

"You're sensitive everywhere, aren't you? That's so fucking hot. I'll be gentle, but this pussy is too pretty not to taste." Cade resumes his tender caress, gently licking and nipping at my core. A strangled cry escapes my mouth as he pulls me into his. I look down my body to watch his head bobbing almost imperceptibly between my legs. He looks as lost in bliss as I feel, and as I climb the precipice, I fight the urge to rock my hips upward to keep from erupting too soon.

As if he can sense my gaze, Cade opens his eyes and stares into mine, never breaking his rhythm. The heat that passes between us is unlike anything I've ever experienced. His touch is decadent, and I can do little else but melt into the mattress as the pressure increases, and he sends me into oblivion.

My hips thrash uncontrollably as my orgasm ripples through me. I scream, or wail, but I can't reconcile the sounds with my body because I've never heard them before. I've never been brought to this state, boneless and spent, yet still on edge, because the man who made me so is looking at me with a hunger I know hasn't been sated.

"That was beautiful, Cora," he says as he kisses his way up my body.

"What about you?" I pant.

"I'm not capable of being done with you yet." He lays next to me, and I feel his hard cock resting against my stomach. "But I can wait for you to recover."

I reach between us and drag a finger up his firm length. It's the first time I've touched him tonight, and I see him shudder from the slight contact.

"Best not to do that until you're ready for me, sweetheart" he says, reaching for my hand. "I'm barely hanging on as it is."

"Sweetheart," I muse. "Is that my new nickname?"

"That depends. Do you object?" His eyes sparkle beneath the wisps of hair covering his forehead.

"Not the way you say it." I pull on my lip with my teeth.

"How do I say it?" A crease separates his brows.

"You don't say it, you growl it. It's kind of possessive."

"You like that?" He seems surprised, and I have to admit, so am I. The way Cade owned my body just now makes the idea of being 'his' sort of appealing. And speaking of how he owned my body, if he can do that with his mouth, I can't wait to see what else he can do.

"I like the way you take control. I want you to do it again." I lean forward to kiss him, and with a strangled groan he gives in and covers my body with his.

Chapter 15

Cade

I haven't even been inside her yet, but I already know it will be near impossible to ever get Cora out of my system.

Once again, she shocked me with her willingness to overlook my past, and her insistence that she wants to be with me. Never in a million years did I expect a woman like her to slum it with a guy like me, much less be so eager to. I mean, she jumped into my arms in the kitchen, which was hot as fuck, and it only got hotter from there.

Not only does she seem to get off on my words, which is fortunate since I'm a vocal lover, she's giving herself completely to me, touching herself as I instruct and screaming when she finds her pleasure. That's so incredibly sexy, I can't believe I haven't gone off yet. I'm desperate to get inside her, but this is going so much faster than I ever expected, and I don't want to screw it up by being too impatient.

My cock is trapped between us as we kiss, her silky little body writhing beneath me, making it near impossible not to glove up and plunge inside her. But I know she's super sensitive, and I suspect that's because she hasn't been touched in a while, so I need to be careful. I slide my hand between us and spread her pussy, needing to know if she's ready for me. My finger slips inside with ease, which makes me unreasonably proud, and eager.

I pull away and reach for my pants to grab a condom, loving the way Cora's eyes never leave my dick. I'm a big guy, so it's a good size, especially for someone as petite as her, and she's eyeing me like she's ready for it. She's definitely wet enough, but I don't want to hurt her.

"You're so sensitive." I drag my finger through her slit with one hand as I stroke myself with the other. "Has it been a while? I need to make sure I'm not too rough."

"I used a vibrator last week." Her beautiful breasts rise and fall hypnotically as she pants in anticipation. And now I have visions of adding toys to the mix. Damn, she's hot. I need to focus.

"I can be a lot rougher than a vibrator, sweetheart." I plan to call her that often in bed since she enjoys it. "I'll try not to be, but you've got me pretty excited." I stroke my length one last time before rolling the condom on.

I crawl over top of her and line myself up to her entrance, brushing the tip of my dick back and forth over her center. The little vixen arches her hips up to meet me, and I sink home, slowly, so she has time to adjust.

The pressure of her taut pussy rolls over me as I press deeper, welcoming me into her slippery heat. When I'm buried to the hilt I pause, waiting to make sure she's comfortable. I've never held myself still inside a woman before, never felt her stretching to accommodate me, and I realize now I've been missing out. Who knew barely moving could feel just as good as urgent thrusting? Tiny little tremors shoot over my cock from root to tip as Cora's body takes me in, almost like little kisses traveling over my length, and I nearly come undone from that alone, which is crazy.

I kind of pride myself on being able to go the distance. Even if I'm just using a woman for sex, I make sure she enjoys it, which means staying in control until she's satisfied. But I'm ready to come apart before I've even begun to move. Holy shit.

"Damn, Cora," I grunt. "I feel you shifting all around me, am I hurting you?"

"No." Her head shakes slightly as she lets out a deep breath "You feel good."

"So, do you." I press a soft kiss to her lips as I pull back slowly, testing to see how she reacts. I'm rewarded with an almost forlorn moan, like she doesn't want me to leave her body.

"Does the ache go away when I'm buried deep?"

"Yes." Her eyes flutter.

I push forward steadily. "Like this?" I circle my hips against her when I can go no deeper.

"Ah," she cries. "Yes."

I circle my hips a few more times before pulling back and thrusting in again, moving as slow as my body will allow so I can memorize every gasp, every sigh, every moan. I want to know what gives her the most pleasure, so I know exactly how to get her off.

I've always believed myself to be a generous lover, observing what a woman likes so I can be sure she gets what she needs during our encounters. But I've never been as fascinated by a woman's reactions as I am right now. I've never paid quite this much attention, so I'd know the difference between the sounds she makes, and how she wants me to respond to them.

Cora gasps when she feels something she enjoys, like when I push all the way inside her. If I do that slowly, it's followed by a sigh, faster a moan. If I hit a particularly sensitive spot, her gasp is high pitched, and the moans turn into breathless cries. She makes the most erotic sounds and exploring them has me imagining all the different ways to fuck her, and the sounds she might treat me to. Before I can get to that, I have to satisfy her now, so I offer her my cock, again and again, to give her what she needs.

As her sweet little moans turn needy, I increase my pace, rolling my hips forward to give her clit some attention. She screams my name, and now, I have the key to her body. I concentrate on hitting that sensitive little bud with each thrust so I can enhance her pleasure, willing my body to outlast her screams. Her pussy constricts around me, a silent plea to move faster, harder, and I oblige.

Cora arches her back, giving me a spectacular view of her gorgeous tits swaying as I drive into her, and I feel my cock go rigid. I need her to come now, because I can't last any longer.

"You feel too good, sweetheart, I can't hold back. Squeeze that pretty pussy hard. Come with me," I ramble as I thrust, feeling her start to clench around me.

"That's it, Cora. Grip my cock. Pull me deeper." And then I feel it. Violent spasms caressing my length as she comes undone, thank fuck. I pound into her one last time to trigger my own release. And holy shit, it guts me.

I hold utterly still, barely even breathing, while my dick bucks inside her. I'm powerless to do anything but come apart as she quakes around me, the pressure of her pussy intensifying the release. Being buried inside her, feeling her clench and pull at me, is fucking euphoric.

When the tremors finally subside, I lay down, careful not to put my full weight on her, as I gasp for breath. I feel her heaving underneath me, her soft breasts brushing against my chest with each inhale, and even though I wouldn't have thought it physically impossible, that excites me. Makes me want more. This woman is something else.

It sounds cliché, but I can't remember a time when I've come so hard, and I can't help but wonder if that's because Cora's more than a casual fuck. Someone I like beyond the bedroom. I was so in tune with her just now, body and mind. I'm not sure how that translated to my pleasure, but that was damn sure the most intense orgasm of my life. Sex with Cora wrecked me in a way I've never felt before. I want to feel that again.

"Did I stop the ache?" I place a chaste kiss on her lips.

"For now." She flashes a playful grin.

I bark out a laugh, a first for me while still buried inside a woman. "You just tell me when you're ready again and I take care of it." The crazy thing is I could probably be ready again in a heartbeat if she wanted it. She's got me that riled.

"It should turn me off that you're so arrogant, but since I think you can actually back that up, I'll give you a pass."

"Damn right," I whisper against her lips, needing to taste her again.

She sighs into me, and damn if that doesn't make me feel almost content. I could stay here like this all night, teasing and kissing while joined together, but this condom won't stay on forever, so I have to get rid of it.

I pull out and go to the bathroom, but before going back to bed, I spot a washcloth, and I grab it on instinct. I've never washed a woman after—I usually just get dressed and leave—but this feels like something I need to do.

Wetting the cloth I bring it back to bed, spreading Cora's legs as I sit next to her. I drag the cloth gently over her skin, wiping away the evidence of our need.

"That's thoughtful of you." She smiles up at me.

"It is?" I ask, because I'm not even sure why I did it.

"I take it you've never done this before?"

"Uh, no." I pull the cloth away and push her legs closed.

"Hmm." She seems puzzled, but I don't understand why.

"What?"

"Well, it seems like you're always doing something thoughtful, so I guess I'm surprised you've never cleaned a woman up...after." She blushes.

"What have I done that's thoughtful?" I lay beside her and prop my head on my hand.

"Lending me your truck, taking care of me after I sprained an ankle, walking me to my car the other night. You do thoughtful things all the time." She runs her finger along my arm.

Ah, now I get it. She's still confusing all that as stuff I did to be nice, not because I'm selfish. "Cora, I've never done any of those things for anyone else. They were all excuses for me to be closer to you without actually asking you to hang out with me, even though I knew I was bad for you. Pretty sure that's selfish, not thoughtful."

"Potato, po-ta-to." She shrugs, and I swear that makes my heart lurch. How is she not disappointed by that admission? How is she so...*good?*

I lean forward and graze my lips over hers. "Why do you refuse to see me as I am?"

"Why do you refuse to see what I see?" She returns the kiss, and damn if that doesn't start to get me excited all over again. But this is supposed to be a date, and I was supposed to feed her before fucking her, so I pull away.

"Get dressed." I take her hand and kiss her knuckles. "We still need to eat."

Cora dons a pair of leggings and some sort of sweatshirt that hangs off one shoulder, minus a bra, which is only slightly less distracting than if she were naked. Even though it takes a lot of willpower not to get distracted by her tempting figure, we have a really great dinner.

We talk about everything and nothing, favorite movies, favorite foods, favorite books...well, hers, since I'm not much of a reader. We talk about why we love the outdoors, and our families. Though our backgrounds are wildly different, hers was privileged while mine was average, we both seem to have parents that are genuinely supportive, even if they don't understand us. For her, that makes it even more important to prove herself and make her parents proud, which contributes to her independent streak. For me, my parents' support is an excuse to act like a kid longer than I should, although I leave that part unspoken, since she's so determined to think I'm a better person than I am. I don't need to ruin the evening with a topic we'll never agree on, especially since I'm still half in shock it's even happening.

After we're finished eating and cleaning up, I'm struggling with whether I'm supposed to stay or go when Cora suggests a movie. She picks something on live TV, a comedy, I think. I'm barely paying attention to the screen because as soon as she sits down, she snuggles into my side, and I can't focus on anything except the sensation of her body next to mine. Her hand resting on my thigh.

I'm not a cuddler. I've never had occasion to just hold someone, and it's not something I ever expected to do, because I didn't think holding someone would feel anywhere near as good as sex, and in my mind if it wasn't as good as sex there wasn't reason to do it. I have to admit though, feeling her soft skin against mine is pleasant. Comfortable. Even though her hand is dangerously close to my junk, and I can still smell the lingering evidence of us on her skin, I'm not doing this movie thing just to bide my time until I can get her naked. I'm content to just keep her close. She isn't though, if her wandering hand is any indication.

I try my hardest to focus on the movie, to make this time with her about her, not sex. But as her fingers hesitantly glide over my thigh, my cock starts to swell. And as soon as she notices that underneath my shorts, she focuses on it, tracing the outline from base to tip and back again. I'm experiencing a whole new sensation, something between relaxation and desire, as Cora delicately explores my body.

I've had a woman take the lead before, but it was always aggressive. Almost desperate. Not slow and curious and sensual. I'm torn between doing nothing and letting her do what she wants to, taking over and doing what I want, or discouraging this so she knows I'm not hanging out with her just to get off.

Okay, who am I kidding? If she wants to initiate this, I'm sure as hell not going to stop her, especially now that she's stopped tracing the outline of my dick and is running her finger over it, causing it to jerk inside my shorts. It feels so good, the pleasure boarders on pain, but in a needy, achy way. I want her to grab me, to squeeze hard and relieve the discomfort, or at the very least take me out so my shorts aren't pinching me, but at the same time she's got me hovering on the edge, and the sweet agony feels phenomenal. Fuck.

I try to sit still, to not rock my hips up into her touch, but I'm losing control over my body. The need is becoming too great.

"You like torturing me, sweetheart?" I clench my teeth together.

"Am I? I thought this would feel good." Her hand stills and she looks up at me, guiltily. *Shit*.

"It feels incredible, it's just getting a little tight down there." I tip her chin up so I can kiss her and disabuse her of the notion that I don't like what she's doing.

"Well, that's easy to fix, right?" She reaches for my shorts and pops open the button before reaching for the zipper.

"Careful," I tell her, because I didn't bother to get all the way dressed before dinner, and zippers are dangerous in my current state.

She slowly drags the zipper down, and my cock stands up as soon as its free. Cora pulls my shorts aside so there's nothing obstructing her view and stares at me, almost fascinated. It's so hot, I feel myself swelling even more, but it also has me confused. I showed her my junk earlier, I fucked her not too long ago, why is she looking at me like that?

"What's on that pretty little mind?" I stroke her hair. "You want to touch me?"

"Yes." She teases the corner of her lip with her teeth.

"You've been touching me all night. Do you think you have to ask now?"

"No...I just...I didn't get to see you very well before, and all the lights are on here and, I...well." She blushes adorably. I hope that means she likes what she sees.

I reach down and stroke myself, needing to take the edge off, and to encourage her not to be shy.

"I like that," she mutters.

"You like me stroking my cock?" I ask, curious.

"Yes." She reaches for me, and I pull my hand back as her finger gently circles my tip. Fuck! My cock lurches toward her touch.

"Good?" She smiles at me, almost like she's proud of herself for giving me pleasure.

"Yeah," I say through gritted teeth.

She trails her finger from the tip down to the base. "And this?"

"Yes." I have to breathe through my nose since my jaw is locked tight.

She wraps her hand around me and gives a gentle squeeze before sliding her fist up and down.

"And that?"

"Fuck yes," I growl. "I like all the ways you touch me."

She smiles mischievously before turning her attention back to my dick. I watch, captivated, as she explores me without abandon. Gentle glides of her finger up and down my length, occasionally circling or flicking the tip. Fisting me in her hand to stroke me slowly. Peppering me with soft, almost innocent kisses. My cock has never been handled so thoroughly. So affectionately, like it's giving her pleasure just to touch it.

Fuck, is that even possible? I know women can get turned on by playing with a guy's junk, but I always thought that was about making it hard enough to ride. A means to an end. Cora seems turned on just by discovering how her touch affects me, kind of like how understanding her sounds made me hot when I was inside her.

Whoa. That's messed up. Or, not messed up exactly, but intense in a way I've never experienced. Are we really getting off on just learning how to touch each other, like that's just as rewarding as the actual finish? I need to find out.

I lift her up and stand her in front of me so I can pull her leggings down. She awkwardly kicks them aside and lets me pull her onto my lap so she's straddling me. Even though I ate this pussy earlier, she's right, I can see it better now, out here where there's more light. It's pink, and plump, and glistening. I drag my finger through her slit. She's *soaked*.

"Did touching me get you excited?" I tease between her legs.

"Yes." She rocks her hips forward to force my finger deeper.

"Why?" I kiss her chin.

"You were holding your breath, and your jaw was locked tight, like you were barely in control." She closes her eyes and sighs as she moves over me.

"I was." I take my slippery finger and circle her clit. She gasps, just like I knew she would. "Having your hands on me felt so good. I wanted you to make me come, but I didn't want you to stop touching me. Did you like doing that to me? Making me so hot I couldn't take it?"

She reaches for my cock and starts stroking it softly while I tease her center. "Yes," she moans.

Damn that's hot. Most women I've been with like knowing they can get me hot, but again it's about reaching the finish. *Our* finish, if not just theirs. And most of the time they used *their* body to get me worked up, showcasing it or touching it, or having me touch it. Few of them focused on touching my body or concentrated on details like how I was breathing when they touched me. They'd stroke or suck until I was hard enough to impale them, but that was the extent of it. Having someone really focus on me is, well, it's intense.

By rights, I shouldn't be the guy getting to touch Cora or have her touch me. I shouldn't be the guy she enjoys touching as much as she enjoys being touched. But since I am, I'm going to do it right.

"Take your shirt off Cora. Let me see you," I tell her.

"You, first." She shakes her head.

I rip my shirt over my head, but instead of losing hers she runs her hand over my chest, down my stomach, mapping each muscle.

"You really are too beautiful without your shirt," she mumbles, and once again she has me laughing in the middle of sex.

"Beautiful?" I cock an eyebrow.

"Yes." She traces her fingers over my skin, and I swear there's not a single part of me that doesn't tingle under her touch.

"You're the beautiful one." I kiss her. "Now show me all of you."

She slowly takes her shirt off, and once again I'm face to face with those incredible breasts. They're so full and soft, creamy. I pull a nipple into my mouth while my finger pushes slowly inside her. Another gasp. Damn this is fun.

I'm not sure how long we stay like that, kissing, sucking, fondling each other leisurely, and on the one hand it feels so good I never want it to end. But on the other I'm desperate to come, and I want to be inside her when I do.

I reach into my pocket for a condom and hand it to her. "Put it on me," I command.

She fumbles with the wrapper, like she's nervous or unfamiliar with how this works, and it's so adorably innocent and hot at the same time I swear that nearly undoes me. I grab my shaft to hold it steady for her while she slowly rolls the latex over my length.

"Ride me," I growl.

She bites her lip as she moves closer, and gently lowers herself onto my cock, going still when I'm fully seated. I brush my thumb over her clit, and she shudders.

"Okay?" I ask.

She nods, then slowly rocks her hips back and forth, getting used to the feel of me inside her. Her movements are slight, almost tentative, like she isn't sure what to do, and I wonder briefly if she's ever ridden a guy before. But since I'm buried deep, I'm content to let her move however she wants, especially since I feel every shift, every clench she makes.

I rest my thumb on her clit so she can feel the friction on that sensitive little nub while she moves. Gradually, she gets used to me and begins to shift her body, raising and lowering herself rhythmically over my length. It feels incredible, and I love being able to see every bit of her while she moves, especially where we're joined.

I reach down with both hands and spread her apart. "Can you see that, Cora? Can you see your pussy sliding over my cock?"

She blushes bright pink as she shakes her head and stills.

"You're blushing, sweetheart." I stroke her cheek. "I thought you liked it when I talked dirty?"

"I do," she whispers. "But...I've never had anyone say...I mean, I've never had anyone watch this...like that..."

"You like it better in the dark..." I wonder aloud, realizing for the first time that maybe it isn't my size that has her acting almost shy, but the fact that we're sort of exposed here in the living room.

"I don't know. I've never not been in the bedroom when..." she trails off.

"When you fucked?"

She bites her lip and nods.

"How come?" I ask, genuinely curious.

"Roommates." Her shoulders rise slightly. "No privacy except the bedroom."

"You're too beautiful to be kept in the dark. And seeing how we fit together is one of the hottest things I've ever seen." I plant a soft kiss on her lips. "But if you want to work up to this we can."

I grab her ass as I stand up to walk us toward the bedroom. She locks her ankles behind my back, pulling me deeper inside her as she does and my entire body threatens to seize at the sensation. I've fucked against walls, on counters, even in a bathroom stall once, but walking around buried inside a woman is a new one for me. With every step, her body shifts and slides over my length, and it takes all my concentration to keep putting one foot in front of the other instead of getting lost in it and pressing her up against the nearest wall.

I take her back to the bedroom and lay her on the edge of the bed, never breaking our connection. Then, with her legs still wrapped around my waist, I thrust deep and hard. Her breasts bounce as I grind into her, and that makes me thrust again, *harder*. She moans.

"Am I too rough?" I pause.

"No," she pants. "More." She unwraps her legs and braces her feet on the edge of the bed, spreading herself out beneath me. I grab her hips to hold her steady and start pumping, fast and steady, driven by her throaty cries.

Chapter 16

Cora

Now that I've got the cover of darkness as a security blanket, I let my body take over, spreading myself wide so Cade can take me hard.

It's not that I'm a prude or embarrassed about my body, but there's something about the dark that's freeing, that lets me give in to the carnal urge instead of getting distracted by what I'm thinking. In the dark, I don't have to wonder if I'm blushing as red as a tomato, or if Cade likes what he sees. I don't get distracted by questioning whether I measure up to his other encounters, or if I'm being too aggressive or too timid.

I just feel.

And it feels *incredible*.

Cade seems to intuitively know how to work my body, sending waves of pleasure rippling through me like a rollercoaster. I don't know how he's already memorized my body, my movements, my cries, like a road map, knowing exactly which touch to take—soft and sweet or hard and unforgiving. He works me into bits, prolonging my bliss, yet kicking me over the edge of insanity.

I suppose it's his vast experience that gives him this knowledge, and in the light, I'd probably freak out about that, but in the dark I don't care. I just take what he gives me and hope I'm giving him something back in return.

Raising my hips, I meet Cade's thrusts, and he answers my unspoken plea, stroking my clit with his thumb as we move together. I feel myself start to contract around him, but before the dam bursts, he pulls out and replaces his thumb with his rigid erection, gliding it slowly over my need. I whimper.

"Don't worry." He leans forward and gives me a chaste kiss. "I'll give you what you need, but if you come on my cock, I won't be able to keep myself at bay, and I'm not finished making you squirm yet." He rocks his hips back and forth, teasing his length over my swollen clit. I can't help it, I pant and gasp and cry with each pass, the friction is too decadent to contain, until finally, mercifully, my release consumes me, and Cade captures my mouth with his, swallowing my cries.

"You're so fucking sexy when you come," Cade mumbles against my lips. "Just watching you is enough to get me off."

His stiffness is trapped between us, and I feel him shifting ever so slightly in an effort to find some relief for the ache he must feel. I rotate my hips slightly to ease his frustration, and my guilt over having found the release he still needs.

"Are you ready again, sweetheart?" He kisses me softly. "I know I'm being selfish, but I have to watch you come one more time."

"How is that selfish?" I pant.

"Because this time I want you on top of me, and I've already abused this gorgeous body so much tonight." He runs his finger between my breasts.

"I'm not complaining," I tell him honestly. "I haven't felt this good in ages. I want you to feel that too."

"I know you do. And I will, when you're ready." He strokes my face gently.

"I'm ready," I say automatically, only to realize it's true, because despite the truly euphoric way he just made me feel, I'm not fully sated, and won't be until he is.

I push gently on his chest, so he moves off me and nudge him toward the head of the bed. He leans against the headboard, his solid cock pointing straight up, waiting for me. I crawl over him and lower myself onto it, pausing a moment when I've engulfed him completely. He sits deeper this way, and even after having an orgasm I need a minute to get used to him before I move.

The moonlight coming through the window gives me the perfect glimpse of Cade's bare skin. While we're still I run my hands over his stomach, up his chest, savoring the feel of his lean muscles underneath my hands. I've never seen such a beautiful body. He's so hard, but soft at the same time. Powerful yet soothing. It's endlessly sexy.

As I explore Cade's body, he does the same to mine, caressing my hips, my stomach, my breasts, which he plays with tenderly, massaging them in his hands as he strokes my nipple with his thumb. Under his hands, I feel the ache building between my legs, and without conscious thought I begin to circle my hips.

Cade moans softly as I begin to move, his hands falling to the bed. I reach behind me to fondle his balls the same way he was just caressing my breasts, and he leans his head back against the headboard, his eyes closed in an expression of pure bliss.

"Do you like that?" I find my voice.

"Fuck yeah," he exhales.

"Do you like it soft like this, or should I squeeze harder?" I don't quite have the dirty words yet, but I figure asking how he likes to be touched is the next best thing.

"I like having you touch my balls, period," he pants. "Rub them, squeeze them, tug on them, I like all of it. Just not too hard."

I increase the pressure a little bit as I circle my hips faster. Cade groans. "Fuck, Cora. You have no idea how good that feels. You better stop touching me or I won't last."

"I don't want you to last."

"I've gotta last as long as you do," he grunts. "But I need you to catch up to me. How can I make you hotter?"

I don't want him worried about me, so I draw his mouth toward my nipple in response. He pulls it between his lips and starts sucking, hard. I can't help the whimper that escapes, and in response Cade grabs my ass and rocks my body firmly over his. I thread my fingers in his hair and hold on while he sucks me into his mouth in rhythm with his thrusting cock.

I thought with me being on top I'd do all the work, but instead I sit motionless, impaled on Cade's dick, and he works me from below, driving me closer and closer to the edge. But as good as this feels, I don't want to take my pleasure from him. I want to give it to him. I pull my breast from his mouth and take his hands off my ass, bracing my hands on his thighs as I arch back so I can lift and lower myself onto his rigid shaft.

"Damn that's hot." Cade runs his hand over my breasts. "I still think you're too beautiful to be kept in the dark, but your tits look spectacular in the moonlight."

Cade's praise empowers me to work my body for his pleasure. I rise up so that I'm kneeling directly over him, the tip of his cock still nestled inside me. Then I lower my body over his shaft until we end, slamming firmly onto him. He groans so deeply he sounds like an animal. I do it again. And again, noticing the way his jaw locks as he battles between letting go and holding out for an even greater release.

I feel my breasts jolt with each bounce, which would normally make me self-conscious, but Cade's expression is so enraptured I don't even care. All that matters is giving to him the bliss he's given to me. And then his earlier words register, that seeing me come gets him excited, and I know how to make this even better for him. I place two fingers on my clit and start rubbing in gentle circles.

"That's it, sweetheart. Touch yourself while you ride me hard. I feel your pussy getting tighter. I want to feel it milking me." His eyes are thick with lust as he groans.

Holy shit. I don't know how or why his words have the power to make my body react, but they do, and just hearing them sends me spiraling out of control. My walls contract, hard, wave after wave of spasms wracking through me. It's so intense, so consuming, I can't even breathe, I can only scream. Yet somehow, despite the pleasure coursing through me, I sense Cade's release gripping him, feel his cock pumping inside me, as he lets out a strangled cry of his own. Oh. My. God.

I don't have the most experience with sex, but I know enough to realize a release like what we just shared isn't typical. I've certainly never felt anything like that before, and by Cade's reaction he hasn't either.

Somehow during that explosion, we shifted to the point where he's lying flat on his back. He's starting straight up at the ceiling, mouth open, chest heaving, like he doesn't have the strength or control to do anything else. It's beautiful.

I reach out to stroke his chest, to ease him down the same way he did for me earlier, but the moment I make contact with his skin I feel his heart pounding, and I can't move. I can only rest my palm on his chest, like I'm holding onto his heart, which is beating just as hard as mine. Feeling that is almost reassuring, because I think it means I'm reading him correctly, and he is just as affected by our encounter as I am.

My touch must rouse him because he uses my hand to pull me forward so I'm lying on him, my head tucked under his chin. He rests his hands on my back, his fingers absently skirting over my skin. He doesn't speak, doesn't do much else but breathe, and hold me against him as if trying to prolong our connection. I don't think this is typical of Cade, in fact I'm sure it's not, but it feels so comfortable, so safe, I let myself melt into his arms.

I must drift off because I'm roused when Cade kisses my forehead and whispers something about needing to clean up. He shifts me off him and starts to rise off the bed, and something about the stilted movement makes me wonder if he's uncomfortable, like he isn't sure if he should stay or go, and what his choice will mean. Just as I overthink things in the light, he's overthinking them in the intimacy of my bedroom. I do the only thing I can think of to calm his mind. I make his decision for him.

"Hurry back," I whisper.

"Back?" he asks softly. "To bed?"

"Yes."

"You want me to stay here?" He sounds hesitant, but whether that's because he's confused or afraid, I don't know.

"Yes. If you'd like to, I mean." I bite my lip.

He smiles affectionately and leans down to kiss my forehead. "Yeah. I would."

I must fall asleep before he makes it back, because I don't remember him getting into bed. But he's there when I wake up, holding me tenderly against him, and even though the room is starting to fill with sunlight I show him just how happy I am to have spent the night in his arms.

***

Over the next week or so Cade and I fall into a comfortable rhythm of working during the day and having dinner together at night, after which he stays over, and we repeat it all the next day. Neither of us consciously decided to organize our schedules that way, I think we just like starting and ending the day together, so that's what we do. Mostly.

There have been a few times I've insisted Cade spend time with Deacon, either for a bike ride or a few beers, before staying the night with me. This gives me additional time to work and keeps the peace between us all. Deacon has been much more accepting of me recently, which may be in part because I always make enough breakfast for him, but I think is also due to the fact that I'm not monopolizing Cade's time. Not completely. And I think a little bit of space is good for us, since we've jumped two feet into this, whatever it is, as soon as Cade told me he wanted to try being with just me.

We haven't really defined anything, and I don't think either of us intend to since we know it's only for the summer, but it feels an awful lot like we're dating. While it makes me smile to know Cade wants to be with only me, it's also a heavy burden, and one I'm doing my best to navigate without anyone getting hurt.

Cade has never had anyone take an interest in him for him, and while we have trouble keeping our hands off each other, I'm careful to make sure sex isn't the only thing we do. We've been on several hikes together, we usually cook together, I've watched him in his workshop finishing Ally's bike, and I try to get him to talk about himself, all so he knows I don't view him as strictly the man sharing my bed. All that means I'm getting to know him on a deeper level, and I really, really, like what I see.

Cade is observant, almost wise, in terms of how he sees and understands the world around him. But he's not afraid to admit what he doesn't know or ask questions, like he does on the rare occasions we talk about my work. I'm increasingly thankful that I didn't listen to my first instinct and dismiss him as nothing more than a flirt and a tease. Not that he isn't a flirt, he definitely has a playful, mischievous side that he shows me when we're alone, particularly in the bedroom. But he doesn't use it as a defense mechanism to keep me at arm's length anymore. Rather, he simply uses it to make me smile and laugh, or turn me on. And wow, does that man turn me on.

I only have to look at Cade and I feel like I'm swooning. He's so beautiful, with that tousled hair, chiseled jaw, and piercing blue eyes. And that body. *Lord* that body. He's so strong, yet he moves with an easy grace that belies his strength. It's totally cliché, I know, but I feel protected and safe next to him even though he can pick me up like a doll despite my being of average height. I actually love when he picks me up, and I think he knows it, because he does it often.

Sometimes, he throws me over his shoulder and carries me to bed amid fits of laughter. Other times, he cradles me in his arms and gently lays me down before him. He's even pinned me against the wall or set me on the counter while he thrusts between my legs, because true to his word he doesn't want to keep me in the dark, and I'm gradually getting comfortable with the idea of letting go in full view of his hungry eyes. No matter where he takes me or how, we always end the night wrapped in each other's arms, until the sun wakes us, and we do it all again.

So, yeah, things between us are comfortable. Familiar. Great even. And that's what worries me, because I'm enjoying this so much, I can't fathom the idea of giving it up. Part of me doesn't want to worry about that at all, to enjoy this to the fullest as long as I can without asking 'what if' along the way. The other part of me, the part that's becoming attached to the idea of sharing my life and my home with someone, is less certain, because I don't think it's so much the idea of sharing my life and home with someone, but sharing them with Cade specifically, that I'm getting attached to.

Aside from the first week or two I was in Katah Vista, I've never lived alone. I grew up with a few siblings and had a roommate all throughout college and grad school, so in essence I've always had someone to share my life and home with. Not romantically, but I certainly wouldn't put myself in the lonely category because I had people around to come home to and talk with.

Yet somehow, after little more than a week of spending time with Cade, the thought of not starting and ending my day with him seems *foreign*.

I know that means I'm getting in too deep. That I should pump the brakes on this thing between us, if not get off the train altogether. And during the day, when Cade isn't with me, I can almost convince myself that's the right thing to do. But as soon as I see him, the part of me that wants to feel instead of think takes over, and I tell myself there's no harm in enjoying this right now as I fall asleep in his arms.

Saturday begins, bright and early, with Cade nuzzling my neck until I open my eyes.

"Morning." I roll over and stretch, and he takes the opportunity to run his hands over my naked body, which he seems to do whenever he has the chance. Usually, it turns into something more, but today we're on a schedule.

"Morning." He grins, planting a quick kiss on a puckered nipple. "We have to stop at my house to grab the bikes, so if you don't want to be late you better put some clothes on."

"What happens if I don't put clothes on?" I trace a finger over his firm pec.

"I'll have to ravage you, which we'd both thoroughly enjoy, but then the whole town would know we were late because I was balls deep in my woman." He licks his lips and gives me a wicked grin.

"*Your* woman?"

"Yeah. *Mine*," he says as he hugs me to him and affectionately bites my neck.

I squeal and roll out of Cade's reach to head for the bathroom, amused and a little shocked by his possessiveness. Then again, I know he still has trouble believing I'm with him for more than sex, so this whole 'mine' thing is probably just based on insecurity. I get that, and even though it can't be permanent, I'm happy to be his while I'm here.

We have a quick breakfast and throw our gear in the truck since we'll be in town all day if not longer, then swing by his house to load up the bikes. We park behind The Underground, and after helping me out of the truck Cade locks his fingers with mine as we walk inside.

It's a simple gesture, but it has my belly doing flips, because it's so uncharacteristic. I mean, Cade likes to touch me when we're together, putting his arm around me while we're on the couch or holding me to him while we sleep, so it's not touching me that's weird, it's touching me when others will see it.

Dex cocks an eyebrow when he notices our clasped hands, but otherwise doesn't say anything. Ally is less discreet. "I knew it," she accuses. "I knew he was the reason you haven't called me to hang out."

Finn clears his throat, for our benefit or Ally's I'm not sure, and Ryder slips a twenty to Deacon, who's smirking knowingly. I swear Dex says something about a dumb bet under his breath.

"I thought he was messing with me," Ryder protests as he flicks Deacon off. "I mean, Cade dating? That's absurd, right?"

"Seriously?" Cade balks. "I'm right here with my girl. Show some respect."

"Sorry," Ryder grumbles, and I find myself trying to stifle a laugh because he really does look guilty.

"It's cool, look she's trying not to laugh." Cade smirks at me. "She knows all about me, but she likes me anyway. Go figure." He squeezes my hand affectionately. I swat him on the chest, because he knows I hate it when he puts himself down.

"Ow. Save that for the bedroom." He winks.

I know what he's doing, resorting to his flirty, nonchalant manner to in order to stave off serious questions about us, and while I normally hate when he does this as a defense mechanism, right now I'm on board with it. I'm not ready to explain this any more than he is, so for now I'll hide behind this wall with him.

"So, this has been going on a while?" Ally crosses her arms and stares us down.

"Sorry," I mumble to Ally. "I meant to call and then, well..." I trail off.

Cade gives my hand a little squeeze, which helps lift the guilt I'm feeling. "I'm much better company," he tells her. "Of course, she'd rather hang out with me."

"Or you have a cock," Ally quips smartly.

"That does work in my favor." He waggles his eyebrows and gives my hand another squeeze. "So, are you really going to parade me around half naked for this race Al? My girl might not like showing me off like that."

Okay, *wow*. That's the third time he's called me his girl today, and I'm starting to like the sound of that. Too much. I know it's part of the act, meant to preemptively control the narrative about us, but the more he says it the more I think I want it to be true. But it can't be true, because that would make this more than the summer fling we were both looking for, and that doesn't work for either of us, right?

I'm all sorts of mixed up right now. It's barely been two weeks since we decided to explore this thing between us, and while I know it's supposed to be temporary, the fact that we've been virtually inseparable makes it hard to remember that. Then there's the hand-holding and him calling me *his girl*. Rationally. I know why he's doing that, but emotionally I'm responding to it. I like having him hold my hand. I like hearing him refer to me as 'his.' And even if those gestures are for show, I find myself wondering if any part of him thinks this is real, the way part of me is starting to.

"Oh please," Ally scoffs, brining me back to the present. "She'll be too busy fending off her own admirers to worry about you."

"Wait." Cade frowns. "I don't like that idea any better. Give her a cloak or something." He says it jokingly, but there almost seems to be a little panic in his eyes. I squeeze his hand, and when he turns to look at me it's gone.

Ally passes out costumes and we all get dressed. I'm still not overly familiar with the show, but it seems to me she's done a great job with the costumes, right down to the wigs some of the guys are wearing. Out of all of us, I think Cade looks the least like his character, because he's not really big enough to be Kahl Drago, but the wig and costume make it evident who he's supposed to be.

Ally makes us all pose for pictures, snapping the first one Cade and I have taken together, and when she's satisfied with the results, we all head out to grab our bikes.

Cade lifts the bikes out of his truck, his lean muscles rippling deliciously in the process, and I do notice the passing stare of several women walking by. The way they're ogling him has me on edge, possessive almost, but that quickly fades when Ally screams in delight.

"Oh my gosh, Cade! It's amazing. This is the perfect solution to keep my dress from getting tangled." She launches herself into his arms and squeezes the life out of him before climbing on the bike. She fluffs her dress over the bustle frame and starts riding around the parking lot in circles, squealing as she goes. "It works!" Cade shakes his head and laughs, amused by her excitement, and I have to admit it is infectious.

Cade hands me a bike, one he was able to borrow from a neighbor, and then we all make our way to the starting gate a few blocks away. We collect our bibs and pin them to our clothes, then line up for the start.

Just as Cade warned me, this isn't a typical race. Not only are we counting laps instead of time, virtually everyone is in costume, most bikes are decorated or re-engineered like Ally's, and entire families including kids on training wheels are taking part. It's fascinating!

There's so much going on that I'm not sure where all to look. One family is dressed like Raggedy Ann and Andy, their kids in matching outfits. A group of twelve or so are all dressed like Waldo, and another group is dressed like Mario Kart characters complete with bikes decorated to resemble the vehicles each of the characters use in the game. The creativity surrounding me is amazing, and I'm starting to see why these events are so much fun.

Once the race begins and we start weaving our way through town, people line the streets to cheer us on, clapping, shouting and ringing cowbells. We wave to the crowd as if we're in a parade, which I guess in a way we are, as we do lap after lap.

It's clear that the entire town is involved one way or another, and that sense of community is almost overwhelming. Not in a bad way, just different, because where I come from you might have a neighborhood or a school come together for a common goal, but you certainly never get the entire town, and while this feels sort of like a big party, it's also heartwarming to see so many people participating in an event that benefits their less fortunate neighbors.

I knew from the first moment I stepped into this town that the sense of unity outweighed anything I'd ever known, but I didn't understand the sheer magnitude of that until today.

Katah Vista isn't wealthy. Wealthy people come here, have second homes here, but the town itself doesn't have money. It has blue-collar, hard-working people. Yet every single one of them is digging deep for this charity event, whether by raising money, donating food or staffing the event. Everyone has a role and is doing their part. Yes, its social and kind of like a giant street party given that most everyone is in costume, but at its core this is an event with a purpose. You might find events like this in bigger cities, though you won't find the entire city participating, and the fact that everyone is involved here makes me want to stay.

Yes, it's small, and that comes with typical small-town issues like a lack of amenities and an abundance of gossip. Yet looking around me, it's clear these are all good-hearted people with a deep sense of affection for each other, and a strong sense of pride in their community. How could I not be drawn to that? To all the generous people I meet, of which there are many.

Throughout the race, we stop at different houses for snacks and drinks, chatting with other racers and spectators while we take a break. At each stop, we're ushered inside as if we've been expected, although from what I can tell there is no schedule. There are hugs and toasts and picture taking and smiles all around, even for me, despite the fact that I don't know anyone.

Although we travel as the *'Game of Thrones'* pack, I'm introduced to dozens of new people as Cade's girl instead of Khaleesi, which unfailingly results in looks of confusion and curiosity. Still, since everyone is so nice, I know that only reflects their surprise, not disapproval. In fact, I'd say most people are accepting, almost happy to see him with someone. And by *with someone*, I mean that Cade is making it evident we're together.

Each time we get off our bikes, he immediately reaches for my hand, brushing his thumb back and forth over my finger. Before we get on again, he gives me a lingering kiss, one that says he wishes we were alone.

Showing this much open affection should give us pause, because it suggests a closer connection than either of us wanted. Instead, it's starting to feel natural. Just as it's starting to feel natural to be here.

Chapter 17

Cade

I've spent my whole life in this town, twenty-six years, and I've done this bike race every single one of them, to the point the monotony of this day was wearing on me. Until this year. Even I'm not dense enough to question why that is.

I fucking loved having Cora next to me all day. Putting aside the fact she's so beautiful and so sweet, she makes everything better just by being there. I don't think she stopped smiling all day long. I couldn't stop myself from smiling when I looked at her, nor could I stop touching her. What's even weirder is that I wasn't touching her to tease her or make her aroused or anything. I just liked the feel of her skin against mine, introducing her as my girl and seeing the way she blushed each time I said it.

Plus, I got to experience this day through her eyes, and that kind of made me love it again. She was so awed by all the costumes, so impressed with the how the whole town got involved, so humbled by how nice everyone was to her. She didn't tell me any of that, not verbally anyway, but I could see it in her eyes. I could see her falling in love with this town, and the selfish bastard that I am makes me wonder if she might like it enough to stay.

I realize that's an absurd thought. She's got big goals for herself, and I'm not sure they can be met here. I'm also not sure she'd be content with the small-town life or could deal with the winters we have. Beyond all that, the thing I'm most unsure about is whether she'd be willing to stay here for me, which I find myself thinking about as we drive back to her place.

Being with Cora feels right in a way nothing else in my life ever has. That makes it sound like I've had a bad life, and that couldn't be further from the truth. My life so far is the stuff other guys dream about; and I'm grateful for that. But it was my life alone. I didn't have anyone to share it with.

A few weeks ago, I didn't think I was capable of feeling this way. That I could commit to one person or that I could be anything more than a good fuck. But instead of feeling confined in this arrangement, like I kind of expected, I feel relaxed. Happy. And while the sex is off the charts, I don't feel like that's all I have to offer Cora, because there are times we hang out without fucking. I think that means I'm starting to fall for her. Or maybe I already have.

That's why I hope she falls in love with this town, because if she does, maybe she'll fall for me too.

I hold on to that fantasy for the drive home, Cora's small hand cradled in mine. But reality sets in as I pull onto her street.

I recognize the silver truck parked behind Cora's Subaru the instant I see it. I had hoped to put this off a bit longer, but in this town that kind of privacy is hard to come by.

Cora's fast asleep when we pull in, so I carefully unfold her hand and walk around to the passenger side to help her out. She leans into me when I open the door, and I scoop her into my arms to carry her inside.

"I'll be back in a minute," I tell my dad, who's now standing in the drive. He nods soberly.

"What?" Cora mumbles dreamily.

"Nothing, sweetheart." I kiss her forehead absently as I walk to the front door and punch in the code. Carrying her down the hall to her bedroom, I lay her down gently to take off her shoes and undress her, then tuck her under the covers.

"Aren't you coming to bed?" she asks as I stand up.

"In a minute." I kiss her softly. "I need to close up the house."

"Hurry back, it's cold without you," she whispers. It's so quiet I can barely make out the words, and I'm not even sure she realizes she said them, because she's already fast asleep. But they give me hope that maybe she's getting just as used to sleeping with me as I am to sleeping with her.

I brush my lips over hers before heading back outside. My dad has closed the door of my truck for me, so the only light is coming from the front porch of the house. It doesn't hide the look of concern on his face as he leans against the railing.

"She's pretty," he begins as I take a seat in one of the rocking chairs.

"She is." I push up on the balls of my feet so the chair starts to sway, an outlet for my restless energy.

"This been going on since you lent her your truck?" He watches me closely.

"No, I really did do that to be nice." He doesn't need to know I was hoping that would help me get closer to her.

He nods his head. "Were you hoping to keep this a secret?"

"No. But I was hoping it'd take longer to get back to you." I rub the back of my neck, dreading where I think this is going. "You here to tell me this is a bad idea?"

"Maybe." He cocks his head. "But not for the reason you think." I'm not expecting this, and I don't have a response for it. The rocking chair stills as I go tense. "You're expecting me to tell you it's a bad idea to get involved with the client's niece? That it could jeopardize business?"

"Isn't that why you're here?"

"That's why I came here, but that's not what had me concerned." He shakes his head slowly.

"What has you concerned?" My heartbeat slows, wondering what else could make him look so grim.

"That you're in love with her," he says matter-of-factly.

"I...what?"

"I see the way you look at her, son." He exhales deeply.

The beat that nearly stopped seconds ago now echoes in my chest. "I...well I like her, yeah," I stutter.

"Give your old man some credit, Cade. I know love when I see it. Now, I admit I came over here expecting to tell you to be careful about having a little fun with the wrong person, and I'm glad to see that's not what this is. I'm glad to see you happy." He smiles, although it looks more sad than pleased. "But that raises a whole new set of concerns for me. If I remember right, she's not staying here past the summer, and I don't want to see you get your heart broken. Does she know how you feel?"

"*I* don't know how I feel," I admit, which seems to shock both of us. I love my dad, and I know he loves me, but we've never really had the kind of relationship where we talked about feelings. Not that we don't talk, we just never really got into the emotional stuff, and we especially didn't get into talk about girls. I don't know how to have this conversation. I don't know what to say.

"You aren't sure if you love her?" Dad asks hesitantly.

"How would I know that?" I throw my hands up. "I've never had a girlfriend before. Until Cora I never even went on a date."

"You went to prom." Dad's brow furrows in confusion.

"In a group, not with one specific girl. I was always more interested in playing on the mountain or playing tour guide than hanging out with one girl." I rub my hand over my face. "Until these last few weeks, I still was."

Dad nods thoughtfully. "So, now you'd rather spend time with her?" he guesses, correctly.

"I still play on the mountain," I protest, thinking about how Cora makes me ride while she finishes her work, and then we hang out after.

"Why are you smiling?" Dad asks.

"I'm smiling?" I wasn't aware I had been.

"You're doing it again," Dad says.

Huh. I lean against the chair and look up at the stars. "Cora makes me ride a few times a week," I tell him. "She doesn't want to keep me from doing that."

"But you would, to spend time with her?" Dad's gaze drifts toward the house.

"Yeah." I nod, keeping my eyes on the sky.

"Then you need to tell her."

"Tell her what, exactly?" I meet his gaze.

"How you feel. That you want her to stay. I assume that's what you want…" he trails off, waiting to see if I'll agree or object.

"She's got plans that don't involve staying here, and I don't have plans to leave. I'm not going to mess up what she's worked for by asking her to stay here." I gesture to the space around us.

"What's wrong with here?"

"She's studying for her PhD, Dad, what could she possibly do with that here?" I shake my head.

"I don't know. But if she knows you want her to stay maybe she'll try to figure that out." He makes it sound so simple.

"And why would she want to figure that out? Because I ask her to stay? I don't know if she feels that way about me." I can't afford to let myself think that way. To get my hopes up.

"She makes you bike a couple times a week," Dad says.

"So?" I set the chair rocking again. Why can't he just drop it?

"So, she doesn't want to get in the way of the things you love, same as you don't want to get in the way of the things she loves. You don't make that effort for another person if you don't care about them."

"Care about me, sure. I know she cares about me. I don't know if that's enough to stay here, though," I exhale.

"That's why you have to tell her how you feel, Cade. Give the two of you a chance."

"You really think she'd do that? That she'd stay for me?" Dammit, now he's got me wondering.

"Only one way to find out, son." He steps to me and claps my shoulder. "Talk to her."

"Yeah, okay," I nod absently. "I'll…I'll do that."

Dad gives my shoulder a firm squeeze. "And bring her over for dinner. Mom will be pissed if you hold out on her much longer."

"True," I chuckle as Dad makes his way to his truck. "Night, Dad."

"Night." He climbs in the cab and drives away.

Well, that was unexpected. Instead of a lecture about being reckless and immature I get a lecture about going after Cora for real. But is it that easy?

Deep down, I know my dad's right about me loving her. I was afraid to admit that to myself since it happened so hard and so fast but hearing him say it out loud, I realize it's true. There's no other way to explain this need to be near her, this desire to have her stay. Could she feel the same?

I understand why my dad thinks I should tell her that I love her. But what if I tell her and she doesn't feel the same? Or what if she does, but she leaves anyway because that's where her career takes her? So, would telling her how I feel make it easier for her to stay, or harder to leave? Until I have a better sense of how she'll respond, telling her might only confuse her, and I don't want to do that.

I head back inside and get undressed to slip into bed. Cora shifts in her sleep and snuggles up against me, exactly where I want her to be. *Always*. Now I have to find when, or if, to tell her that.

***

I'm not sure what wakes me, Cora's feather light touch mapping my chest, or my throbbing dick, which is no doubt a result of her gently caressing me. Either way, I have the strangest sensation of being relaxed and aroused at the same time, and I'm torn between wanting to stay still and needing to move. It's the look on her face when I open my eyes that gives me my answer.

Cora watches intently, almost mesmerized, as her finger glides over my body, outlining the muscles that are visible beneath my skin. She's so focused I don't think she realizes I'm awake, and I fight to stay still as her fingers roam over my stomach, my pecs, grazing a nipple before drifting down to where my shaft is straining to break free of my shorts.

Her touch is so slight I almost have to concentrate to feel it, but that somehow makes it more potent. More erotic. And that makes my cock twitch visibly.

She starts when the movement catches her eye, and her gaze darts to mine. "Morning," she blushes.

I reach out to tuck a strand of hair behind her ear. "Morning."

"Sorry I woke you," she half whispers.

"I'm not. I like waking up with your hands on me."

Her eyes dart to my cock, and I see a mixture of curiosity and lust in them. We've explored each other's bodies thoroughly at this point, but Cora seems to like when I tell her how to touch me, almost like she needs permission to be bold and aggressive. Not that she's a timid person by nature, but when it comes to sex, she's almost shy, to the point that when she takes the lead, she's a little tentative. I'm guessing that's because she worries about her lack of experience compared to mine, and while I know she's kind of embarrassed by her shyness, I find it sexy as fuck.

"You don't have to ask, Cora. Take what you want. Use me," I reassure her.

She tugs the waistband of my shorts up and over my swollen cock, sliding them down my legs until it's unrestrained. It stands straight up, long and thick, and primed for her touch.

Cora drags her fingers up and over my length, circling the thick ring of skin at the tip before taking me firmly in her fist and stroking me down to the base. The groan that escapes me sounds more like a feral growl even to my own ears, and Cora smiles in response. Then she leans forward and takes me into her mouth for the first time.

It's takes every ounce of control I have to not burst right here and now. The heat of her mouth, her slick tongue circling my tip, my cock disappearing inch by inch between those sultry lips. And her eyes, closed peacefully, like she enjoys the feel of me in her mouth.

She works me slowly, affectionately, licking and sucking and stroking me to the brink of ecstasy without ever letting me fall over the edge. But she's not toying with me, not trying to withhold my release. She's simply exploring my body in a different way, oblivious to the fact that she holds so much power over me.

Her innocence is so fucking sexy, I want to stay here forever, watching her touch and taste me so thoroughly. Feeling her hot little mouth suck me, that wet tongue flicking over my tip. It feels so incredible I can't speak, can do little else but grunt and groan as she uses my body to push her limits and get bolder.

When her head starts to bob rhythmically, I brace myself and hold my breath. I know she's worked herself up to this, and I want her to feel confident enough to touch me whenever she wants, however she wants, without relying on my commands. But once my cock hits the back of her throat, I know I won't last, and I lift her off me.

"I can't take any more or I'll come in your mouth," I shudder.

"Isn't that the idea?" A tiny little crease appears between her brows.

"Maybe another time." I pull her forward and kiss her deeply, my finger seeking her slick channel so I can give her a taste of the pleasure she's given me. She's fucking drenched.

"I want to be inside your pussy when I come, sweetheart, so I can feel you coming with me." Circling her clit with her essence, my girl gives me a throaty, sultry moan that I feel in my balls. Teasing her opening, I coat my fingers with her juices and spread it over her folds. I love the way her arousal feels against my skin, all slippery and silky and hot.

Dipping my finger inside, I stroke her walls and pump slowly, watching her breasts heave as her breathing quickens. I withdraw my finger to reach for a condom, but before I do, I spread her arousal on my dick, needing to feel some of that wet heat on my skin. My finger glides effortlessly over my cock, and that slippery contact feels so good I can't help but moan.

Cora takes it all in and mimics my movement while I reach for the condom, slicking her essence over my erection with her fingertips. It feels phenomenal, almost as good as her hot little mouth. I moan again.

"You like this?" she whispers as she does it again.

"Fuck yes," I groan. "It's so hot to feel your fingers gliding over me."

"Would it feel like this without..." she trails off.

"You mean bare?" I freeze, my hand halfway to the nightstand.

"Yes," she whispers as she strokes me again. "I'm on the pill."

Not gonna lie the thought of being inside Cora bare, her slick pussy sliding back and forth over my length, is tempting as fuck. Though I can't do that to her.

"You shouldn't let me in your body bare, sweetheart." I pull her finger to my mouth to suck it clean.

"You don't want that?" she pants.

"Of course, I do." I kiss her softly. "But it wouldn't be fair to take you that way."

"Why not?" she breathes. "Are you...have you not been safe?"

"I've always been safe," I tell her honestly. "But going bare isn't the kind of thing you do on a whim."

"You think this is a whim?" Her lips turn down.

"I think we're both desperate for each other, and I don't want you to do something in the heat of the moment you might regret later." I caress her cheek.

"Why would I regret it?" She strokes me again, and I exhale a shaky breath.

"You know why, Cora," I whisper, cupping her face in my hands to kiss her slowly. "Just because you don't care about my past doesn't mean you shouldn't. A guy like me doesn't deserve to be inside you bare."

Her eyes flash with disappointment. Or is it anger?

"I decide what I deserve." She pushes me to my back and climbs on top of me, and I swear I fall even more in love with her as I watch her overcome her bashfulness and take charge. I want to kiss the fuck out of her for being brave and determined enough to tell me what to do. Before I can touch my lips to hers, she guides my cock to her entrance and sinks onto me, and every doubt I had is erased by the sheer bliss of feeling her slippery walls engulf me.

"Oh God," I groan, arching my hips up to feel more of her. "Fuck."

"This feels good?" She starts to rock her hips slowly.

"Fuck yes. It feels amazing, Cora. But why? Why let me do this?" I strain to get the words out.

"Because I want to give you something you've never had before, the same way you do for me."

"What do I do for you?" I exhale as she slides her sweet pussy up and down my now slippery cock.

"You make me feel sexy."

"You are sexy." I put my hands on her hips to slow her movements, buying myself some time before I totally lose control.

"I mean sexy like brave, or uninhibited. Not sweet or cute." She rocks against me.

"You're all of those." I sit up so I can tease her nipple with my tongue. "It's hot as fuck when you let me take control and push your boundaries, and when you push your own." I cup her tits and massage them in my hands while she rides me slowly. "Everything about you turns me on."

"You're doing it again," she breathes. "You make me feel good. I want to make you feel as good as you make me feel."

"You don't have to fuck me bare to make me feel good," I grunt, my control waning.

"I know. But do you?" She's moving a little faster now, taking me slightly deeper. I feel my jaw tense it's locked so hard.

"Do I what?" I grit.

"Do you like it?"

"I fucking love it," I blurt, unable to hold back any longer. "I feel your pussy everywhere. It's so hot, so wet. And my cock is drenched. I fucking love it," I repeat.

Cora smiles, but whether she's relieved or satisfied I can't tell because my control is gone, and I can't hold back. I crush my mouth to hers as I flip us over and plunge deep.

I'm desperately trying not to take her like an animal, but fuck, the feel of her slick walls rubbing against me, the sound of our skin slapping together, her breathy cries. I'm so lost.

"Damn, Cora. You feel so good. I need you with me, but I can't hold back." I'm rambling as I thrust, rolling my hips with each pass to give her clit some attention. "Tell me you're close, sweetheart. Tell me how to make you come with me."

"This," she heaves. "Just like this."

I pump as long and slow as my body will allow, but I'm too close, barely able to control my movements. My cock needs to move, and I give in, thrusting faster and deeper, desperately trying to take her over the edge before my own release consumes me. And then I feel it, the tiny kiss of her pussy starting to tighten around me, and I let myself come apart, my dick pumping into her as she grips me hungrily.

Oh. My. God.

My body is utterly spent. I couldn't move if I tried, and I don't have to, because without a condom I can linger inside Cora while we come down together. Maybe we can stay like this long enough to go again. I'm seriously into that idea before the magnitude of what just happened hits me. I took her bare, and in the process, I lost all control.

"Cora." She's still gasping for breath beneath me, and I shift my weight to give her more air. "Cora." I kiss her softly. "Are you okay, sweetheart? Did I hurt you? I tried not to, but you felt so good and I...are you okay?"

Her eyes flutter as a small smile plays on her lips. "I'm perfect. That was perfect," she sighs.

"It was," I agree, kissing her again, before I can blurt out what I really feel.

Chapter 18

Cora

"Mmm, my favorite," I roll over and stretch as Cade sets a steaming cup of coffee and a toasted bagel on the nightstand.

"I know." He takes a seat on the bed and gives me a quick kiss.

"Does breakfast in bed mean we're spending the entire day in bed again?" I lick my lips before taking a bite.

"Think you could handle that?" Cade drags his finger up my leg and toward my core.

"I want to say yes." I close my eyes, remembering how much I enjoyed lounging around in bed, talking, teasing, fucking. "But I think you wore me out."

"Rain check then," Cade laughs. "Besides, I have to work."

"Ugh, me too. And I have lunch with Ally and Lennon"

"You're ditching me for the girls?" His puppy dog eyes peek through his shaggy locks.

"Only for lunch." I give him a toothy grin.

"I guess I can live with that. Hey, that reminds me." He twirls a lock of my hair in his fingers. "My parents want us to go over for dinner. Think you can do that tonight?"

I freeze, coffee halfway to my mouth, as I replay those words in my head. Did he really just invite me to a family dinner?

"Isn't that...I mean...you want me to meet your parents? Already?" I sputter.

"Small town, Cora." He exhales heavily, letting my hair drop. "As soon as we went out together word spread. They're curious."

"Okay. Wow. I mean...you told me this would happen, but I guess I wasn't thinking word would get back to your parents." I feel my face heating.

"This is why I didn't want to say anything too soon." He offers a weak smile. "The town sort of takes over and makes it hard to have any sense of privacy. But we don't have to do it. They'll understand if I tell them it's too much."

"It's not that," I blink, "I've just never met anyone's parents before. I'm not sure what to expect."

"You've never met a guy's parents before?" He looks confused.

"Well, I didn't really date much in high school, and in college no one's parents were around so, no." I give a little shrug. "I don't really know how this works."

"I've never brought a girl home before, so I don't know how it works either. And I know it's...weird to do this already, but, seeing as most of the town has already met you, it's kind of weird that my parents haven't, if that makes sense." He rubs his neck, looking adorably flustered.

"I guess." I trap my lips between my teeth. I know word travels in a small town, but what sort of word has made its way back to them? Does the town see me as the helpless visitor Cade's watching over? Do they worry that I'm using him for the summer? Do they know he stays here every night?

"What's wrong, Cora?" Cade threads his fingers through mine. "You got sort of pale there for a second."

"What do you think your parents have heard about me?"

"Nothing bad." He gives my fingers a squeeze.

"Do you think they know...I mean...does the town know that you stay here..." Now I'm definitely red.

"Do they know we're sleeping together? I assume so," Cade smirks. "My dad was here when we got back from the race, he saw me carry you inside."

"Oh. Well, do they know you stay here every night?" I hold my breath bracing for the answer.

"Probably. My truck has been a permanent fixture in the driveway for a few weeks." He shrugs like that's no big deal at all.

"Oh my gosh." I fan my face. "That's...how am I supposed to have a meal with them if they know..."

"Cora," he interrupts. "I know I'm new to this, but I'm pretty sure sex is a normal when two people are hanging out. Even if we were in a big city, people would assume we're sleeping together, right?"

"Yes, but in this town, they don't have to assume, they know. Isn't it weird that your parents probably know you stay here every night?"

"Cora, I'm no saint, remember?" He brushes my hair back from my face. "Besides, they'd probably rather have me sleeping with you than with a bunch of random tourists."

Oh wow. That's an angle I hadn't thought of before, and it kind of knocks the wind out of me. I don't care about his past, though I do care that people might make assumptions about me because of it. Especially his parents.

"Cora, you're looking pale again." He cups my cheek.

"Your parents know? I mean, they know your...*history*?" I swallow.

"They don't know details." He rolls his eyes. "But it's no secret that I spent lots of my time with the visitors who came through town."

"Won't they think I'm another visitor?" I squeak, and immediately regret it. We haven't had any conversations about what's happening with us, and it sounds like I'm fishing for confirmation that I'm somehow different. Even though I know I am, at least in the sense that he's spending time with only me, I wasn't trying to push him for anything more. Not deliberately anyway.

"You're...I...Maybe this is a bad idea. I didn't mean to put you on the spot." Cade's eyes drop to the floor.

"You didn't." I clutch his hand, hoping that lapse in judgment didn't just push him away. "I'm just not used to being under a microscope. We've spent so much time here in our own little bubble, I guess I convinced myself no one noticed, least of all your parents."

"Shit," he mutters. "You're right. I've kept you holed up here, so we didn't have to face the town. I've never even taken you on a real date. I can't believe I forgot to do that." He rubs his forehead. "I should've at least taken you to breakfast or dinner or something."

"That never even occurred to me." I squeeze his fingers. "I'm actually kind of glad we stayed holed up here. It gave me the illusion we weren't a topic of conversation, and I think I needed that."

"So, are you okay with it now? Being talked about, I mean?" He watches me skeptically.

"It's still weird. And I do wonder what your parents have heard and what they'll think, but you said not to worry about it, right? That you don't survive in a town this small if you worry about what everyone thinks?" I offer a weak smile. "I have to try not to worry about it."

"Now you're getting the hang of it." His wary expression eases into a smile. "And don't worry about my parents. They won't think anything one way or another. They just don't want to be the only people who haven't met the girl I'm sleeping with." He arches his brows suggestively.

"Well, when you put it that way how can I refuse?" I roll my eyes.

"That's the spirit." Cade leans in to kiss me, more tenderly than I expected given the way he was just teasing me, then heads outside, giving me some much-needed time alone. Not that I'm tired of having him around or anything, the opposite actually, which is why it's good for me to have a little space to sort things out.

He hasn't said anything specific, but between his actions at the bike race, spending the day in bed yesterday, and now dinner with his parents, I get the sense things have taken a more serious turn. I mean, small town gossip aside, if I was just the summer fling would he really bother introducing me to his parents? My gut says no. But if I'm not a summer fling, what am I?

The fact that we're basically living together is no doubt complicating things. I know that I'm putting my heart at risk by immersing myself in him so completely. But I can't seem to pull back, which is why dinner with his parents scares me.

Cade wouldn't go through with dinner if I was just a fling, but just because I'm not a fling doesn't mean he's falling for me the way I'm falling for him. After all, this is the guy who's never been on a date, who I'm not even sure has been with the same woman twice, so believing that he could actually fall for the first girl he tries a relationship with is a stretch.

He may care about me in a way he didn't let himself care about other women, but as much as I want to believe that makes this thing with us real, unless he actually says that I have to operate under the assumption that Cade is simply living in the moment. That he isn't reading anything into the fact that he spends the night every night, or that he's going to introduce me to his parents. He's simply making the most of this experience while it lasts, because we still have an end date.

I try not to dwell on that thought as I get ready for lunch. After all, it's not like the idea of an end date should surprise me. I always knew there'd be one, and it's not fair to Cade to expect him to think differently just because he's too inexperienced at dating to realize he's treating me like an actual girlfriend.

I park on one of the side streets and walk the two blocks to the cheery patio where they're waiting for me.

"I want to know all the details, now!" Ally's eyes twinkle as I sit down.

"What's there to tell?" I feel myself blush under her curious gaze.

"Oh, come on." Lennon rolls her eyes. "Who made a move on who, how long has this been going on, are you guys really living together?"

"Oh my gosh, is that what people think?" I squeal, my cheeks heating. "We just started hanging out, no one can possibly believe we live together, right?"

"Deacon says his truck is parked in the exact same spot every morning, like it never moves." Ally waves her hand airily.

"So that means he moved in? Do either of us seem like the type to move in with someone so soon?" I ask with more composure than I feel.

"Stranger things have happened." Lennon sips on the water in front of her.

"Like what?" My eyes grow wide, wondering what news she's going to share.

"Like Cade having a girlfriend," she deadpans.

I stick out my tongue.

"Cute," she harrumphs.

"He wouldn't call me that." I pick up the menu and pretend to be bored with this conversation.

"What would he call you then?" Ally presses.

"I don't know." I flip it over to read the other side. "We haven't really defined it." The waitress picks that inopportune moment to stop by our table.

"Oh, you're Cade's girl." She smiles warmly. "You make a pretty convincing Khaleesi, except your hair's more golden than platinum, and I think you're taller." She chews on her pen. "But overall, pretty convincing."

"I...thank you."

"I'm Meredith. I was Princess Peach in the Mario Kart group." She extends her hand.

I take it and give it a shake. "Oh, of course. Sorry. I didn't recognize you."

"I'd be surprised if you could recognize anyone without their costume. So, what can I get for Cade's girl?"

I give her my order, trying to ignore the knowing smirks beside me. "You were saying." Lennon grins when Meredith moves to another table.

"I was saying we haven't defined anything. I can't help if the town thinks different." I know I sound defensive, but it's strange to have the town give me a label Cade hasn't.

"The only reason they think different is because they saw the two of you together at the race. And he did introduce you as his girl." Ally pins me with a look that dares me to object.

"Yes, but was that part of the costume or Cade just being the flirt he normally is?" I deflect.

"Or maybe he meant every word of it," she counters.

I'm tempted to agree with her on that point, but that's more because I want it to be true than because it is. And even if it is, there's still the matter of me being a temporary resident that throws a big wrinkle into things.

"So." Ally leans forward, lowering her voice slightly. "You still haven't given us the deets."

I give them the Cliffs notes version of the last few weeks as we eat, starting with how Cade and I got to know each other a bit after I sprained my ankle, and culminating with how we both agreed there was enough chemistry between us to explore hanging out together. They're visibly disappointed that I'm not willing to share more personal details, like when we started having sex, and whether Cade's 'vast' experience translates into any tips or tricks I might be able to share with her and Finn, though overall, I have a good time and find it a bit of a relief to have someone to talk to about Cade.

I'm not seeking advice about him, nor are they offering any, but over the past few weeks he's become a big part of my life, and until now I didn't have anyone to share that with. I'm not going to tell my parents or my uncle about our involvement, because they'd only worry about me getting hurt when the summer is over, and even my roommate Tara would probably share their concern, so none of them know about him.

Cade would probably attribute my silence to a need to make my friends and family proud of me, and a summer fling might not earn their respect. I can't deny that's part of it, because flings aren't generally in my nature, and I haven't quite mastered the ability to ignore what other people think. But I think an even bigger part is that whatever I say out loud becomes real, and if I talk to my family or to Tara, I won't be able to pretend I haven't fallen in love with him. As much as I like the girls, I don't know them well enough to get into feelings of love, so it somehow feels safer to talk to them.

"Sounds like you two have really hit your groove." Lennon nudges my arm when I finish recounting the past few weeks.

"Our groove?" I balk, pushing my salad around with my fork. "Not sure we can have that after only a few weeks. We're just having fun."

"Romantic hikes, making dinner together, passionate sex, wake up and repeat. Am I wrong?" She arches a brow, daring me to disagree.

"I didn't say anything about romantic hikes or passionate sex." I spear a tomato.

"She filled in the blanks." Ally pops a fry into her mouth. "The point is the two of you click so well you're kind of inseparable. No wonder we all think you live together."

"Please tell me that's not the rumor. I don't think I can go through with meeting his parents if they think we're living together." I drop my head in my hands.

"You're meeting his parents?" Ally claps, her eyes wide with excitement.

"It's not like that," I protest. "It's not," I reiterate when she raises an eyebrow. "After the bike race word got back to his parents. Cade feels like he has to introduce us since I met most of the town."

"You really believe that?" Lennon shakes her head.

"It's what he told me, why wouldn't I believe it?" I ask, keenly aware that they're observing my every move.

I like the girls, and I'd like to be friends with them. But the whole 'no privacy' thing has me a little guarded, so I'm reluctant to confide in them completely. I'm happy to give facts, like how much I enjoy Cade's company, but I'm not ready to speculate about his motives. Not when I'm questioning them myself.

"I can't claim to know everything about Cade, but one thing I do know is he doesn't do anything he doesn't want to. If he tells people you're his girl, which you clearly are by the way," Ally points her fry at me, "it's because that's how he sees you. If he's taking you to meet his parents, it's because he wants you all to meet."

"I can only go by what Cade tells me." I toss my napkin in my empty bowl. "Guessing is how rumors get started, and in this town, I'm not going to throw gas on that fire."

"Fine," Ally huffs. "But you should know that in this town rumors are usually rooted in fact. It's a fact that Cade does what he wants, not what he's told, and the whole town knows it."

"You're saying the whole town knows he wants me to meet his parents?" My eyes involuntarily search the patio to see who might have heard this conversation.

"She's saying, the whole town recognizes that Cade is acting differently, and he wouldn't do that unless he wanted to. That's why everyone seems to be in your business. They aren't trying to start rumors about what's happening with you two, they recognize that something *is* happening. That's a big deal for him, Cora." Lennon's tone turns softer. Serious. "He might downplay it, try to pass things like dinner off as something he *has* to do, but deep down the reality is he wants it. He wants you."

***

I'm fidgety as we make the drive to Cade's parents, but not because I'm about to meet them. Well, not entirely. I still think meeting the parents is kind of a big deal, though what really has my mind spinning is what the girls told me at lunch. Cade may try to downplay things or pass them off as an obligation, but he only does what he wants. So, somewhere in his mind, in his heart, he wants me to meet his parents. The question is why.

They think he wants me, which I know is true because he admitted as much himself. But I know when he said that he was talking about a summer fling, the chance to explore something more than a one-night stand. They're insinuating that he wants me in a more permanent sense. They've known him longer, so I can't totally dismiss what they're saying, but I still feel like I have to go off what Cade tells me, not what other people insinuate. So far that means we still have an end date, and this is nothing more than a courtesy for his parents, right?

We pull up to a ranch-style house on a flat plot of land next to a stream that carries the snow melt off the mountain. It's clearly an older house, though it's well maintained, and with the wide walkway up to a large porch it looks inviting.

"You grew up here?" I ask as the truck rolls to a stop.

"Yep. This was one of the first houses dad built here, and mom loved it so much she claimed it as hers instead of letting him sell it. Come on." He exits the truck and walks around to help me out, then guides me to the front door.

From the front entry, you can see straight through the house, past the living room to a wall of windows that frame the mountain range in the distance, and I immediately see why Cade's mom fell in love with this house. Right now, the view is a lush green dotted with reds and yellows and purples from all the wildflowers. In the winter, I imagine it's a pristine white surrounded by a rich blue sky. It's breathtaking.

He takes my hand and leads me through the living room to the deck out back where his parents are lounging on a couch. A coffee table holds a few plates of snacks, and a grill sizzles off to the side with what I presume is dinner.

Cade's parents turn to look at us as we enter, and I notice right away he's the spitting image of his dad. An inch or two shorter and slightly thicker, his dad has the same strong jaw and blue eyes that first drew me to Cade. His mom is also tall and slender, her sandy brown hair matching her son's, perfectly. Both of them have lines around the mouth and eyes, the kind you get when you smile often, which calms my nerves.

They rise off the couch to greet us as Cade makes introductions. "Cora, these are my folks, Charles and Jessica. They go by Chuck and Jessie."

"It's lovely to meet you." I shake their hands. "Thank you for having me."

"It's lovely to meet you too," Jessie says. "Can we get you something to drink?"

"Whatever you're having." I smile. Chuck hands me a glass of white wine and Cade grabs a beer, then leads me over to the couch where we all sit, his fingers loosely intertwined with mine. I know our joined hands don't go unnoticed, but I convince myself if Cade's comfortable with it then I should be too.

"How are you enjoying your stay so far?" Chuck asks.

"Oh, it's great," I gush, hoping I don't sound overly enthusiastic. "The weather's been cooperating, and the scenery is unbelievable. Even better than I remembered."

"You've been here before?" Jessie pauses with her glass halfway to her mouth and gives me a confused look.

"Years ago." I wave my hand. "That's what led me to believe it would be the perfect spot to get some work done."

"Cade mentioned you were working on a PhD?" Chuck moves us past that awkward exchange.

"Yes, in environmental science," I say proudly. I don't miss Cade's reassuring wink, and I have to admit it feels good to own that instead of dwelling on how it sets me apart from the rest of my family.

"What's your thesis on?" Jessie leans forward.

"Mom's a teacher at school." Cade's silky voice draws my gaze to his. "Science."

"Oh," I exclaim, turning back to his mom. "I'm focusing on alternative energies. Specifically, water, and how we can harness its power without negatively impacting the ecosystems that it supports."

I notice Cade picking at a spot on his shorts as I talk, like he's uncomfortable. We rarely talk about my work, and not in explicit detail. He's attentive and asks questions when we do, which I appreciate, but I think that's more to be polite than because he's really interested. I get it, the subject isn't for everyone, so I haven't tried to force it. I can't help but wonder if it bothers him that he's learning some of this at the same time his parents are. If anyone else notices they don't say anything.

"That would make Katah Vista a good resource as well as a good spot to work I imagine," Chuck wonders aloud. Cade seems to perk up a bit at that.

"It would." I try to focus on the conversation. "Observing how water acts as it melts helps us understand the impact it could have if we alter that behavior or try to harness it, although much of the work currently being done in this area is on the coast."

After a few follow-up questions, the conversation drifts towards lighter subjects like favorite movies, foods and places to travel. Over burgers, Cade and his dad debate the pros and cons of a former ski racer buying the resort. Apparently, everyone is a little apprehensive about the son of a wealthy man getting handed the reigns, even if his background is in the sport. Since that topic doesn't apply to me, Jessie and I chat about her work at the school, what lessons she teaches her students, and even the history of the area.

"Did you know the mountain runoff follows the same path today that it has for centuries?" she asks me.

"I knew the path had never been deliberately altered, but I didn't know it's the same it's always been." I shake my head.

"There's less of it now. That stream over there used to be several feet wider and higher." She points to the edge of their yard, "and some years it's little more than a trickle, but that's the same riverbed that existed when the Native Americans first settled here. That's how the area got its name."

"From the riverbed?"

"No, from the mountain. Katah is short for Katahdin, the Native American term for 'Great Mountain.'"

"Mom, no history lessons tonight," Cade groans. "Cora has enough school during the day."

"Then no business talk for you two," she admonishes the men with a grin in my direction.

We cap off dinner by roasting marshmallows over the fire pit, with Cade teasing me that the light brown shade I prefer isn't melty enough just before he takes a bite of his crisp marshmallow and dribbles the sticky mess all over his face. I help him wipe it off before realizing his parents are watching us with contented smiles. I feel myself blushing under their gaze and am grateful for the dark that hopefully hides it.

Cade's parents refuse my offer to clean up, so he takes me to his old room while they put the leftovers away. It looks exactly like you would expect a teen boy's room to look, a double bed with a plaid comforter in the center of the room, sports and band posters all over the walls, samples of what I assume are his earliest attempts at welding on a bookshelf.

"When was the last time you stayed in this room?" I run my finger along the edge of the dresser.

"I usually stay Christmas Eve so I'm here when I wake up, but I haven't lived here since I was twenty."

"You're really close with your parents." It's more of an observation than a question.

"Yeah. Hard not to be when I work for my dad. Plus, I bump into them around town a lot. You're not close with your parents?" He sits on the bed to watch me wander around his room.

"Yes and no." I pick up a little figurine that resembles a bike. "I don't bump into them around town so the only contact we have is when we schedule it. And even though they support what I want to do the fact that I didn't go into the family business puts some distance between us. Not bad, but it's there. Your parents are nice." I change the subject.

"They're pretty easy to hang out with." He leans back so he's resting on his forearms.

"They are. And they didn't give me the third degree which was nice. I was sort of bracing for that." I pick up a different piece, a candleholder maybe?

"That's not really their style. They just wanted to meet you." His eyes track me as I set the candleholder down.

"If you ever met my parents, you'd definitely get the third degree," I say without thinking. Dammit, why do I keep saying things that seem to hint at a future?

"Yeah?" he seems curious. "That does sound uncomfortable. Now I get why you were worried about coming here."

"I wasn't...yeah, okay. I was worried." I smile sheepishly. "But I shouldn't have been. This was fun."

"They like you, you know." he sits up and pulls me to him, setting his hands on my hips.

"How can you tell?" I lay my hands on his shoulders.

"Just a feeling." He shrugs before gently touching his lips to mine. "You know," he whispers against my mouth, "I've never shown a woman my room before. Never christened this bed." He trails his fingertip along the waistband of my skirt.

Something about our conversation must've spooked him since he's reverting to his flirty persona. But since being with his parents felt so easy, I'm a little spooked too, and I retreat to the physical with him.

"You want to do that now, with your parents here?" I slide my hands under his shirt and worry a nipple. I'm absolutely not doing that, but I don't mind teasing him a little.

"No. You're a screamer. So, I'm thinking I should get you home." He nibbles at my ear.

"I'm not a screamer." I pinch him.

"You will be tonight." He kisses me deeply.

We stop by the kitchen to thank his parents, then he takes me home, where he makes good on his promise.

Chapter 19

Cade

It's been a week since dinner with my parents, and ever since then I've alternated between ridiculously happy and totally depressed.

There are times Cora fits so perfectly into my life it almost scares me. I fucking love falling asleep and waking up with her every day. With or without sex, sharing a bed every night is amazing, and I can't see myself getting tired of that. I love knowing that I'll see her after work, and we'll go explore some trails or wander around town before eating dinner together and going to sleep. Even dinner with my parents felt so natural it's like she belonged there with me. But as perfect as that dinner was, it's also the reason I get depressed, because that's when the topic of her thesis came up.

Since then, she's talked more about her work with me, and while I always knew Cora was smart, she's on a whole other level than I realized. Why she finds a guy like me worth talking to is crazy, because I don't get half the stuff that excites her, and while I'm happy to listen, it only makes the differences between us more obvious. The things she's studying, the stuff she can do with that knowledge, well, they shouldn't be confined to this town, or this guy. She needs someone as brilliant as she is.

I know it was for my benefit when my dad got her to admit that Katah Vista was a great place to do her work, and I can see how that's true right now. But long term? There's no way she could have the career she wants in this little corner of the earth, and there's no way I could be the guy who supports her given that her interests are so far outside my grasp.

That's why I waver between happy and depressed. That's why I haven't taken my dad's advice and told her how I feel. All I'm going to get is this summer. I have to make the best of it.

"Tell me again why we're here," Deacon interrupts the thoughts that have been playing on repeat. "The parade starts in less than two hours."

It's the Fourth of July, one of the busiest days of the year because of the parade we host, and it's getting so popular you have to get there early to get a good spot.

"Tiff needs my truck to pull her float. I need to get all these tools out." I gesture to the boxes in the bed. Normally, I keep my tools in my garage, but since I've been staying with Cora it's easier to leave them in the truck. Now that her uncle's garage is nearly done, I can stick them in there while giving Tiff more room.

"We couldn't have done this yesterday?" Deacon grunts.

"Didn't think about it until this morning." I scratch my head, realizing I need a haircut.

"Too busy thinking with your dick," Deacon mutters under his breath, just loud enough for me to hear him.

"What's that mean?" I turn to face him, gritting my teeth.

"You're still staying here every night, and today is the Fourth, the day you hyped all last year as being the perfect time to find a bunch of hot women wearing skimpy outfits," he complains.

This is another popular day for costumes, and while I draw the line at wearing a flag, I'm playing along and wearing a royal blue velvety shirt that matches Cora's stars and stripes dress.

"It is, so you'll have plenty of opportunity." I lift one of the boxes off the truck.

"But I won't have a wingman." Deacon scowls as he lifts another.

"Get Ryder. Or Blake. You don't need me." I walk toward the garage, hoping that's the end of it.

"I know. But I envisioned this summer going much differently." He follows me. "We were supposed to hang out and go crazy the way you always bragged about, and instead you're spending all your time with Cora. I like her and all, but I thought you were going to fuck her out of your system and move on."

"Those are your words cousin, not mine." I shoot him a warning look. "I said I couldn't get her out of my head and was tired of fighting it."

"So, haven't you got her out of your head yet?" Deacon scoffs.

"Not even close." I set my box down and open the door, holding it ajar so he can pass.

"But you've been practically inseparable. How is that possible?" He steps inside and sets the toolbox on the floor.

"I don't know," I fib, because no way I'm telling Deacon how I really feel. "It's like the more time I spend with her the more I want to be with her."

"That's not like, boring, or anything? The same woman every night?" He looks at me skeptically. I know it wasn't all that long ago that I thought that same way, but right now I struggle to believe I ever thought one woman could be boring.

"Honestly, I think it's better with one." That's as close as I'm going to let him near the truth.

"Dude, you're kind of scaring me with that talk." I swear he actually shivers.

"Then don't listen." I haul my box inside and turn to leave. "If you want a bunch of different women, go to the parade and find a few. You won't have any trouble."

I send Deacon on his way with a promise to find him in town. I know I'm disappointing him by not being there for him this summer, and I feel bad about that. Not bad enough to waste any of the time I have with Cora, though. I'll always have Deacon, but I may not always have her.

Cora and I make the short drive to town and deliver my truck to Tiff in the parking lot where they're staging the parade. We make plans to meet at The Underground later so I can get the keys back, but Cora and I head there now since Dex usually sets aside a spot for us right out front.

The crew is already there when we arrive, and I pour Cora a mimosa from one of the pitchers Ally brought with her in a little camping wagon.

"Wow, you guys come prepared." She takes the plastic cup I hand her.

"We've been doing this a long time." Dex lifts his cup. "Tradition."

"Yep." Ally nods. "Breakfast and drinks along the parade route, lunch at Ryder's since his house is just a few blocks away, fireworks in the park, finish at The Underground." She toasts Cora.

"What is it with this town and your all-day parties?" Cora wonders aloud. "I don't know where you find the stamina."

"Tradition," Dex says again.

"Pace yourself," I whisper to Cora with a quick kiss to her temple.

We have an hour before the parade starts so I grab a camping stool and pull Cora to sit on my lap while we wait. An endless stream of friends and neighbors pass by on their way to find a spot, and normally, I'd get up and talk to each and every one to pass the time, but right now I'm content to just nod hello while I hold Cora to me and run my finger along the smooth skin of her thigh. Not to tease her, but to commit the feel of her to memory.

"Have you ever been in the parade yourself?" Cora absently runs her fingers through my hair as we watch people pass.

"A few times. Mostly as a kid when different classes or clubs made a float. I drove Tiff's float a few years ago, but then you don't get to just enjoy the day, so now I lend her the truck every year."

"Is she an only child, too?"

"Yep. I used to get stuck watching her when our parents would hang out, and she'd make me play dolls and tea party." I pretend to shudder.

"I can see how that would make her like the sister you never had." Her fingers dance over the back of my neck.

"She's a good kid. I tease her about being like my annoying little sister, but I love her like she really is." That's the first time I admitted to anyone, including myself, how deep my affection for Tiff is. It's kind of a big deal since I've never really been a 'feelings' guy, and Cora must realize it because she rescues me before I can analyze that.

"Next you're going to tell me you actually liked playing dolls and tea party," she whispers against my ear.

"Tell anyone and I'll have to make out with you right here where the whole town watches," I whisper back.

Her panicked blush is adorable, but she recovers faster than I anticipate. "They already think we're living together, what could a little PDA hurt?"

I bark out a laugh. That's not at all the response I'm expecting, and that little show of bravado has me both amused and proud. Before

I realize it, I'm holding her face in my hands, trying to reign in my laughter. "God, I love y...our spunk," I amend right before I kiss her.

Damn that was close. I almost told her I loved her. I'm not even sure what I actually said, just that something came after love, and hopefully if it didn't make sense that kiss distracted her.

"Get a room," Ryder snorts.

I flick him off. That was definitely a PG kiss, but I pull back anyway, afraid of the expression I'm going to see on her face.

"Spunk?" She scrunches her nose.

Huh? Not the best choice of words, but I can work with it. At least she heard that instead of what I almost said. "Yeah, you know. Spirit. Courage. How you don't back down when I bait you, even if it makes you a little nervous. Spunk."

"Oh. Well, when you put it that way it sounds like a compliment." She smiles warmly.

"It is a compliment." I plant a brief kiss on those soft lips. "Come on, parade's about to start."

I help her to stand as I rise off the stool and set it aside so people can crowd together for a better view. I put Cora in front of me and wrap my arm around her shoulders, so she's pressed against my chest. She folds her hand over my forearm, and I swear that gesture damn near makes my heart beat out of my chest. I can't get enough of this woman. Touching her, talking to her, laughing with her, I'm like a fucking junkie hoarding everything I can get, and it's not enough. It's never enough.

Cora squeals and claps as the floats roll by, not bothered in the least that the floats are really just trailers decorated with streamers and poster board, most carrying little kids in costume.

There's a float for the little mountain bikers club with kids in helmets and pads, there's one for the wildflower club with kids dressed as flowers, and Tiff's little dance float is full of girls in pink frilly costumes who are spinning and twirling randomly. There's also a firetruck, a float with all the town veterans, and one from the local gift store that's tossing out candy to the kids. In other words, there's nothing really spectacular about this parade, but Cora's smile is so big it's like she's at Disney Land.

When the parade is over, Cora and Ally fall into deep conversation about what their favorite floats were and how cute all the little kids looked. I catch Finn's eye and he gives me a helpless little shrug along with a knowing grin, and in that moment, I realize that he's probably the only one of my friends who gets me right now. He realizes the women are way too excited over that goofy parade but seeing them this happy is better than an epic bike ride and the perfect powder day combined. He knows that I get that now, which means he also knows how I feel about Cora. I close my eyes and exhale, acknowledging my feelings, then shake my head slightly to let him know this stays between us. He nods in return before reaching for Ally and pulling her to his side. I do the same to Cora, because I can't stand not touching her.

"Ready to head over to Ryder's?" Finn plants a kiss on Ally's forehead.

"Yeah. You guys are coming, right?" she demands, turning to me and Cora.

I let my arm slip from Cora's shoulder and thread my fingers with hers. "Yep, as soon as I get my keys from Tiff. She should be bringing them along any minute and then we'll meet you there."

Right then, a pair of arms are flung around my neck, and I'm tugged slightly downward for a suffocating hug.

"Cade where have you been? I've been looking everywhere. I've even been to your house the past three days, but you were never there."

I pull the arms from my neck with my left hand, since I'm still holding Cora with my right, and stand to my full height, looking down on the beautiful brunette who, until this year, was my go-to fling on the Fourth. I totally forgot about her.

"Ashley, hey." I nod.

I notice my friends all rooted in place around me, their eyes darting between the two women, waiting to see how this will play out. I admit it's not ideal to run into Ashley right now, but I'm not worried about it since I don't have any secrets from Cora.

"Happy Fourth. We were just heading out." I give Cora's hand a squeeze and start to tug her with me toward the bar.

"You can't leave now that I've found you. Where have you been anyway? You usually aren't this hard to find." She reaches out to stroke my chest, apparently oblivious to the fact Cora's hand is still tucked in mine. I'm stunned silent, not because I don't know how to answer but because I can't believe Ashley would touch me when I'm clearly with another woman. I take a step out of reach and open my mouth to speak, but it's not my voice that comes out.

"I'm sorry, I guess you didn't realize. Cade moved in with me." Cora leans into my side, and I dislodge our fingers so I can wrap my arm around her and pull her closer. "I suppose we have been sort of hibernating at home, haven't we?" She smiles up at me as she wraps her arms around my waist.

Damn she's beautiful, looking up at me like I'm her world. This is a side of Cora I've never seen, and it gives me hope that she's not claiming me just for the day or the summer. I still don't have any words, so I do the only thing I can think of. I kiss her.

"Who's this?" Ashley gapes.

"This is my girl," I answer as I look at Cora. Her eyes light up brighter than I've ever seen them. I can't help it, I kiss her again. I'm vaguely aware of Ashley watching in disbelief, but I can't bring myself to care. Maybe that makes me a dick, but all that matters right now is Cora, and making sure she knows she's the only woman I want.

By now our friends have drifted, realizing there isn't anything to be concerned about. I break away long enough to tell Ashley to have a nice visit, then I pull Cora with me into The Underground. The moment we're through the door, I press her up against the wall and kiss the fuck out of her, getting lost in her lush mouth, the thrill of my girl claiming me, fueling my need.

"That was so fucking hot," I mumble against her lips. "I like this possessive side of you."

"I'm not possessive," she protests. I cock an eyebrow. "Okay, maybe I was a little. But she was rude. And forward."

"Probably my fault." I rub the back of my neck. "Ashley comes here every year for the Fourth. It didn't even occur to me that she'd be here. I'm sorry."

"It's not your fault she was forward. What kind of woman comes onto a guy while he's holding hands with another woman?" she rants, her cheeks getting pinker by the second.

"Shocked the hell out of me too. But it was kind of worth it to see you stake your claim on me." I press my body to hers so she can feel how much I liked that.

"Of course, that makes you hot." Cora rolls her eyes. "I guess I should be glad you didn't suggest sleeping with both of us since you apparently like women fighting over you."

Cora's not usually sarcastic, so I'm not sure if she's making light of Ashley's advances, or if me wanting other women is something she's worried about. I need to make sure she knows my dick isn't the only part of me that likes what she just did.

I cup her chin in my hand and force her to look in my eyes. "I don't like women fighting over me. I like *one* woman fighting *for* me. There's a difference."

She snorts.

"I'm serious." I stroke her chin with my thumb. "It's like I told Deacon, I'd rather have one woman that many."

"Oh my gosh, you talked to Deacon about us. About...why would you do that?" She frowns, pushing at my chest.

I capture her hands in mine and hold them between us. "First, I wasn't just talking about sex. I was talking about everything we do together, whether it's just sitting at home or watching a parade. I only want to do that with you. Second, I didn't tell him anything private, and I wouldn't. All I told him is, I prefer to sleep with only one woman instead of a bunch of different women. It's less distant, more intense."

"You really believe that?" she asks nervously.

"I do," I tell her, knowing full well that's only true for her, because of how I feel about her. Since I can't say that all I can do is relate it to sex, the one language I can speak freely. "Deacon thinks variety is what makes sex fun, and I admit I used to think that. Now, I know different. I know every inch of this body, Cora." I drag my finger up her side, skirting her breast. She sucks in a breath. I lean into her so I can whisper in her ear. "I know how to make you gasp. I know how to make you moan. I know how to make you scream. I know what to say to make you wet, and I know what kind of touch to use to take you over the edge. I can make this body do whatever I want, and that gives me more pleasure than I've ever had with a woman."

"Oh," she sighs, her eyes glued to my lips.

"Yeah, 'oh.' That made you wet, didn't it? Thinking about how good I can make you feel. All the sounds I can get you to make," I growl in her ear as I slide my finger under the hem of her dress. Her hips roll towards me, and I let my finger drift to her center, which is soaked. I slide her panties off her hips, so I have room to maneuver, and rub her clit.

"Do you have any idea how hot it makes me to see the way your body responds to mine?" I groan.

"It does?" she inhales sharply.

"Hell, yes." I grind against her thigh as I slide my finger inside her. She leans her forehead against my shoulder and moans.

"Should we be doing this here?" She pants as I stroke her.

"Want me to stop?" I pull my finger out and tease her sensitive core.

"No." She clings to me.

"Good, I wasn't going to." I nuzzle her neck.

"What if someone comes in?" Her eyes dart to the door.

I reach over to the door and twist the lock. "They won't. Now stop worrying about what we're doing and just feel. Feel my fingers sliding inside you. My thumb rubbing that swollen little clit. Your pussy grip my fingers."

She whimpers as I take her higher, her hips rocking into my hand to increase the friction between her legs.

"So beautiful," I mumble. "I never get tired of watching you chase your release. Don't hold back, Cora. Let me see it. Let me feel you come all over my fingers."

As intended, my words push her over the edge, and I feel her body clenching all around me. Her fingers dig into my shoulders as she leans her head against the wall, her sultry cries growing louder as I pump through the contractions. I cover her mouth with mine to muffle the noise, drinking in her ecstasy. She gasps for air between kisses, her soft breasts heaving against my chest as she rides the waves of pleasure coursing through her. *Fucking perfect.*

I still my hand as her orgasm wanes, our kisses morphing from urgent and needy to slow and gentle as her heartbeat returns to normal. When I'm sure she's steady, I pull my fingers out and bring them to my lips, sucking them, one by one. I think I moan myself when I taste her.

"You really like that?" She scrunches up her nose, studying me.

"Like what? How you taste?" I lick the last finger.

She nods, her hands drifting from my shoulders to my waist.

"Hell, yeah I like it." My cock presses painfully against my shorts.

"Why?"

"I don't know. Turns me on." I glance down, knowing she'll do the same and see what she does to me.

"Do all women taste the same?" She lets her fingers wander along my waistband.

"No."

"Do you like the way all women taste?" She holds her breath.

"In general, yes. But some taste better than others. You taste the best." I grin and give her a soft kiss.

"I'm serious." Those beautiful brown eyes plead with me not to tease her.

"So am I." I cup her face. "In general, I like the taste of a woman's arousal, but I react differently to yours."

"How?"

"It makes me so hard I can barely function." I rock my hips forward to show her the proof. She seems to ponder this, chewing on her lip. "What's with all the questions?" I stroke her cheek. Cora may not care about my past, but I think sometimes it intimidates her, and that kills me because no one in my past comes close to what I have with her.

"I haven't tasted you yet, and...I never really liked the taste of guys finishing before, but I'm wondering if you'll taste different? Like I taste different to you?" Her pretty eyes slay me with their sincerity.

"You don't have to taste me, sweetheart. You don't have to do anything you aren't comfortable with." I shake my head slowly.

"I want to," she protests. I feel her finger tracing my dick over my shorts, and damn if that doesn't nearly undo me right then. I lean my forehead against hers and take a deep breath, unsure of what to say. She really doesn't have to do this for me, but I'd be lying if I said the thought didn't intrigue me. She's had me in her mouth before, but not to completion, and what guy doesn't want to be taken to the finish line?

I shouldn't let her do this here. Only, before I can pull away, I feel cool air hit my throbbing cock, and I realize while I was wavering, she took charge.

Cora pulls me out and starts stroking me slowly but firmly. I can't deny it feels incredible, nor can I contain the groan that rumbles from my throat as she fists me. All I can do is mumble a weak "Are you sure?" to which she nods her head and grips me tighter.

I'm dying to feel her mouth on me, but what shocks me even more is that I just want to kiss her. So, I do. Long and slow and deep, I kiss her with all the passion and desire and need and love I feel but can't say. I hold her face in my hands and pour my soul into her, the feel of her lips against mine, offering just as much bliss as her hand on my cock.

I'm lost in a mixture of ecstasy and need, content with what I'm feeling yet somehow wanting more, when she drops to her knees and takes me in her mouth. Time seems to stop the minute her lips close. I hold my breath as her mouth slides over my length, her tongue dragging lightly over my skin with each pass. When she pulls back and sucks on just the tip, my knees start to buckle, and I brace my hands on the wall to stay upright.

I look down and watch Cora's fist sliding over me as she takes me into her mouth. Her eyes are cast down, her attention so focused on her actions she's oblivious to the pleasure she's giving me. It's so erotic I can't stay still. I rock my hips gently, pushing my cock deeper so I can feel more of her on me. Watching my dick disappear inside her pretty mouth, feeling her tongue sliding over me, it's too much. I fight the urge to thrust hard and deep and instead pump shallow and fast, rubbing my length over her lips and tongue.

"Grab my balls," I grunt as I thrust. "Squeeze them in your hand. That's it," I groan as she complies. "Fuck Cora. Fuck. That pretty mouth feels so good. It's too much sweetheart. I won't last," I babble as she drives me toward the edge.

"I'm gonna come, sweetheart. Are you sure you want this? Are you ready?"

She moans what I think is supposed to be a yes, and the vibrations from her throat tip me over. "I'm coming. Oh shit, Cora."

I try not to pump my hips as my release bursts into her mouth, but my body convulses on its own accord. I look down at Cora, eyes closed, swallowing what she pulls from me as her hand coaxes out every last drop.

I'm gutted.

Cora releases me with a soft kiss to the tip of my dick. I pull her up and lean my forehead against hers, too weak to do anything else but melt into her.

I bring a shaky hand up to her face to make sure I haven't left any traces of myself on her, then kiss her softly. My musk lingers on her lips, and I find that strangely satisfying.

"Well?" I prompt softly. "Did you like that or hate it?"

"I didn't hate it." She gives a quick little shake of her head. "But I think maybe it's an acquired taste. I liked seeing you lose control though."

"That's what you do to me. You make me lose control." I lean in to kiss her again but am halted by movement at the door. A rattle, and when it doesn't open a loud knock. "Shit," I mutter as I put my cock away and fasten my shorts.

"You good?" I look to Cora as she puts her panties back in place. Her eyes meet mine and I read the panic there, and while I know no one will be able to tell what we just did I give her an out anyway. "Go sit at the bar. Grab a drink if you want."

She rushes off while I unlock the door for Tiff.

"Sorry Tiff, didn't realize that was locked." I open the door so she can step inside, positioning myself between the door and the bar so she can't see Cora.

She gives me a skeptical once over before handing me my keys. "Thanks again for the truck. I left it in the public lot. Where is everyone?" She tries to peek around me, but I don't think she can see the bar where Cora's recovering.

"Ryder's. We're headed there now if you want to come with us." I pocket the keys.

"Maybe I'll stop by later. I still have some cleanup to finish from the parade." She jerks her thumb over her shoulder and starts to turn toward the door.

My memory drifts back to what I told Cora at the parade, and I wonder briefly if Tiff knows I'm not teasing when I say she's like my little sister. I should probably tell her, but I've never specifically said that before, and I'm not sure how to. So, I say the first thing that comes to mind. "Float looked good this year."

She stops cold and turns. "Since when do you pay attention to the floats?" Tiff knows all too well that I'm usually socializing or drinking during the parade, and don't often notice much else. I can tell she's a little stunned.

"Uh, since Cora really enjoyed it." I rub the back of my neck.

"That's what I thought." she grins knowingly.

I can't talk about this, not with Cora in earshot, so I step to her and pull her in for a hug. "Happy Fourth, Tiff."

"I like what you've done with him, Cora." Tiff hollers over my shoulder.

"Brat." I tug her ponytail. "Get out of here."

"See you around." She smiles affectionately as she heads for the door.

I grin as I watch her go. I kind of like what Cora's done with me, too.

***

Cora and Ally are huddled together talking about god knows what as we wait for the fireworks to start, but I'm doing my best to give her some space. Not that she's asked for any, but because I think I need it.

Today has been perfect, so much so, that I don't want it to end, and that's a dangerous way to think when I know our time is limited. But dammit, if I can turn off the voice that's trying to convince me this is real.

I got so wrapped up in the moment earlier, I almost told her I loved her, and I flat out admitted that I like how she got possessive over me. Plus, after foregoing condoms, meeting my parents, and what we did in the bar earlier, I know she's giving me the kind of firsts a girl like her normally saves for someone special. All of that makes it so tempting to believe I won't lose her to her career, but she hasn't given me any indication she wants me to be part of her life, and unless she does, I don't see how I can mess with her dreams. So, I'm trying to put a little distance between us right now to regroup and get my mind right. I'm hoping this will make it easier to get through the fireworks, which I know she'll watch from my arms.

"Just tell her already," Finn says quietly as he hands me a beer.

"Not that easy." I shake my head as I accept it.

"Not that hard either." He looks at me pointedly.

"Maybe not for you, but Ally wasn't chasing a big-time career she'd have to put on hold to be with you." I nod subtly towards the girls.

"Sure, she was." He takes a sip of his beer. "She wanted to be a fashion designer, and instead she owns a boutique."

I didn't know that, but I press on, undeterred.

"She can design stuff anywhere though, right?" I raise my eyebrows.

"True, but it's a harder path to do it alone than to work under a big label and build up your references."

"I hear you, but I'm not sure Cora can do all her science stuff from here. It's not like there's a lab around town." I stare at the ground so he can't see how much that bugs me.

"What do you mean, science stuff?" He cocks his head.

"Oh, uh, Climate change, alternative energy, monitoring plants." I lift a shoulder, realizing that since I've been so consumed with Cora, I've never actually talked to the guys about what she's doing here. What she wants to do.

"I'm no scientist, but I would think you could do all that stuff anywhere." Finn sips his drink.

"She wants to do stuff with water. We don't have water around here we have snow. She needs to be by a big river. Or an ocean."

"Snow becomes water," Finn deadpans.

"Pretty sure it's not the same thing." I roll my eyes.

"Okay, what if you went where she needed to go. You can do construction anywhere, right?" I know he thinks he's helping, but that's not actually a solution.

"Leave Katah Vista? Who will take over my dad's company?"

"You say that like you're thinking of taking it over. You've never been interested in it before."

He's got me there.

"Still not. Yet, I always knew it would happen one day though. I just didn't feel the need to rush into it," I admit what I've never really said aloud.

"So, what are you saying? You want to stay here and take over?" He seems surprised.

I guess after years of shunning responsibility I get that.

"That's the plan." I sip my beer.

"But would you be happy?" He frowns.

"Sure. Why not?" I stuff my free hand in my pocket. I may have been putting it off, but I resigned myself to this fate long ago.

"The only thing I've seen you really truly happy about is Cora, and if she's not here I'm not sure your nice setup will cut it." He actually looks worried. Shit.

Finn isn't telling me anything I haven't thought about already but hearing it out loud has a way of making it real. So real, the thought of living here without her makes it hard to breathe, and that feeling doesn't go away until she's sitting between my legs with my arms wrapped around her as we watch the fireworks.

Chapter 20

Cora

"Where is he taking you?" Ally's eyes sparkle as she hands me a dress to try.

"He didn't say, he just said to wear a nice dress." Cade woke me up this morning with instructions to be ready at five, and to wear a nice dress. Then he took off to help out at a different job site, leaving me without any other information.

"So mysterious." Ally murmurs, passing me another one.

I look at the little black number she handed me and shake my head. "This feels too fancy."

"What do you mean?" Ally frowns.

"I mean it's the kind of dress you wear when the man has on a suit. I don't even think Cade owns a suit." I haven't looked in his closet or anything, but he doesn't strike me as the suit type.

"Good point." Ally takes that dress back and gives me another one. It's all red with exposed shoulders, cinched at the waist but loose at the ankle, making it more bohemian than formal. I know right away this is the one.

When I emerge from the dressing room Ally squeals. "Oh my gosh, he's going to die when he sees you in that. The red makes your tan glow, and your shoulders are so sexy all bare. Here." She thrusts a black wrap at me. "Add this so you have something for those shoulders if you get cold. The black will make the red pop even more."

I put the wrap on and realize she's right. It's dramatic without being too fancy. Practical yet pretty. "This is perfect," I tell her.

"You really have no idea what his plans are?" Ally asks as she rings up my purchase.

"None." I shake my head. "I assume it involves a nice restaurant since I'm supposed to wear a dress, but that's just a guess. Is there anywhere in town where you have to dress up to eat?"

"Not really." She scrunches her lips together. "I mean, there are nice places and people sometimes dress up to go there, especially up at the resort, but there isn't a dress code or anything. People go there in their ski gear in the winter."

"Well, I'm officially stumped then." I put my credit card back in my wallet.

"I'm officially jealous," Ally says. "I'd love if Finn surprised me with a dress up night. I can't believe I'm saying this, but I may have to tell him to get some date night pointers from Cade. No offense."

"None taken." I laugh. "I know it's not really in his nature to do dates and things."

"It's really not. Just goes to show what the right woman will do."

"What?" I gasp.

"Oh, come on. Don't tell me you're unaware of how monumental this is for Cade." She gives me a disappointed look.

"Taking me on a date?"

"That, sure. And putting so much effort into it. You've turned that man upside down and inside out, Cora. I know you know that." She passes me the bag.

"I know he's out of his element, sure," I agree. "But that doesn't mean he's all turned around."

"What would you call it then?"

"I don't know. Living in the moment." I grasp.

"Please," she scoffs, putting my signed receipt in the register. "Cade wouldn't go through the trouble of planning a special date for just anyone. That man cares about you. A lot."

"I know that," I insist. "But this is the man who's never really dated before, so that just makes anything he plans seem like a big deal."

"You're totally going to ignore that part about you guys caring for each other?" She frowns, hurt.

"I'm not ignoring it." I shake my head vigorously. "Of course, we care about each other. We wouldn't be spending so much time together if we didn't. But you're trying to make it more than that."

"Are you telling me it isn't?" she presses. "Are you telling me he's not in love with you? Or you with him?"

"I'm telling you he hasn't said that, and I won't put words in his mouth." I set my mouth in a firm line to avoid giving anything away.

"Fine. Then tell me how *you* feel." She crosses her arms and waits for my response.

I hold my breath, trying to decide how to answer that. I like Ally, and I want to be honest. But I don't want to fuel town gossip that might put Cade in an awkward position, and I don't feel right telling her things I haven't told Cade.

"Cora, I'm not trying to pry." Ally seems to read my mind. "I'm only trying to point out that you two have something real. Something that makes you both happy."

"He does make me happy."

"And," she prompts. "Is that all, or do you want more?"

"For now, happy is enough," I say. "Anything more is up to him."

Ally sighs and offers me a weak smile. "Okay, I'll drop it. I didn't mean to take the fun out of shopping for your date. I just want to see my two friends happy."

"I know," I tell her. "I promise, we are."

"Ally, I need an interview outfit, stat!"

I turn to see a stunning brunette woman barreling through the door, cheeks flushed and eyes sparkling with excitement.

"Lennon was only kidding about you interviewing for that waitress job. It's yours if you want it." Ally gives me an apologetic smile then turns back to the brunette. "You don't need an interview outfit."

"I do when the interview is for the resort," the woman beams.

"You scored a meeting with the team doctor?" Ally steps to the woman and clasps her hands, bouncing with excitement.

"No." The brunette deflates a little. "The spa at the resort. But massage is a foot in the door."

"People don't go to the spa for physical therapy." Ally gives the hands she's holding a little squeeze before dropping them.

"Tourists might. And at least they'll have my name on the payroll." The brunette seems determined to stay upbeat.

Ally seems ready to respond when she catches sight of me. "Oh, I'm sorry. Cora, this is my sister, Sloane. Sloane, Cora." She gestures between the two of us. "Sloane just moved here to pursue a job in physical therapy. She's hoping to work for the ski team."

I shake hands with Ally's sister, finding it impossible not to get caught up in her excitement.

"A job at the resort sounds like a good start," I encourage her.

"Right!" Sloane exclaims. "It'll put me closer to the team and give me a chance to perfect my massage techniques. Win, win."

"The spa doesn't pay as well as the doctor would." Ally shoots me a worried look.

"Then I'll take the serving job too. Lennon said she'd hire me, right?"

"Finn might need that job with Carter Quinn taking over the resort." Ally crosses her arms in a huff. "I wish that man would make up his mind about what he's going to do with the existing staff."

"He can't get rid of everyone and still run a resort." Sloane rolls her eyes when she thinks Ally can't see it. "Besides, Finn has been here forever and knows the mountain inside and out. This Carter guy would be a fool to get rid of him."

"I hope you're right." Ally worries her lip with her teeth until she catches sight of my bags. "Oh my gosh, what are you doing here listening to us babble. Go have an amazing time with your man." She gives me a hug.

I'm tempted to stay and offer support, but I catch Sloane's eye and she gives me a thumbs up, signaling she's got this.

"I will." I say goodbye to them both and head home to get ready for my first date with Cade.

***

"Holy shit. Uh, I mean, wow," Cade says when I open the door. "You look beautiful."

"You look pretty handsome yourself." I blush as I look him over. He's wearing a pair black slacks and a gray button-down shirt, rolled up to the elbow. "I have to admit, I wasn't sure what to expect."

He looks down at his outfit. "You mean you weren't sure if I even owned nice clothes?" He tosses me a coy grin.

"Exactly." I laugh.

"I might break out in hives if I wear them too long, but you're worth it." He leans in to give me a gentle kiss.

"You didn't have to do this you know." I gesture to our outfits.

"I know, but I want to. You deserve a nice date once in a while." He takes my hand.

"There you go with that whole *deserving* thing again."

"I'm not taking it back this time. Besides, this is just as much for me as it is for you." He leads me to the truck.

"Really?" I wrinkle my nose, baffled.

"Of course. I get to look at you in this dress all night. Totally worth the discomfort of wearing a shirt with a collar." He helps me climb in the truck, so I don't step on my dress.

"Do I get to find out where we're going now?" I ask as he pulls into the street.

"There's a reservoir about 45 minutes away. A really nice Italian restaurant is on the bank, and I thought we could sit outside and watch the sunset." He pulls my hand into his.

"That sounds perfect."

Cade points out different landmarks as we drive, teaching me the names of different peaks or pointing out where he likes to camp and or fish. Seeing this helps me understand why he refers to the area as every guy's dream backyard. It really is endless, with an infinite amount of things to do.

When we get to the restaurant, we're shown to a table in a quiet corner, overlooking a vast lake. The water itself is a deep blue, but the bright green peaks that seem to rise out of it are what make it striking.

"It's beautiful," I gasp, stepping up to the railing for a better look.

A minute later, I feel Cade's heat against my back as he runs his hands over my bare arms. "Not as much as you," he whispers.

Cade turns and pulls out a chair for me so I can take a seat. When we're both settled and have a glass of wine, he tells me a little more about the area, including how before the reservoir was built a small town existed here, and in the past, severe droughts forced the water level low enough that you can see some of the buildings.

"That must be strange, to see the remains of a town." I try to imagine what it would be like to see roofs poking out of the water.

"It is, especially because lots of the buildings are still pretty intact," he says. "Like they're frozen in time."

"Speaking of building, what's the new project you have?" We don't spend much time talking about Cade's work, since up until now, I've had a front row seat to it, but I'm curious to know more about the business. What else he works on.

"Just a house." He gives a little half shrug as he twirls the stem of his wineglass.

I roll my eyes. "Big house, small house, custom, something else? I know it can't be *just* a house, not after I've seen what you're doing at my uncle's."

"It's nothing special." He offers a weak smile. "Five bedrooms, chef's kitchen, vaulted ceilings. The normal stuff people want in a dream house."

"Do you enjoy it?"

"Enjoy what?" He looks at me blankly.

"Building." I nudge his foot under the table. "I know it's the family business and you'll inherit it, but do you enjoy it?"

"Mostly. I'm not much of a desk guy, so I like the building part of the business. The operations stuff I'm not too keen on, but Dad sees it as his legacy to pass on, so it'll be my job eventually." He rubs his neck.

"I can't tell if you think that's a good thing or a bad thing." I watch his face for a reaction that doesn't come.

"Probably a little of both." He sips his wine absently before focusing on me. "I'm fortunate to have something stable, something I can do year-round as opposed to the seasonal jobs most other people have. And I guess it'll be nice to work for myself instead of someone else, but I'm not in a hurry to be the guy in charge."

"Does he want you to be? In charge, I mean?" I take a sip of my wine.

"Not yet. He's not ready to retire, and he'll want to make sure I'm all set long before he calls it quits. I'm sure he'd prefer I start learning the ropes sooner rather than later, though." The corner of his lip pulls up just slightly before it settles back into a thin line.

"It means a lot to him to have you take over?"

"Yeah. He took over from my grandpa," he trails off, looking out at the water.

"The fat happy guy?" I hint.

"That's the one." He finally cracks a full smile. "I think it's a pride thing to be able to pass it on, you know?"

After a second, I nod my head, because I do understand family pride and being able to leave your kids with something. I also understand that can be both a blessing and a curse. In my case, the pressure for me to go into the family business isn't as encompassing since I have siblings and cousins who are happy to get involved, leaving me free to pursue what I want. For Cade, I sense it's a bit of both, he appreciates it, but it might not have been his first choice of careers. I respect him more than ever for his inability to walk away from it, and if anything, it just makes him look even more selfless in my eyes...It just means his future is here, and only here.

It's never been a secret, but having it confirmed still makes my chest ache, because up until now, a part of me wondered if he'd ever consider leaving. Whether his feelings for me might outweigh his love for his hometown.

I'd never ask him to leave, of course, though I thought if he'd be willing to leave maybe I'd be a little more forthcoming with my feelings. But in addition to not knowing exactly how he feels, I could never ask him to turn down the legacy his family wants to leave him. Which means, when I leave in a few weeks, he'll stay here. Permanently.

That makes this whole evening bittersweet. It's such a thoughtful gesture, to get dressed up and take me out for a special evening, highlighting how much he really does care about me. And like I told Ally, it's clear that we both do truly care about one another. Yet our lives seem to be on separate paths, which is what makes this evening just as sad as it is special. He'll never leave Katah Vista, and my career path doesn't encourage me to stay.

That's not to say I couldn't work here. Environmental scientists are used everywhere, particularly where people and nature form a delicate balance like in Katah Vista. But I've poked around to see what sort of opportunities exist, and right now there aren't any. Besides, it'd be presumptuous of me to get a job and stay here when he hasn't indicated that's what he wants. He may care about me, but that doesn't mean he wants me to be a permanent fixture in his life.

I need to be content with the time we have instead of spending it wishing for more.

"If your other clients rave about your work as much as my uncle does, they're leaving you with a nice legacy." I try to sound positive.

"They are," he agrees.

"And I bet in some ways it's nice not to have to question your future. I envy you that, since I still don't know where I'll be working after I finish my thesis." I play with the stem of my wine glass.

"Wherever it is, I'm sure you'll make an impact. You're the most brilliant person I've ever met." He's giving me a compliment, and while his intense gaze tells me he's serious, he almost seems sad about it. I'm not sure what I've done to make him lose the giddy smile he had earlier, but I don't want the evening to end on a negative note.

"You know you don't have to compliment me to get me into bed, right?" I whisper. "I'm a sure thing."

That earns me the chuckle I was going for.

"I didn't bring you here to get you into bed." He bumps my leg with his under the table.

"Why did you bring me here?" I ask. "I mean, you mentioned about me deserving a nice date, but why here? Why not somewhere in town?"

"If we went somewhere in town, I'd have to share you, especially dressed like that. Everyone would stop by to say hello, they'd want to know what the occasion was, and they'd make it impossible to eat in peace. I didn't want to share you tonight. Is that okay?" He looks slightly panicked, like he made the wrong decision.

"Of course." I reach out to grab his hand, threading my fingers with his. "Don't get me wrong, I love the town and all your friends, but I like that's it's just the two of us right now. Sometimes, I don't want to share you either. Especially when almost every woman we see looks at you like a piece of meat."

"You don't have to worry about them Cora." He rubs the back of my hand with his thumb. "I don't want anything to do with them."

"I know that," I tell him honestly. "But I don't want them to even look at what's mine." That last slipped out before I could stop myself, but the wave of heat that washes over his face has me clenching my thighs together.

"I don't want another man looking at what's mine either. Especially in that sexy red dress." Cade signals for the check.

Chapter 21

Cade

We're mostly silent on the drive home, with our interlaced fingers doing the talking, driving up the sexual tension.

Cora's thumb slides over the back of my hand, feather-light, yet just as potent as if she was stroking my chest, or my cock. Everywhere she touches me, every way she touches me, ignites such an intense response. I'm helpless against it. I'm helpless against her.

She's part of me now, and I know that won't change even after she's gone. That thought puts a bit of a damper on an otherwise perfect night, because we're inching closer to the day when she'll leave for good, and there's nothing I can do to stop it.

Tonight was sort of a last-ditch effort to see if there might be a future with her. I wanted to give her a traditional date, show her how special she is to me, and I hoped by doing so she'd decide to pick me instead of her career. I can't outright ask her to do that. It's too selfish, even for me.

I figured if she came to that decision on her own, I could live with myself. So, I went all out, getting dressed up, taking her to a fancy restaurant, the whole nine yards. And I can tell she loved it. But not enough, since she mentioned not knowing what her future holds after she finishes her thesis.

I knew it was futile to hope she'd pick me after all the work she's put towards her dream, though I still hoped for that anyway. It fucking crushed me to have her confirm she's still leaving, but then she turned around and laid claim to me, and I'm still kind of riding that high right now. It's probably temporary, I think she still plans to give me up when she leaves, although if dinner didn't convince her to stay maybe sex will.

That makes it sound like I'm reverting to old habits, but nothing could be further from the truth. Sex is totally different for me now than it was before, and while I have so much more than just sex with Cora, there's no denying that the two of us together is something special. At this point, I'm so desperate to have her choose me I'm not above using any means necessary, including sex, to nudge her toward that decision.

By the time we get home, her sweet little touches have made me hard as a rock, and I have the overwhelming urge to throw her on the bed and take her. But I force myself to go slow, to savor every moment of this, and show her what she means to me since I can't tell her.

I take her hand and lead her to the bedroom, standing her before me so I can drink her in. She's just as stunning as she always is, but tonight she looks so sultry with that pretty little dress hanging off her shoulders. I trace my finger along the exposed skin, over her collarbone, down to where the fabric meets her chest.

"Beautiful," I whisper as I cup her face in my hands and kiss her softly.

Cora reaches out to undo the buttons on my shirt, one by one, pushing it off my shoulders to run her hands over my chest, down my stomach, teasing along the waistband of my pants. I give her dress a gentle tug and it falls to the floor, leaving her standing before me in nothing but her matching red panties.

I want to capture the image before me, commit it to memory, but the need to touch her is too great. I pull her close, her breasts pressing against me, as I wrap my arms around her and capture her mouth. Our tongues meet in a sensual dance, giving and taking and savoring this moment where our passion for each other is the only thing that exists.

"I need you," Cora whispers against my lips, and damn if that doesn't make my heart ache just a little. I know she means she needs me physically, but a month ago she wouldn't have been bold enough to say that, and it makes me both proud and sad that she's comfortable enough to do it now.

Stripping off my pants, I pick her up and set her gently on the bed so I can run my fingers over her curves. Her breathing turns heavy, and goose bumps rise to the surface of her arms. Her nipples pucker even though I haven't touched them, and when I slip my finger inside her panties, I find her warm and wet.

I dip my finger inside and stroke her slowly.

"Cade," she whimpers. "You're supposed to me inside me. We're supposed to come together."

"We will." I place a quick kiss on her soft lips. "But you, first."

She rocks her hips into my hand, forcing my fingers deeper and I press the palm of my hand against her clit to increase her pleasure. She's so primed that's all it takes before the bliss overtakes her and she cries out, her orgasm rippling along my fingers.

Cora coming is a beautiful thing. Her hands grip the sheets, knuckles white. Her back arches as her hips buck. Her breasts heave as she cries out. *Fucking beautiful.*

I hold still until the tremors stop, the withdraw my fingers to lick her essence off them. "You're such a selfless lover." I brush my thumb over her lip before I give her a chaste kiss.

"How can you say that when you haven't come yet?" she pants. "You're giving me twice as many orgasms as I've given you."

"I get pleasure out of watching you. Feeling you. It makes me so hot. So hard." I press my dick against her hip so she can see just how hot she makes me. She fists me and gives me long, slow stroke.

I'm tempted to linger here, to let her fondle me as she recovers. But my cock is throbbing, and it needs relief. Pinning Cora underneath me, I rock my hips against hers.

"No more waiting, sweetheart. I need to feel you. This time we'll come together."

I push slowly inside her, and the ecstasy consumes us both.

***

"What're you looking at?" Deacon asks as he comes to sit next to me.

I turn the screen off before he gets close enough to see that I was staring at a picture of Cora. It's the only one I have of just her, taken at our sunset dinner, when she was standing at the rail looking over the water.

Her back is to the camera, bare shoulders looking almost like caramel next to the vivid red dress, hair glowing in the sunlight. Her head is turned to the side, looking at something in the distance with a wistful expression. I don't know what possessed me to take the picture, but I look at it every chance I get.

"Nothing, just a list of what's left to finish." The lie rolls off my tongue so easily I think I get away with it, until Deacon snorts.

"Right. A list of what's left to do is what's giving you that sad puppy face, not the fact that your girl is leaving."

"We should be done in the next day or so." I ignore him, because I don't want to have this conversation. I know my life is about to change for the worse, and don't need Deacon to point it out.

"You don't have to pretend," he continues. "You look fucking miserable, and I know it's because of her."

"It's not because of her." I shove my phone in my pocket.

"Of course, it is. Instead of getting her out of your system, you managed to get her stuck in it." He shakes his head, looking at me like I'm pathetic. I probably am.

"That's not her fault."

"Maybe, maybe not. Look," he exhales, "I know I wasn't your biggest supporter this summer, or hers, but I'd rather have no wingman than a depressed one, and if you're this depressed now, I hate to think what you're gonna be like after she leaves."

"What's your point?" I rub a hand over my face.

"Don't let her leave," he says matter-of-factly.

I hate how everyone thinks it's that easy. My dad, Finn, now Deacon. They all think my feelings have the power to keep Cora here, and that I can completely ignore the fact that she'd be giving up everything she's ever worked for. Her dreams. Her ambitions. And sure, maybe I can convince her to stay now, but she'll grow to hate me for it when she regrets abandoning her goals in life to date me. I'd rather miss her like crazy than have her resent me one day.

"Whether she stays or goes isn't my call." I sink to the retaining wall as my energy wanes.

"Let's try this another way," he starts. "Do you think she'd want to stay? She's obviously as interested in you as you are her."

I close my eyes and shake my head slowly. "Wasn't that long ago she mentioned not knowing what she'll do after she's done with her thesis. If staying here was on her radar I'm sure she would've said something."

Deacon blows out a breath. "That sucks, cousin. I'm sorry."

"It is what it is." I shrug, trying to downplay how sick I feel at the thought of her leaving. "I knew this had an expiration date."

"Yeah, but you didn't expect to fall for her, did you?" He sounds almost sympathetic.

"No, that part was a surprise." I sigh, feeling somewhat relieved to admit that.

"Shit. I'm never gonna fall for a girl like that. If this is what it does to you it's not worth it," Deacon shakes his head.

"This part sucks, that's for sure. But there were good parts too. Great parts." I smile up at him sadly.

"Like sleeping with only one woman?" I can't tell if he's being genuinely curious, or sarcastic, like he's trying to cheer me up by implying I can go back to sleeping around.

"Don't knock it til you try it, cousin. Fucking phenomenal."

"Pfft." He waves his hand dismissively. "Not from where I'm sitting. No woman is worth the way you look right now. And before you jump down my throat, I like Cora, really. But if this is what a woman does to you, I want no part of it." He shudders.

"I hear you. I used to think that too. But the right woman has a way of making you think differently. The right woman makes everything feel like it fits." I lean forward and rest my arms on my knees, too tired and depressed to sit straight.

"Everything?" Deacon takes a seat next to me with a sly grin.

"I'm not talking about sex." I give his shoulder a quick shove. "I'm talking about all of it. Hanging out together, talking, sleeping next to someone. Before you have someone to do that stuff with you don't realize you're missing anything, but after, it's almost like..." I stare towards the mountains that always used to make things seem okay. "It's almost like before I had the illusion of things being complete, and now I realize they weren't. At this point, I think Cora knows me better than anyone else, and that feels right. Like now, I'm whole. I don't know any other way to explain it." I slump forward.

I see Deacon from the corner of my eye, staring at me with his mouth hanging open, like he can't believe that sappy shit just came out of my mouth. Truth is, neither can I, but that doesn't make it any less true.

"You'll get it one day," I say to him even though I'm staring at the ground. "And I'm going to enjoy saying 'I told you so' when it happens."

"No way," he protests. "After seeing you like this, there's no way I'm ever dating someone seriously. And I wish I'd never suggested you try it either."

"I don't. I wouldn't change a thing," I say quietly.

"How can you say that?" Deacon scoffs. "She's not even gone yet and you're already moping. You wouldn't change that if you could?"

"Nope. I fucking hate that she's leaving, and I know when she does, I'm gonna feel like shit for a long time. But I don't regret any of it. I'd do it all over again. The good parts were that good." I sound like a fucking sap. I don't care.

Deacon shakes his head in disbelief. I know he doesn't understand me right now. Pities me even. But I've never really worried about what other people think, and I'm not going to start now. I'll never regret my time with Cora, even knowing I'll be wrecked when she leaves, because letting her go is the right thing to do. Even if it breaks me.

Chapter 22

Cora

I wake around dawn, too restless to sleep. My departure is just hours away, which has me feeling depressed over the coming changes, though I'm trying to focus on being grateful for the good times.

My summer couldn't have been more perfect. Filled with hikes, barbeques, bike rides and summer concerts, there was always another adventure, and I loved every minute of it, loved experiencing Katah Vista the way Cade sees it. But I confess my favorite part has been the lazy evenings we spent at home, where it was just the two of us, and we talked and made love into the night.

Since our very first night together, we haven't been apart, and as the minutes tick closer to my departure, I'm not sure how either of us will handle being alone. We have such a comfortable rhythm, our separate lives fitting together effortlessly, that I wonder if returning to the life I had before is even possible.

Cade fills the voids I didn't even realize I had in my life, and now that I know what it's like to connect with someone so completely, I'm not sure how to be normal without it. Or if I can be content with being singularly focused on my career.

I feel like that's the future I'm heading for, since we never talked about ignoring our end date. We seemed to have an unspoken agreement not to discuss it, to just live in the moment, but now that the end is in sight, I'm finding it harder and harder to ignore the fact that being with Cade feels right, in a permanent sort of way.

There are times I think he feels the same, like when I catch him staring at me when he thinks I'm not looking, a sort of forlorn look on his face. Or when he cradles me to him in bed like he's trying to prolong every opportunity to hold me. He makes me feel loved, although, if he did really love me, wouldn't he have said it?

I know that makes me sort of a hypocrite, since I haven't told him how I feel either, but by his own admission he doesn't know how relationships work, and I don't want him thinking he's obligated to feel the same way I do just because we're together. Whatever his feelings for me are, I want him to express them in his own accord without any influence from me. Otherwise, I'd wonder if I pushed him to say something he wasn't ready to say. And since he's never brought up how he feels or what he wants, that means we have just a few short hours left together.

I snuggle closer to Cade as the sunlight creeps into the room, and feel his arm pull tighter around my waist.

"Morning beautiful." His voice is thick with sleep, but other parts of him feel like they're awake.

"Feels like you've been *up* for a while." As far as dirty talk goes, I'm still a novice, but my words tend to make him chuckle, which he seems to appreciate.

"There is no better way to wake up than to feel your sweet little ass rubbing against me." He nuzzles the back of my neck. "I'm kind of getting attached to it."

It's not a declaration of love, but this may be all he's capable of, so I'll take it. I'll make the most of it.

"You're getting attached to my ass?" I wiggle against him.

"Sweetheart, there isn't a spot on your body I'm not attached to." He kisses my shoulder.

For a brief moment, my chest feels hollow, wishing his attachment applied to more than my body, but I push it back as Cade's hand starts to caress my breast. In my heart, I know there's a connection between us, something more than just sex. It just doesn't outweigh the physical component behind what's happening. Not for Cade. I always knew that might happen, so I have to accept it.

Despite his inability to see beyond the physical, I don't regret my time with him. Cade has brought me more pleasure than I ever imagined was possible, and I wouldn't trade that for a different ending. I value what's happened between us too much. I do regret that he can't see beyond this moment, but I don't fault him for that. So, I do what I always do when he touches me. I focus on how it feels to have his hands on me, giving myself over to this moment in time so I can't think about what comes next.

Cade's finger circles my nipple, coaxing it to attention, which doesn't take long because my body is so in tune with his. I know that's because we share more than just sex, but I let him believe it's because he's such a good lover. He prides himself on taking care of me in bed, and while I think he finally sees himself as more than just a good fuck, there's no denying he has the skill to own my body.

As my nipple hardens Cade teases it tenderly, pinching and flicking and rubbing so the pleasure shoots from my breasts straight to my core.

"These pretty tits of yours are so sensitive." He cups one and molds it to his touch. "I bet your pussy is already soaked, just from me playing with them." He glides his hand down my chest, over my stomach, to my naked folds. He doesn't part me, just runs his finger along my seam, groaning when he feels the juices seeping from within.

Cade teases me, spreading my arousal around my lips, over my clit. His movements are unhurried. Casual. Not designed to bring me closer to release because he doesn't want me there yet. What he's doing right now is for him, to satisfy his appetite for foreplay while we have the time to indulge. His goal is to coat himself in my essence, because he delights in making me wet.

"How should I fuck you, Cora?" he asks as he covers my pussy in my essence. "With my fingers? My mouth? My cock?" He kisses my jaw where it meets my ear, his lips as light on my skin as his finger is on my clit.

"However you want," I gasp.

"Uh, uh. Ladies' choice." He sucks my earlobe into his mouth.

I feel how hard his cock is, trapped between our bodies. He wants to focus on my pleasure, but I can't deny him his. "With your cock."

"Sweet girl, always thinking about both of us." He pinches my clit and my hips buck of their own accord. "Soon, sweetheart. I'll give you my cock soon. Do you want it slow and sweet, or fast and hard?"

The truth is, I love all the ways Cade fucks me, but if I choose slow and sweet that will only confuse me more. "Fast and hard," I breathe.

"As you wish. But I'm gonna need this hand to hold you steady, "he pinches my clit again, "so you'll have to play with this for me." He takes my hand and guides it to my pussy, then grabs my hip and plunges inside me. I'm practically dripping, so he seats himself to the hilt in one thrust.

"Oh fuck, Cora. That first push nearly undoes me every time. You're so wet. Damn you feel good," he groans.

Cade tightens his hold on my hip as he starts to pump, fast and hard, just like I requested. My body lurches as we slap together, my breasts jiggling freely. He can't get as deep from this angle, but the tip of his cock feels incredible where it rubs deep inside me behind my core. I circle it firmly as he thrusts.

"Rub your clit again sweetheart," Cade doesn't miss a thing. "Your pussy clenches down on me when you do, and it feels so good."

I do what he asks, and he groans in response, which gives me a certain amount of pride too, because I love hearing him turned on.

He increases his pace, losing himself completely to the feel of my body sliding over his. I pant and cry his name as he takes me, urging him on as he drives us both to the edge. And when I can't hold out any longer, I pinch my center between my fingers, pushing my body over.

My walls constrict a split second before I burst. The contractions ripple through me and over Cade's cock, pulling and gripping as he buries it inside me, his own release pulsing in rhythm with mine.

As the tremors subside, he loosens his grip on my hip and pulls me to his chest, cradling me in his arms. It's a tender gesture after our frantic coupling and undoes the separation I sought when I told him I wanted it hard and fast.

I should move, leave his arms so I don't fool myself into thinking his hold on me is anything more than exhaustion, but I can't bring myself to do it. I drift off to sleep with our bodies still joined, wishing this wasn't our last morning together.

***

I blink furiously to keep the tears at bay as I put the last of my clothes into my suitcase. I want to get this finished while Cade's in the shower and can't see me, because my tears will make him feel guilty, and he doesn't deserve that. It's not his fault I fell in love with him, and it's not his fault he doesn't love me back, so I need to keep the tears to myself. Or at the very least, get them under control.

He saw me tear up last night at my going away party, so if worse comes to worse, I can probably play this off as an extension of what he saw last night, when I said goodbye to everyone, but especially Ally. I couldn't hold them back with her, in part because she's become a good friend, and in part because she's the only one who knows how I feel, and I just couldn't keep up the ruse in front of her any longer.

"Tell him," she implored last night, during a rare moment when Cade wasn't by my side. *"If the way he looks at you is any indication, he feels the same way."* But he hasn't said it and I won't force him to.

Ally went on to defend him saying, *"That's what stopping you? No offense but Cade isn't the brightest bulb when it comes to relationships, he's going to have to take some cues from you."* Which is exactly why I can't tell him. He'd follow my leave, regardless of whatever he feels, and I'd never know if he genuinely loves me or if he just said it back to make me feel better. I wouldn't put it past him to spare my feelings, and if he truly did love me, he would've said it already.

And of course, Dex took notice of my tears and had come over to cheer me up, saying "It's a going away party, not a goodbye party." Then, he spat me his best line yet and that's when I realized the tears last night weren't just about Cade, but the entire group. "We are great, which is why I know you'll come be back one day. Now come on Angel Tits, your Cock Sucking Cowboy wants a Wet Pussy tonight, not wet eyes. He'll have a case of Blue Balls soon enough, so be a Porn star and give him a Blow Job before the night's over. I'm sure he'll return the favor with a Screaming Orgasm."

I'm pretty sure my jaw hit the floor when he called Cade a Cock-Sucking Cowboy. It's absolutely impossible to not laugh at that. Too bad Dex is the judge and not a contestant, because seven drinks and an insult to Cade's manhood would have won him the record.

I snorted through the tears and accepted one of the several shots he suggested and managed to get through the rest of the night without thinking about the fact that it was my last. But now that I'm packing, I can't pretend anymore.

I'm going to miss this place, *these people,* desperately.

Before coming here, I didn't know it was possible to form attachments so quickly, not just to people but to the town itself. Everyone has been so welcoming, and while I know a big part of that is due to Cade, that's also just the way this town is. Humble, friendly, supportive, generous, accepting…pick an adjective and it can be used to describe this place and the people who live here.

I've never experienced such an intense feeling of belonging, even though I've only been here a couple months. It's hard to walk away from that. It's even harder to walk away from Cade. But like I told Ally, I won't put him in the position to feel obligated to me, so the best thing to do is get on with my life.

The water turns off and I take a deep breath, trying to get my emotions under control. It works for about ten seconds, when Cade walks out of the bathroom wrapped in just a towel.

I hold my breath, too afraid that if I let it out the tears will come with it. And if my vision isn't marred by my tears, I can get one last look at the glorious body that brought so much pleasure and comfort to mine.

The broad shoulders that carried me.

The strong arms that held me tight.

The lean, muscled torso that made my knees weak.

The rough fingers that touched me so gently. And the eyes, those piercing blue eyes that I got lost in when he looked at me.

Physically, Cade surpasses every fantasy man I've ever conjured, and in that respect, I doubt I'll ever be as attracted to another as much as I am to the guy in front of me. But what I feel for him goes beyond the physical. He's the first person to take my choices at face value and support them unconditionally. And he's the first person to make me feel truly beautiful, just as I am. Sexy even. I don't have worlds of experience with men, but Cade is nothing like men I've dated in the past, which makes me fairly certain that I'm getting the last look at the man who will prove to be the love of my life.

I take a fortifying breath and try to keep my emotions in check by taking a page from Cade's book. "I'm going to miss this view." I lick my lips as my gaze roams over him.

"I knew it, you wanted me for my body all along," he responds in kind. He knows I'm joking to keep things light, but there must be some part of him that's going to miss this, or he wouldn't be flirting without abandon. I take some comfort in knowing that even if he doesn't love me, he cares enough to be sad I'm leaving, and he's trying to cover that by flirting.

Suddenly, he strides toward me and engulfs me in a hug, guiding my head to rest against his chest. I take a moment to savor the feel of hard muscle covered by smooth skin, the faint smell of soap. Cade rests one hand on my back and strokes my hair with the other. We both know this is the last intimate embrace we'll share, and neither of us seems ready to let go. But if I can't live my life with Cade I need to move forward. That means I have a plane to catch.

I kiss his pec softly before pulling back and returning to my suitcase. I watch him dress and toss his clothes in a duffel bag from the corner of my eye as I finish my packing, trying to make myself believe we're packing for a trip instead of the return to our separate lives. When there's nothing left, we close up the house, parking my uncle's Subaru in its new garage home, and head to the truck so Cade can drive me to the airport.

It's not a quick drive, but it's mostly silent. We don't have future plans to talk about, like what we want to do for dinner, or how we want to spend the weekend, topics that might otherwise come up. We don't even hold hands like we normally do. He does ask about the process to finish my thesis, and I tell him about having to present and defend my conclusions to my professors, but that topic seems to make him uncomfortable, and we quickly revert to silence.

I've never felt this uncomfortable with Cade, not even during our earliest encounters when he flirted outrageously and put me on the defensive. At least the banter we had then was playful, not awkward like this silence is. As much as I don't want to leave, I can't wait to be out of the car. I don't want this strange feeling to be my last memory of our time together.

When we get to the airport, Cade takes me to the passenger drop off instead of parking to accompany me inside, and I'm oddly relieved that our goodbye will be over soon instead of drawn out at the ticket counter or the security gate. He pulls my bags from the trunk and passes them over to the attendant who checks me in.

And then it's here. My final goodbye.

Cade stands before me, hands buried in his pockets. My fingers fiddle with the strap of my purse. And even though this moment is as awkward as the car ride, I don't want it to end, because when it does our time together really will be over.

I'm not sure how long we stand there, acting more like strangers than lovers, before I finally find my voice. "You gave me the perfect summer, Cade." I feel a tear slide down my cheek, but I make no move to stop it. It will only trigger more. "Thank you."

He nods his head, lips pressed in a firm line.

"Maybe I'll see you around?" I say lamely.

Cade seems to start, like my words have only just reached him. "Here." He presses something cold and hard into my hand. "This belongs to you."

I look down and see the flower we made together in his shop.

"I realized this morning I never did get you flowers." He shrugs, a sad smile on his face. "I should've, but I can at least give you this."

"Thank you," I whisper as another tear falls. He steps to me and cradles my face in his hands, wiping away my tear. Then he touches his lips to mine, giving me a kiss so tender and delicate I very nearly say the words I promised not to say unless he did. But he speaks first.

"Take care of yourself, Solo," he whispers.

My heart plummets to my stomach. I know he's trying to make this easier, but the nickname causes the cracks in my heart fracture completely. I need to break away before I break down.

"Goodbye Cade." I press my lips to his one last time, letting myself linger for just a second before I turn and head into the airport, the tears flowing freely. I can't look back.

Three hours later, Tara picks me up at the airport and drives us back to our apartment. She's upset we didn't talk more while I was away and wants to hear everything. I feign exhaustion and promise to fill her in tomorrow, because my heartache is too fresh to talk about right now. I retreat to my bedroom, lay the flower Cade made me on the nightstand, and cry myself to sleep.

Chapter 23

Cade

Nights are the hardest. That's when the loneliness is the most crushing, because now all the things I used to do with Cora I have to do alone. Even though that was the case before she came into my life, and it never bothered me, I hate it now.

Deacon and the guys think hanging out with them will make it all better, divert my attention or something. That only makes me miss her more, because as much as I like those guys, their antics don't interest me the way they used to. I couldn't care less about chasing girls. I couldn't care less about getting drunk. I couldn't care less about what's happening around town. Besides, going anywhere would only expose me to the talk I know is going around, and for the first time in my life I can't stomach that.

Cora may not have realized I was in love with her, but there's no doubt the whole town knew. They saw the changes in me, and I know they were happy for us and now, that's turned into sympathy and pity and that makes me stomach churn. They don't mean anything by it but seeing the sorrow mirrored back at me over and over again is too much. So, I don't go out anymore. Not to The Underground, not to the concerts and end-of-summer festivals, not even to do my errands.

I drive to the next town over for those, where I'm less likely to run into anyone I know. Or anyone I know well enough to ask about Cora anyway, because if someone did, I don't have an answer to give.

We haven't communicated at all since she left. Total radio silence. I guess I should be glad she's making a clean break, not drawing things out and making it even more difficult to get over her. I might resent it a little though, because she's apparently fine without me, and I'm wrecked without her. Barely surviving and keeping it together by staying busy so I don't have time to think—to remember.

I hope closing the books on her uncle's project today will help with that, because I can't stand to be at this place without her. Normally, I'd leave this part to my dad, but without Cora here, I've started to take on a bigger role in the business, and given that this was my job site, Dad wants me to go. It makes me antsy, waiting on the front porch of the place I was basically living in a few weeks ago.

"I know, you've never been good at sitting still," Dad says, "but you're driving me nuts."

"Sorry." I stop pacing and take a seat on one of the chairs to wait for Rick.

"You never told her how you feel, did you?" He sounds disappointed.

"I couldn't do that to her." I rest my arms on my knees and shake my head.

"Do what exactly? Make her happy? Because she looked pretty damn happy when I saw her." He rocks back and forth in his chair.

"For the summer, yeah. But long term? She's too smart and driven to be happy with a guy like me," I say softly.

"Was that really your decision to make?" He stares at me pointedly.

"Yes," I insist. "I'd just hold her back."

"Why, because you don't have a PhD?"

DISTRACTION

"Among other things," I snap.

"Don't tell me you're intimated by the fact that she's smart."

"Of course not. We don't exactly boast a lot of jobs that she'd feel fulfilled in here. There are no labs, and nothing for a distinguished scientist like Cora. Let alone that fact that I have absolutely no idea what she's talking about when she discusses her work. It sounds like a foreign language to me and the best I've got to add to the conversation is the occasional head nod. I'm not foolish enough to think that at some point she'll want to be with someone who understands what she does." I stand up to pace again, unable to sit still.

"Do you think I understand what your mother does?" Dad frowns, his eyes tracking me as I move.

That's not at all what I was expecting him to say. "Don't you?" I ask.

"Hell no. I'm a builder, same as you. I find what she does interesting, but I can't talk to her intelligently about it. I can't give her advice or input about her job any more than she can give those things to me, although I like to think that the questions I ask help her do her job better." He winks. "Either way, what we do for a living doesn't have any bearing on how we feel about each other."

I admit I hadn't considered my parents' ability to make things work despite being in two wildly different fields, but the type of work Cora does or the fact that she's brilliant was never my major hang up. Sure, I worry that she'd get bored with a guy like me, but I was more concerned with her ability to do what she loves here in Katah Vista. Mom doesn't need a lab to do her job, she's fine with a couple scales and microscopes. I doubt Cora could say the same.

A car pulls into the drive, ending our conversation. Which is for the best considering that I've thought through all this already, and I don't need to go through it again, even with my dad. I doubt he could change my mind anyway. Rick exits and gives the driver a tip before turning to get his first look at what we've done, and from the look on his face he likes what he sees. We were able to blend the new garage with the original structure in a way that makes the house seem like it still has its original footprint, but whereas before the garage faced the driveway, now it's sort of tucked behind the house, connected by the new, oversized mudroom.

"I'm speechless guys, it looks amazing." He steps up to shake first Dad's hand, then mine.

"Which part do you want to see first?" Dad beams.

"The garage. Definitely the garage." Rick's eyes light up as he looks at it.

Rick and Dad follow me to the first of three bay doors, where I enter a code into the keypad. The door slides upward to reveal the Subaru that's been parked there since Cora's departure. It's the first time I've seen that car since she left, and it hits me harder than I expected to see it sitting there untouched. It makes the air leave my lungs for a minute, and I have to take a shallow breath to shake off the memories before I lead them inside, hoping they didn't notice my hesitation.

Rick likes his toys, so we've set him up with storage for everything from skis to bikes and tools. The car has always been here, but once we finished the garage, we retrieved all his items from the storage locker he rented and put everything away. You wouldn't know it given the lack of visible evidence, but this garage is holding a shit ton of gear.

"I can't believe how clean it looks. You guys made storage for everything," he marvels as he opens and shuts cabinets.

Dad beams at the compliment. I should too, since it's actually my work, but I just can't bring myself to get that excited. Dad looks at me with raised eyebrows, and I reluctantly make the rounds to show Rick each and every nook and cranny he has to store stuff, first in the garage, then the mud room. When he's explored every inch, we head to the patio so he can take that in.

Outside, I can breathe a little better but I still can't muster a lot of enthusiasm, even when Rick discovers the sculpture I hung on the garage. I can't look at the copper mountain-scape mimicking the view from Cora's favorite hike without feeling like my chest is about to cave in. I look everywhere else while he asks about it, doing my best to answer his questions without sounding like an asshole.

"I never would've thought to hang anything here, but that sculpture makes this feel like another room, not a patio. And I love how it's suspended on the wall, so it looks three dimensional even though it's flat. And you say it will change over time?" He turns to me.

"The patina will change, yeah," I mutter.

He and my dad exchange a look, and I know I'm not doing a good job of sounding pleasant.

"It'll become a little more weathered, but not smudged like silver gets," I add, trying to sound informative instead of bored. It's not Rick's fault I can't wait to get out of here.

"Did you get this piece locally? I'd love to put something like this over the fireplace inside too." He turns back to admire the sculpture.

"I made that with a few copper scraps I found." I rub the back of my neck, wishing he hadn't asked that. I don't want to get into how I came up with the design.

"You made this? With *scraps*?" He traces the edge of the mountain-scape with his finger.

I nod, wondering if his surprise means he's disappointed or impressed.

"Wow, I never would've guessed. You know, this reminds me of this little flower Cora has. It's made out of a gear and, some sort of metal pipe, I think. From a distance it looks like an ordinary flower, but up close you can see the size of the leaves are slightly different, sort of imperfect, which she says makes it more real because nothing is perfect. But now I'm wondering if that was the intent, or if that's just what the artist had available." He stares at me knowingly as he finishes talking, and even though this is her uncle, I can't help but wonder if maybe her ability to see inside me and understand me better than anyone else comes from him, because it sure feels like he knows me too well right now. It was oddly reassuring when Cora did it, but it's kind of intimidating coming from Rick. Shit.

I've always liked Rick, and I'm not going to insult him by playing dumb. But I don't know how much Cora has said about her summer, and I don't feel right talking to him about us, so I'm not going to volunteer anything more than I have to.

"It's what I had available," I confirm evenly.

"Why does it say, *'our first flower?'*" he presses, his tone decidedly less friendly than it was when we were looking at the garage.

"Come again?" I frown, confused. It didn't say anything the last time I saw it, and while Cora knows I'd never made a flower until that day, that doesn't explain why it says 'our.' Unless it's because she worked on it too? Damn, I'd almost forgot about that day. I was so nervous standing close to her, worrying that I couldn't keep my hand steady with the welder because my heart was beating out of control. That was right before I kissed her for the first time.

"It's in a frame on her desk that says, *'our first flower.'*" He crosses his arms and stares pointedly at me.

She framed it? With the caption 'our first flower?' That's...what's the word I want? Sweet? Nah. I mean, it is sweet, but that's not quite right. Sentimental? It's that too, but that's not right either. Adorable. It's fucking adorable, just like she is. Damn I miss seeing that.

Oh shit, Rick's still staring at me. Am I smiling? Or staring at nothing? Even good memories of Cora can leave me feeling empty, so I have no idea what expression he sees right now. I try to make my face blank.

"Well, that was her first attempt at welding, and I helped her with it, so I guess we did make it together." That's sounds like an excuse, a dismissal, even to my ears, despite the fact that every word is true. But I won't say more because it's not my place to tell him what she might have been thinking when she framed that. Or what I wish she was thinking.

"You know, Cade," Rick glowers, "I'm tempted to deck you right now for taking her smile away, but since you look just as miserable as she does, I'm guessing she isn't the only one with a broken heart. What the hell happened?"

Dad's eyes dart back and forth between me and Rick, like he's not sure whether to be alarmed by this confrontation, but I'm too distracted by what Rick said to think about his anger. A broken heart? That doesn't make any sense.

"You think she has a broken heart?" It comes out as barely a whisper.

"She's not the same person she used to be, and I can't think of another explanation for that. So, are you going to tell me what happened?" he demands, fisting his hands on his hips.

"Nothing happened." I clear my throat. "Not like you're thinking anyway."

"What am I thinking?"

"That we had a fight or parted on bad terms or something. But it's nothing like that. She came here with a goal, and she finished it. Now she has an amazing career ahead of her." I try to sound happy. Optimistic on her behalf. I don't think it works.

"I suppose that's true." He nods slowly, his jaw locked firm. "That still doesn't explain why you're both lonely and miserable."

"She's lonely?" I wince.

"And miserable," he adds.

I'm not sure how to react to this. I assumed the reason I didn't hear from her was because she was able to put me out of her mind, not because she was miserable. Did I really cause her to feel that way? Did I end up being the distraction I always swore I wouldn't become? If so, I may have put her career in jeopardy. Shit.

"Did she pass her thesis?" I cringe, waiting for the answer.

"Yes," he says curtly.

"What's she going to do now?" I ask softly.

"I don't know. I don't think she knows. We've all been wondering why that is, when she was so driven before. Now I understand." He eyes me critically.

"I'm sorry." I hang my head. It's not enough, but I don't know what else to say. I'm not sure there's anything you can say when you screw up someone's future. I never should've let myself get close to her.

"Sorry for what? Sorry you let her go? Or sorry she fell in love with you?"

"You think she's in love with me?" I blink as my jaw drops.

"It would explain how she's acting."

For a moment, the weight in my chest vanishes. Cora in love with me are the words I've wanted to hear for so long, and even though it's not her saying them, it makes me so fucking relieved to hear it. But all too soon the weight comes crashing down again. Even if it's true, it doesn't change anything.

"I'm sorry, Rick, I don't think that's right," I choke. "She never told me that."

"Cade, I'd be remiss if I didn't point out here that you're in love with her, and you didn't tell her how you felt either," Dad says, almost guiltily. Rick looks at me with raised eyebrows.

"I didn't tell her because she deserves the best, and that's not me or this town. Not for someone like her," I say firmly.

"Someone like her?" Rick prompts.

"Yeah. Someone who's brilliant and wants to do good things with that knowledge. She should be surrounded by people who can help her do that. None of that applies to Katah Vista or to me. She deserves better." I'm practically shouting at this point, but I'm damn tired of having to justify why she's better without me.

"Forget about what she deserves," Rick scoffs. "Think about what she wants. Do you even know what that is?"

"Do you?" I retort.

"I used to," Rick insists. "But like I said, she's different now. She's different since she met you. I think the only way to know what she wants is to ask her."

I stare at him, dumbfounded. "What, just call her up out of the blue and ask what she wants to do with her life? Ask if she wants me to be part of it? Is that what you're saying?"

"Yes," he shouts, startling both of us. He shakes his head, takes a deep breath, and continues. "I appreciate that you're trying to think of what's best for her, but that's not your decision to make. It's hers."

"Can't you see, by not asking her, I'm keeping her from making a bad decision?" I reason. "How could I live with myself if she gave up her dream career for me?"

"From where I'm standing, it looks like you'd sacrifice anything for her. I fail to see how that makes you a bad decision." He crosses his arms, almost daring me to object, which makes no sense considering he seemed pissed at me just a few minutes ago.

What the hell? Why is everyone hell bent on me trying to make things work with Cora? Can't they see that's a selfish thing to do? I don't want to be the selfish bastard anymore. I don't want to be the guy who thinks of himself at the expense of others. I'm finally putting someone else's needs before my own, and even though it's gutting me to live without her, I'd rather do that than be the reason she loses her dream.

I hate that Cora's hurting, and I'd do anything to take that away. Anything but what Rick's asking. She had goals before she met me, and she'll remember that if I'm not there to distract her.

"We're talking in circles here Rick," I exhale, shaking my head in defeat. "I'm not going to give Cora a reason to mess up her future."

"Even though you love her?" He arches a thick brow.

"Because I love her," I say softly.

Rick throws his hands in the air and turns to my dad. "Is he always this stubborn?"

"Not usually, no." Dad sounds almost sad. Hopeless, even. *Fuck*.

I storm off before I can hear Rick's response. I can't stand here and talk about Cora anymore or listen to Rick and my dad talk about me. I don't care that Rick's the client and I'm supposed to be nice to him, I don't care that I'm walking out on my dad, I can't be here anymore. All I care about is erasing this day from memory in the nearest bottle. Maybe then, I'll forget what Rick said about Cora loving me.

Chapter 24

Cora

My heart beats wildly as I sit on the front step, waiting.

I can't remember the last time I was this nervous. Even presenting my thesis didn't leave me this jumpy. I wipe my sweaty palms on my pants, cursing the fact that my anxiety can't be limited to a racing heart and a queasy stomach. Sweaty palms are so embarrassing.

Not for the first time, I wonder if I'm doing the right thing. My heart says yes, but my mind isn't as sure. I replay the events that led me here, hoping they'll give me some reassurance...

"Uncle Rick?" I mutter as I open the door.

"That doesn't sound like you're happy to see me." He steps inside to give me a hug.

"Just surprised. I thought you were in Katah Vista to see the work on the house." I close the door and lead him to the living room to sit down. "Do you want something to drink?"

"No, I can't stay very long." He sits at one end of the couch while I take the other. "I probably shouldn't be here at all," he continues, "but I'd feel guilty if I never said anything."

"Said anything about what?" I'm suddenly very nervous. Rick and I are close, but this is a little out of character for him.

He braces his arms on his legs, wrings his hands together nervously. *"I saw Cade,"* he blurts.

At the mention of his name, I freeze. I've thought about him daily, all-day every-day more accurately, but I haven't heard anyone say his name since I got home. It has a bigger impact than I expected.

"Why didn't you say anything?" Rick meets my eyes, his own a mixture of confusion and sadness.

"What do you mean?" I say cautiously. I haven't told anyone about Cade, except Tara, and I'm not sure what Rick's getting at.

"Cora, you've been different since you got back. I couldn't figure out why, none of us could. Then I saw Cade. You're in love with him, aren't you?"

I'm afraid if I try to speak, I'll end up crying, so I nod instead.

Rick sighs. *"That's what I thought. You didn't tell him?"*

"I didn't want him to feel obligated to say it back," I exhale. *"He'd never been in a relationship before, and I didn't want my feelings to influence his. That was the only way I'd know if they were genuine."*

"Okay." Rick nods, turning my words over in his mind. *"I can see that. But if he had been the first to admit his feelings would that make yours any less genuine?"*

"I...you're making it sound like you know what his feelings are," I venture.

"Picked up on that, did you?" He smirks. *"Yes, I know how he feels. I also know he's as stubborn as you are, which is probably how you two ended up in this mess."*

"What do you mean, stubborn?" I frown. *"That doesn't sound like Cade."*

"Apparently, it's a new trait he's picked up, but he's already a pro." Rick shakes his head, frustrated. I still don't follow what he's getting at. *"He's bound and determined to believe that being with him means you'd be giving up your career,"* he exhales deeply.

"That doesn't make any sense," I protest. *"I wouldn't have to give it up completely. It just might look different in Katah Vista than it would in a place with more resources."*

"Well, he doesn't see it that way." Rick shrugs. *"And I'm pretty sure he won't unless he hears it from you."*

"Hears what from me? That being with him doesn't mean giving up my career? Or that I love him?" I ask cautiously.

"Either. Both."

"I'm just supposed to show up out of the blue and tell him that?" My eyes bug out.

"If that's how you feel, then yes." Rick nods.

I let myself imagine for a minute that I could, that if I showed up at his house and told him how I feel we'd get our happily ever after. Only I know it's not that simple. Cade won't leave Katah Vista, and while I'm sure I could find something to do there, it would undoubtedly look different than what I originally envisioned for myself. I can live with that, but could Cade? Or would he constantly blame himself for forcing me to go in a different direction, even if I was happy to do it? I'd have to convince him he's more important to me than my career, and he's never been good about believing he's important.

"What if he can't accept that?" I whisper.

"Then he's not the man I think he is," Rick says matter-of-factly. *"Just think about it, Cora. I hate to see you unhappy."*

"Okay." I hear myself agree even though I don't know that I can.

Rick stands to leave, but before he heads to the door, he reaches into his jacket pocket. *"I saw this on my trip. I thought it might interest you."*

I look at the printout he hands me. It's an advertisement for a job. An environmental science position. My jaw drops to the floor as I look to him for confirmation.

"You heard about the new owner at the ski resort?" he prompts.

I think back to my dinner with Cade's parents, and shopping with Ally. I do recall talk about a new owner. I'm ashamed to admit I haven't thought about how that might affect the people in town, especially the ones I'd grown close to.

"Yes," I reply.

"He's talking about doing some new development at the resort. That'll require a lot of study before anything can begin, I imagine." He winks at me as he heads for the door...

And now here I am, waiting for Cade to get home, so I can pour my heart out in a last-ditch effort to see if we have a future together. If he wants one.

The crunch of tires on gravel pulls my gaze to the driveway, where Cade's truck is rolling to a stop. The engine goes quiet, but the driver's door stays shut. There's no movement inside the cab, and because of the sun's reflection on the glass I can't see Cade's face to know what sort of expression he's wearing. I take a shaky breath, force a smile to my face, and wipe my palms again as I stand up.

The door creaks as it opens, echoing in the relative silence around us. Cade steps out but makes no attempt to move away from the truck. Instead, he stands there with a confused look in his eyes, like he can't make sense of what he's seeing.

His face is just as beautiful as I remember, but the mischievous spark I grew so fond of is gone, replaced with an almost vacant air. He's here, but somehow not. Detached almost. Lost. It breaks my heart to see him like this.

"Cora?" He blinks. It's barely louder than a whisper.

"Hi." I give a lame little wave since he makes no move to welcome me into his arms.

"What are you doing here?" He sounds more disoriented than happy or sad, leaving me to question again whether this was a bad idea.

"I...wanted to see you," I falter.

He's still standing by the truck, using it like a shield, or maybe a support. I'm usually better at interpreting his movements, but right now he feels like a stranger. God this is awkward.

"I'm sorry," I blurt. "I shouldn't have just shown up like this. I'll go." I look around for an escape, but Uncle Rick dropped me off, so I either have to call him for a ride or walk. I'm leaning toward the latter and step off the porch when Cade seems to wake from his stupor.

"Don't leave." He finally shuts the door and comes toward me. "I didn't expect to see you, that's all. Come here."

He opens his arms so I can step into them, and the moment we connect all the tension and anxiety evaporate. A huge sense of calm washes over me, and from the way Cade sighs I'm sure he feels it too.

We cling to each other and just breathe, and for a moment time seems to stop. My mind goes quiet. His touch shuts out all the doubts, the fears, the what ifs. I know this doesn't mean we're magically okay, we still have things to talk about, but as long as we can hold on to this, to how right it feels to be together, I have to believe we'll figure it out.

"Come inside," he whispers, taking my hand and pulling me with him toward the front door.

As we step into the living room Cade drops my hand and starts rushing around, picking things up, and I'm reminded of the lost look he had earlier. We didn't spend much time at his house over the summer, but I was here enough to know he keeps it fairly clean, and just like his expression, this clutter is something about him I don't recognize. I'm not sure whether to feel guilty that my silence led to this, or hopeful that I can fix it by telling him the truth.

"Sorry about the mess," he says. "I haven't...I've been working a lot," he amends as he clears a spot for me to sit on the couch.

He takes a seat on the opposite end, and once again I start to lose my nerve, the distance between us making me wonder if he's ready to hear what I have to say. I won't change my mind, but I can't just blurt it out. Not when he's clearly confused about how he should act. I'll have to ease into this.

"Work?" I ask. "Another build?"

"I've been doing some more with the business. Managing stuff." He meets my eyes briefly as he speaks, then averts them again. Usually, when he doesn't know what to say he flirts outrageously, but this Cade is subdued. Almost timid. I hope I'm not too late.

"Your dad must be glad to have the help," I offer.

He nods absently. "I heard you passed your thesis. Congratulations."

For the first time since he pulled up, my smile isn't forced. "I did. Thank you."

"Does that mean you have a job lined up? You stopped by to tell me where you're off to?" He doesn't look at me when he asks.

"No job," I say softly. It's now or never. "But I did apply for one.. .*Here*."

"Here?" He meets my eyes again, but this time he doesn't look away. He studies them, searching. Hopeful almost. "In Katah Vista?"

"Not Katah Vista, specifically. The whole county. There's talk about more development around the mountain, and the kind of infrastructure needed to support that. The environmental impact for that would have to be carefully studied. I'm more than qualified, and there's a lot of work to do. *Years* of work..." I trail off, not sure how to finish.

"That's not the alternative energy you wanted to focus on," he says sadly.

"Not exclusively," I agree. "But energy resources are part of any development, so I'd still be able to work in that specialty, maybe even with water as a resource."

"Why?" He shakes his head in disbelief.

He doesn't have to elaborate. I know exactly why he's asking that question.

"I could live anywhere in the county. Even right here," it's barely a whisper.

"Don't do this for me, Cora." He closes his eyes, an almost pained expression on his face. "Don't give up on your dreams for me."

"I'm not," I say evenly.

"You are." He looks at me sadly. "Katah Vista was never part of your future."

"You weren't supposed to be either," I shrug. "Plans change."

"They shouldn't. Not for me," he insists. "You deserve better."

I was hoping after a summer together Cade would be able to accept how important he is to me, but I see now he still needs convincing.

"I'm not changing my plans for you. I'm doing it for me." I take a deep breath and continue. "This is what I want. To be here. Besides, didn't we agree you were going to stop worrying about what I deserve?" I bite my lip, waiting for his answer.

"We did." A hint of a smile plays on his lips though his eyes are still sad.

"Good." That near smile gives me the confidence to continue. "Because the only thing I deserve is to be happy, and the thing that makes me happiest is you."

"Me?" he winces.

"Is that so hard to believe?"

"Yes. I'm the local playboy. I don't know how to be a boyfriend or support your career. I'll only hold you back." He looks at me sadly.

"I disagree," I say as calmly as possible. "You were a great boyfriend all summer. You gave me endless support to write my thesis. And you taught me to enjoy the moment. You didn't hold me back, Cade, you taught me what's important in life." I look straight into his eyes, willing him to understand my meaning.

"Don't say it, Cora. Don't say *I'm* what's important." He shakes his head.

"You *are* important," I insist. "When are you going to see yourself the way I see you?"

"You see the best in everyone, Cora. But what you think you see isn't there," he pleads.

"Let me tell you what I see." I scoot towards him and take his hand, hoping that the contact will bring back the calm we felt outside, and give me the courage to say what I came here to say. He looks down at our joined fingers.

"I see a man who's humble, honest, and supportive. I see a man who loves to have fun yet puts his responsibilities first. I see a man who acts carefree but feels deeply. And I see a man who's so selfless he'd give up his own happiness to see someone else find theirs. I know men who possess one or two of those qualities, but not all of them, and none of them make my panties wet when I look at them the way you do." That earns me a weak laugh, just as I'd hoped for, but he still won't meet my eyes.

Stroking over his thumb, I try to give him time to process, but when he stays silent, I try again, "There isn't a better man on Earth than the one sitting in front of me, and I don't care if I deserve him or not. I want him. I want you, Cade. I love you."

He inhales sharply and holds his breath, his eyes darting from our joined fingers to meet mine, and I swear they almost look a little glassy.

"And years from now? When you're still focused on the development of this town instead of making groundbreaking discoveries in a state-of-the-art lab, will you still want me then? Will you be happy you chose me?" His voice cracks.

"There isn't any other choice." I feel my own eyes turning glassy.

Cade reaches up to cup my cheek. "I really can't convince you to walk away?"

"No," I whisper.

"Thank God," he exhales, "because I'm damn tired of trying to convince myself that I'm okay without you." He leans his forehead against mine and threads his fingers in my hair. "I love you, Cora Gerome. I love you so fucking much I haven't taken a full breath since you left. I've never felt as empty as I did without you here, like a piece of me was missing. I don't ever want to feel that again."

"You won't." I wrap my hands around his neck so I don't collapse as the nervous tension that was holding me up seeps out of me.

"Good," Cade whispers, right before he touches his lips reverently to mine, and my heart beats for what feels like the first time in a month. This, in Cade's arms, is where I've always belonged.

"God, I've missed you Cora," he mumbles against my lips. "I missed holding you. Touching you." His kisses morph from tender and loving to firm, insistent. Making up for lost time.

"I missed you too." Heat explodes throughout my body as his tongue drives inside my mouth to find mine. We cling together, tongues clashing, urgent, searching, as our hands fumble to get rid of our clothes.

Our lovemaking is urgent yet tender, carnal but passionate, both of us starved for each other but conscious of the magnitude of this moment. For the first time, Cade's allowing himself to believe he has value, that he deserves me just as much as I deserve him. It's everything I was afraid to hope for, and now it's real. *We're real*.

After our need has been temporarily sated, Cade cradles me against his chest, stroking my back as our breathing returns to normal.

"How did I get so lucky—to get this second chance?" he mumbles against my forehead.

"Uncle Rick," I say automatically.

"Did you seriously just mention your Uncle?" Cade groans. "I'm still inside you Cora, you can't say another man's name while I'm inside you, especially your uncle's."

"Well, you asked," I giggle.

"That was rhetorical, sweetheart," he chuckles. "Although, I do appreciate your ability to make me laugh in bed." He wraps his arms around me and hugs me deeply.

"I'm glad to be back in your bed." I sigh into his neck. "I was so sure I'd lost you forever."

"You never lost me, Cora. Even when you weren't here, I still belonged to you." He tucks his finger under my chin and pulls my lips to his for a soft kiss. "From the moment I blocked your car in, I've belonged to you, and I always will."

Reaching up to kiss his cheek and whisper in his ear, I say, "I guess I'm no longer *Solo* anymore, huh? You'll have to find a new nickname."

Chapter 25

Epilogue

Cade

Cora got the job with the county. No surprise really, because she's brilliant, and just as she predicted it does include some work on energy resources. That eases some of the guilt I still feel about everything she sacrificed to be with me, but since she lights up like a star when she talks about work, I know she doesn't think she's sacrificed anything. Plus, alternative energy is becoming a popular business, and sometimes her family's investment firm gets approached to back these new technologies, and they always ask for her input. That keeps her on the cutting edge of what's going on.

Watching her inspired me to focus on what I love, which isn't construction. Managing it anyway. After trying to get involved in the operations of the company, I confirmed what I'd always suspected, that I'm not really a desk guy. After a good talk with my dad, we came up with a future plan that doesn't involve me doing the paperwork. When he's ready to retire we'll either outsource things like payroll and accounting or bring in an office manager, so I can concentrate on building. That will also give me the freedom to continue welding.

Rick wasn't just fishing for confirmation of my feelings for Cora when he was talking to me about my work. He commissioned a piece for above the fireplace, and he's recommended me to several friends and clients looking for unique pieces. Now, I have a little side business making metal art, which gives me the opportunity to experiment in the studio and brings in enough extra cash that I was able to buy Cora the perfect engagement ring.

Deacon worries that this is happening too fast, first moving Cora in with me and then getting engaged a few months later, but that month I spent without her was the worst in my life, and I wasn't going to go through that again. I know now that keeping my feelings to myself can have dire consequences, and I'm not going to make the same mistake twice. In a few short minutes, she'll be my wife. I cannot fucking wait.

There are still days when I wonder what I did to deserve her. I've stopped admitting that to her, because she thinks I'm putting myself down when I say that, but I'm not. Not anymore. I remember what she said about all the good things she sees in me, and when I stopped beating myself up for wanting to have fun, I realized she was right. As a neighbor, as a friend, as her future husband, I do have good qualities. I'm honest and responsible. I'm supportive. And I definitely care deeply about the people around me. She helped me understand that. So, when I wonder what I did to deserve her, it's not about putting myself down or questioning what she sees in me, it's about the fact that I got lucky enough to find the person that helped me see those things about myself. The person who makes me whole. I know how special that is, and I'm grateful for it every day.

I follow the minister to the arbor at the rim of the scenic overlook with the Katah Vista mountains as a backdrop. I offered to get married wherever Cora wanted, thinking she'd pick her oceanside hometown, but she said she wanted the ceremony in the spot we were going to build our life together, so she could see it every day. My girl's a fucking romantic.

The guys follow me to the front of the crowd, first Deacon as my best man, followed by Dex, Finn, Ryder, Blake and Cora's brother. When the music starts, Cora's friend Tara walks down the aisle first, then Ally, followed by her sister. Lastly, her two cousins come down the aisle, Rick's daughters, and my palms grow sweaty, knowing it won't be long before I see my bride. Cora starts down the aisle with her dad and I forget how to breathe.

She's fucking stunning. She's wearing this long cream dress that clings to her figure without being too tight, like she's wrapped in silk. The dress itself is basic. Plain even. The only notable thing about it is that Cora is in it, and that's perfect, because she should make the dress, not the other way around.

Her long blonde hair is pulled up in an elegant knot, showing off her slender shoulders. She's holding a bouquet of flowers in front of her, a splash of pink that matches the blush in her cheeks. But it's her face that captivates me. Soulful brown eyes that glisten with unshed tears, and a smile so bright it guts me with the knowledge that I'm the one who put it there. God, I love this woman.

Cora and her father reach the arbor, and he shakes my hand and gives me a hug before placing her hand in mine. I'm vaguely aware of both our mothers smiling through their own tears as I clasp her hands, and because I'm so overwhelmed, I do the only thing that's ever come naturally when it comes to Cora. I kiss her and feel her smile against my lips.

"Ahem," the minister clears his through. "You're skipping ahead son."

"Sorry." I shrug as the guests try to stifle their laughter. "I'm ready to start calling her my wife."

Cora turns red, but her smile tells me she feels the same.

"I understand." The minister smiles warmly. "Dearly beloved," he bellows to the guests, and my future begins.

***

Sloane

He slips into the back row just before the procession starts, and instead of focusing on the bride, I focus on him. I moved in with my sister, Ally, about the same time he moved to town, though until last week I hadn't seen him in person. This makes two Carter sightings in two weeks. What are the odds?

He's mesmerizing in his charcoal suit and black tie. I'd say that's because he's the only guy here in a full suit, but it's more the way he fills out that suit that catches my eye. It's clearly not something he bought off the rack, clinging to his frame in a way that accentuates his trim physique.

I'm not really the kind of girl who goes for suits. In my experience most guys look uncomfortable in them, like they're pretending to be an adult. Lumberjack is more my style, or it was before today, when I saw how Carter fits in his.

He was wearing a suit the day I was summoned to his office to give him what turned out to be an *awkward* massage. Or suit pants anyway, so I didn't get the full effect. With the jacket and tie he looks both graceful and powerful, though the hint of late-day stubble adds a bit of rustic appeal.

I sneak another peek at him just as Cora passes my row, beaming in her elegant gown as she makes her way to the front of the church. His expression is blank, his posture stiff, though his eyes look a little less serious today than they did in his office. In fact, they almost look warm, making me wonder what's going through his mind.

There's no denying Carter's mystery is part of his appeal. Cora seems to like him, but of all the people I know in town she's the only one to have any regular contact with him. No one knows why he picked this ski resort to purchase or what his plans are for it, except maybe Cora, but she's under contract and can't share details of her work.

Similarly, no one knows anything personal about him, like what his hobbies are, what foods he likes or whether he has a girlfriend. He so rarely leaves his office at the resort that sightings have become a bit of a game, a 'Where's Waldo' CEO edition.

The ceremony begins with a laugh—Cade jumps the gun and kisses his bride before the officiant tells him to—which seems fitting based on what I know of the guy. Before long I'm wiping away tears, as I watch them take their vows. If ever there was an underdog to root for it's Cade, the guy who once seemed allergic to relationships and felt that made him unworthy to be in one. Fortunately, Cora didn't judge him based on his past, and now they're the perfect couple.

Once the ceremony ends people file out of their chairs and head toward the reception tent. I lose track of Carter in the crowd when I try to wipe away the evidence of my happy tears, but my curiosity has me casually meandering through the guests, turning my head from side to side in a lame attempt to catch another glimpse. After the massage debacle, this might be my last chance to see him in person, and I don't want to miss it. Unfortunately, the man is elusive.

I'm about to give up my search when something pulls my eyes toward the gift table. I look up to find Carter staring in my direction, lips pressed in a firm line, offering no clue to what he's thinking or feeling. Yet the intensity in his gaze suggests there's some deep thoughts behind the expressionless mask, and I have a sudden desire to discover every one of them. *Get it together, Sloane. This is still your boss.*

Heart pounding, I hold my ground, willing myself not to blink. I don't know what's happening, what this little staring contest means, but I'm determined not to be as flustered as I was the other day. I still don't know what prompted the episode in his office—I don't have any illusions that it was me he was responding to—I simply don't want to give the impression he makes me as nervous as I must have appeared. And I want to commit him to memory in case this is my last interaction with him.

As the seconds tick by and we hold each other's gaze, my mind registers the need to move, to do something other than stand frozen in place. My hand drifts up to offer a tiny wave just as he drops an envelope on the table and spins toward the exit. *Guess I should've kept playing statue.*

Deflated, I head to the bar for a drink, telling myself this is probably for the best. After all, fantasizing about your boss can only lead to trouble, and in a town this small, trouble is the last thing I need.

***

If you enjoyed Cade and Cora's story, please leave a review. Want more from the town of Katah Vista? The mysterious Carter Quinn is faced with overlapping personal and professional desires in Validation. Visit my website www.mlenardromance.com and sign up for my newsletter to receive updates on my next series.

The Elevation Series

Distraction

Validation

Revelation

Liberation

Absolution

Exception

You can also check out my contemporary romances in Mile High Romance, a collection of steamy stories about finding love when your career sometimes gets it the way. Set in Denver, Colorado, this series features sports, workplace and forbidden romances, with a flawed yet lovable "relationship whisperer" who is surprisingly good at offering advice that he doesn't know how to take, until its his turn to fall hard.

Books in the Mile High Romance series

Not So Friendly Intent

Purely Novel Intent

Totally Inevitable Intent

Willfully Malicious Intent

Thoroughly Innocent Intent

Strictly Forbidden Intent

For the latest updates on other releases join my VIP reader group.

Acknowledgments: Thanks to my critique group, Janie and Amanda, without whom I wouldn't be whole. You two have challenged me as a writer, and helped me improve my meager design skills. Cover design by Sweet N Spicy Designs.

Read on for a sneak peek at the short story, The Long Route.

Chapter 26

The Long Route

The stunning brunette jogs by right on time, her long ponytail swishing with each step. As she passes me, I catch a whiff of something floral. Roses maybe? Lavender? Whatever it is it reminds me of summer, and the flowers that grew just outside my bedroom window.

Having it open was a compromise I made with my mother, who insisted I get fresh air if I wasn't going to play outside with my brother. As a kid I didn't really care what was growing out there, but I liked the smells that came in with the breeze, faint, just the way they are when my runner dashes by and the scent floats past.

Of course, it's not only this girl's scent that has me intrigued. It's the lean legs poking out from her tiny running shorts. They're the perfect mix of grace and power, and as a fellow runner I appreciate that combination.

Running was another compromise. Dad would have preferred I play a sport to stay active, football or soccer like my brother, but my hand-eye coordination is somewhat
lacking, and no one wants a guy who misses the ball on their team.

It worked out in the end because I enjoy running, and still do it to this day, although I prefer early mornings instead of early evening. I suppose if I switched to an early evening schedule that would give me a reason to approach this woman, or at the very least signal to her that we have something in common, but I'm afraid that might change the interaction we have now, and I like what we have now.

Each day she passes by with barely more than a glance in my direction, although after that glance she bashfully averts her eyes. Sometimes she'll glance over a second time, a little longer, and we'll lock eyes. It's brief, just long enough to acknowledge that we see each other, but it feels more significant than that. Like we're the only two people in the park. But she keeps running, and I keep letting her go without trying to talk to her.

I sling my bag over my shoulder and jog toward the south quad, hoping I'm not too late. Class ran over because the professor was a little late, which normally wouldn't bother me since I love class, but this time it interfered with my only window to see my runner. Since I don't know anything else about her, like her name or where she lives, getting to the bench before she passes it is the only way I can be sure to see her.

She's nowhere in sight by the time I get there, and I drop my bag on the bench in frustration. I don't know how or why this whole 'look but don't touch' thing we have going on gets me so excited, but I can't get enough of it. Maybe the game speaks to my introverted personality, which she must have as well, because we both seem determined to be approached instead of doing the approaching. Ah well, maybe we'll get another round tomorrow.

I reach for my bag and start to turn back towards my apartment, colliding with another body mid-spin. On instinct my arms shoot out to steady whoever I bumped into, and I find myself face to face with my runner.

"Whoa there. Sorry. Are you okay?"

"Didn't you hear me coming?" She rests her hands on her hips, brow arched, though not in an irritated way. Inquisitive maybe. Or assessing. It makes me feel like I'm being scolded, and I've never been one to need scolding. It's kind of exhilarating.

I pull my earbuds from my ears. "Didn't you see me standing here?" I answer her question with one of my own, hoping my smile tells her I'm only kidding.

"I expected you to sit down. This is your usual spot, right?"

"You noticed?" I'm sure it's not very suave to keep smiling like a loon, but her admission makes my day.

She rolls her pretty brown eyes. "Of course I noticed. I also noticed you watching me during my run the past few weeks." Her voice rises a bit, almost like she's hinting at something. It suddenly occurs to me that my attention may have been unwanted. What if she was only paying attention to me because she was wary, not interested.

"Oh... I uh." I push my glasses higher. "I mean...yes I watched you – you're very beautiful – but I would never have approached you. I wouldn't want to make you uncomfortable."

"Well that's a shame."

"Excuse me?"

"I sort of wanted you to approach me." She kicks at the ground with her tennis shoe.

"You did?"

"Why do you think I ran into you? You didn't leave me any other choice, although that might have been a bad one." She rubs her arm. "You're sturdier than a brick wall."

I glance down at myself. At nearly six-two I am pretty solid. Wait – she ran into me on purpose?

"Are you hurt?" I start to reach for her arm then pull back, unsure if my grip might hurt her more.

"Nothing permanent." She smiles timidly and glances at the ground before meeting my gaze again, some of her earlier bravado giving way to uncertainty. It's cute.

Flirtatious even.

"So, it's okay that I like watching you run?" The corner of my mouth pulls up as I watch her fidget.

"Oh no." Her brown doe eyes blink innocently, although her soft lips fight a smirk. "It's rude to watch, unless you're planning to ask me out?"

Yep, flirting. I'm rusty, but I can do this. "I can't ask you out if I don't know your name."

"Brynn." She bites her lip as she offers me her hand.

"Charlie." I take it, her delicate grip sending a bolt of electricity up my arm. That's unexpected, but not unwelcome. I think I'm smiling like a loon again. Chris would be mortified to call me his brother.

"So Charlie." She bounces on the balls of her feet to keep her muscles warmed up. "When do I get to see you again?"

"What's wrong with now?" I ask boldly. That would make Chris proud.

"I have class."

"In the evening?"

"Twice a week." She nods. "But at least it's Tuesday/Thursday and not Friday."

"They're playing a movie on the South Quad Friday. Would you like to go?"

"What movie?"

"Come to think of it I don't actually know." I adjust my glasses.

"Hmm, that's an enticing offer." Her eyes sparkle. "The movie 'I don't actually know.'"

"We could do something different, if you don't like movies." I feel my ears turning red.

"I like movies," she giggles. "I'd love to go to the mystery movie with you. Let me give you my number." She gestures to the phone in my left hand.

I pass it to her and watch her fingers peck away at the keys. She hands it back with another bashful smile.

"Talk to you soon." She gives me a little wave and continues on her run.

The breath I didn't know I was holding comes rushing out. I have a date. Holy shit, I have a date! I need to talk to Chris, ASAP.

Read the conclusion at www.mlenardromance.com.

Made in the USA
Monee, IL
22 July 2023